HOUSE ON FIRE

THE SECOND EDITION

ANNA BOWMAN THRILLERS
BOOK TWO

Westley Enterprises Publishing
Helena, Montana
www.westleyenterprises.com

SECOND EDITION
ISBN 979-8-9916308-8-7 (Paperback)
ISBN 979-8-9916308-9-4 (eBook)

*Dedicated to the smart little man who
inspired Fernando Serna.*

You're the nicest evil dictator I've ever met.

ALSO BY AK WELLER

Enemy Closer

House on Fire

Bigger Fish

No Port in a Storm

The Lost Portrait

CONTENTS

HOUSE ON FIRE

1

Saturday, December 26, 2020
London

I struggled to my knees on the ribbed metal floor of the cargo van. My arms, zip tied at the wrist behind me, were no help. The van turned sharply to the right, throwing me against exposed metal wall behind the driver while I stared stupidly at the man in the passenger seat.

Luke.

I turned away from him far too late to hide my recognition, and I locked eyes with the man riding it out in the empty cargo area with me.

"A familiar face, eh?" he taunted, English with a thick French accent.

Lacking any coherent or helpful response to that, I settled for kicking him in the jaw as hard as I could. While he recovered, I struggled on my knees toward the rear of the van in a wild bid for freedom, but he tackled me from behind. Gripping me by the hair, he swung my head toward the bulging wheel well.

The impact knocked me senseless, but only for a moment. I could tell very little time had passed because the Frenchman was still breathing heavily, swearing at me under his breath, as I came to. I remained motionless, wondering if he'd kill me if I kept fighting.

"What're you trying to do, kill her?" Luke complained, echoing my thoughts.

His voice sounded too far away, as though my hearing had been impaired. He was speaking French, and to my ears it was indistinguishable from any native French-speaker. He spoke better French than I did.

"She kicked me! She nearly broke my jaw!" the man whined.

"Well, maybe next time you won't forget about her feet," Luke shot back.

I rolled onto my back as the Frenchman began patting himself down, searching his pockets for more zip ties. The driver remained silent, only his right ear visible to me. Luke was again absorbed in the windshield, his jaw set.

Rage surged through me and I screamed, "You lying scumbag! Where is Alice? *Where is she?*"

I caught a flash of the driver's profile as he turned sharply, silently, to Luke. A hand closed over my right ankle, distracting me. I met the Frenchman's eyes and saw a satisfying gleam of apprehension. He tightened his grip, and I jerked my knee toward my chest, dragging him forward. He toppled forward onto my stomach.

As I tightened my thighs around his neck, thinking I might

be angry enough to actually kill the guy, the driver finally spoke.

"For God's sake, Giles," he sighed. "Luke, do something about her."

With a grunt, Luke climbed into the back and knelt beside me. He and I watched Giles' face turning purple for a moment before Luke pried my knees apart and allowed him to slither backward, gasping for air.

Luke leaned over me to mutter in English, "Anna, stop it. Please."

Giles hacked, coughed, and snapped, "You do it, then."

A thick, black zip tie flew at Luke's face. He caught it, then met my eyes again. My brain had caught up enough to keep my most pressing questions to myself: Why are you helping them? Why aren't you rescuing Alice like you said you would? Why did you let me go to the museum if you knew this was going to happen?

As Luke formed the tie into a loop to secure my ankles together, I considered what would happen if I attacked him. I knew enough jujitsu now to grapple most people into submission, but I'd learned it from Luke. And it was two against one. And my arms were still tied together. Luke and Giles would put a quick end to my struggles, and I'd end up taking a nap. I didn't want to lose consciousness. I'd heard on TV that it's bad for you.

Luke rolled me over onto my stomach, bent my knees toward him, and slipped the zip tie over my shoes. I let him do it, telling myself I was waiting my turn rather than letting my last chance slip away because I was too afraid to fight a superior opponent.

Where had I gone wrong? What was it my Krav Maga teacher always said? "Don't go stupid places to do stupid things with stupid people." Something like that. Well, I didn't know any particularly stupid people, and I'd never understood what he meant by "stupid places." It wasn't like I made a habit of visiting bad neighborhoods at midnight. So that left doing stupid things. What one stupid thing had I done to start the chain reaction of events that ended in London in this van with these three men?

After a too-quick mental review—sometimes known as one's life flashing before one's eyes—I had to conclude I'd made a serious mistake when I fell in love with fireworks as a child. That was the beginning of the end. Had I not become obsessed with fireworks, I'd have skipped out on the Independence Day show when I was 17 and no one else in my family wanted to go with me. Then I never would have met my high school boyfriend; gotten pregnant; been effectively spayed by said boyfriend; become a barren social cast off in my tiny, backward hometown of Manchester, Texas; and ended up desperate enough to marry Aaron Oakley when I was only 19.

Then I never would have fled to an internship with the FBI in Washington, DC to get away from Manchester and my violently abusive husband. Without the FBI, there would certainly be no Agent James (Jim) Camposanto in my life.

Jim never would have picked me out of a stack of wannabe agents (for God only knew what reason) to be his mole inside the undercover operation of his nemesis, Agent Philip Levin. Wherever I might have ended up on February 15, 2020, it wouldn't have been a warehouse in Houston where my partner,

Tommy, was killed and Luke Jackson assassinated a Tres Islas Cartel (TIC) money guy named Francisco Lira.

Had I not been involved in that ill-fated operation, I never would have been sent to Colorado to find Luke and question him about what happened that night. I wouldn't have built between us the bond of affection and attraction that goaded Luke to tell me he was coming to London. He wouldn't have invited me to come find him here, so I wouldn't have. I never would have been sucked into Luke's world where these wretched creatures dwelt.

Contrary to an earlier assumption that Luke was involved with the TIC, he appeared to be working for a totally unrelated criminal syndicate represented by the two Frenchmen in the van with us. The only one missing was their brother, who was recovering in the hospital after being stabbed by my flatmate, Alice Murphy, who may or may not be dead.

Oh, God, Alice…

I was jerked back to reality by something cold and hard pressing into my knee. I realized the Frenchman was about to put a retaliatory bullet into my knee cap, and terror erupted inside me.

Luke noticed, too, because he snarled, "Put that away, you petty little idiot."

"What do you care, it's just her knee."

"Giles, I will tear you apart if you hurt her."

At least Luke was partially on my side. The pressure disappeared from my leg, the roar of the axle beneath me drowning out my sob of relief.

Into the relative silence that followed Luke's threat, the driver of the van spoke again.

"Luke."

He conveyed a lot with that one word. I felt tension swell, tightening Luke's voice as he answered, "You said she wouldn't get hurt."

Disregarding this, the driver asked, "Did anyone see you at the museum, Giles?"

"No."

"You're sure?"

"Positive."

Luke climbed back into the passenger seat. I wormed around on the floor, ignoring the Frenchman's smirk, until I was seated with my legs stretched toward him and my back against the wall. I hoped to hear more crosstalk, but all three men were silent for the remainder of the ride. Through the windshield, I saw nothing but overcast skies.

I reviewed what I knew about the Frenchmen so far: Luke had told me the three Marchand brothers were named Marcel, Giles, and David. Marcel was the eldest, the one in charge. I couldn't remember if Luke had explicitly said that, or if I'd inferred it, but I felt it was true. Giles and David were the two who'd been casing the pub where Alice and I worked, so David must be the one out of commission thanks to Alice's impressively gritty kitchen knife stab to the neck. David was either dead or receiving medical treatment somewhere. Marcel, then, was the driver. The three of them represented the shady import-export company Frères Enterprises.

Jim. That *liar*. He was the real reason I was tied up in the back of a van. Hadn't he told me to look for Luke in locations associated with import-export companies? He definitely had not told me about Frères Enterprises specifically, no more than Luke had. I'd worked that out on my own, and it hadn't been easy. Could Jim have known that the eponymous frères were the Marchand brothers, the very people who sent Luke to kill Francisco Lira in Houston in the first place? Would it have killed him to give me a heads up?

Before I'd left for the museum, which I'd only done to comply with Alice's kidnapper's demands, Luke had told me he would find Alice. He was supposed to rescue her while I was at the museum doing my best impression of a worm on a hook. Either that was still in the works, his plan had taken a left turn, or that had never been his plan at all.

I'd lost track of time. By my best guess, I had about two hours until I was supposed to check in with Jim. The chances of that happening were remote enough to be counted as impossible. Even if I could get to a phone, it would only be to sound the S-O-S. An hour after the missed call, Jim would put the wheels in motion to track me down and send someone to my aid. How long that would take, if anyone could even find me, I had no clue.

When I judged we'd been driving for about an hour, the van took a right turn and slowed considerably. Fifteen minutes later, another right turn put us on a gravel road. Through the windshield, I could see trees arching over us. The already dim, gray light became dimmer still. I stopped hearing other cars around us.

A long, slow left turn, possibly around a circular driveway, finally brought the trip to an end. The van lurched to a stop, and Marcel instructed, "Luke, I'd like to speak to you inside. Giles, see to our guest."

Evidently Giles wasn't that keen on taking orders. He opened the side door and climbed out without a word or a glance, slamming the door shut and leaving me alone in the van. I heard an indistinguishable shout from Giles, an answering bark from Luke.

I peered around the dark interior of the van, looking for a weapon of any sort. Tie-down straps, a packing blanket, and a ripped corner of a cardboard box comprised the entire contents of the van. The heavy hook at the end of the straps would have made a handy bludgeon, but that required hands. I inched my way toward the passenger seat, saw the face of a stone mansion to the right of the van, and was eyeing the glove compartment when the side door slid open again.

"Oh, no you don't," Luke cried, grabbing me by the tail of my sweater and hauling me backward. I grunted my annoyance as he threw me over his shoulder and headed towards the house. He asked, "Are you an idiot, or are you trying to let her get away?"

I realized he wasn't talking to me when Giles answered, "She's too heavy."

"It's no wonder you two needed my help. Couldn't even handle a tiny little pub wench."

"Ah, shut up."

Up a short flight of stairs, through a tall doorway, and

across a marble foyer, Luke carried me, finally depositing me onto a hard, narrow couch in an old-fashioned sitting room. Marcel and Giles were there, the latter getting a fire going while the former stared motionlessly through a picture window that looked out over the driveway and front lawn.

Like his brothers, Marcel was of average height and stocky build, his short hair slightly darker and peppered with white at the temples. Luke interrupted my study by stepping between us and helping me into a sitting position. I watched his face, trying to pick up on some kind of clue about how I should be reacting to him while he cut away the zip tie around my ankles. He left my wrists bound, shot me one totally indecipherable glance, and left to help Giles with the fire.

Marcel turned around, and I found myself staring up at the type of face for which the paradoxical 'nondescript' had been coined. If one could create a mental picture of dark brown hair, matching eyes, exactly one nose, one mouth, and two ears, they'd have as good a grasp on Marcel as I did. Even his expression was hypotonic, and as he stared at me I couldn't decide whether he was planning to make me a sandwich or put a bullet between my eyes. I figured after all the cloak-and-dagger nonsense to get me here, an immediate execution probably wasn't anything to worry about.

"Hello, Anna," he said in French with neither a friendly nor a threatening tone. His voice was soft, as though he were unwilling to expend the energy required to speak at a normal volume. He sat down in an armchair across from the sofa. "I'm Marcel, and this is my brother, Giles. Luke you already know. I hope

Giles wasn't too hard on you. He has a capricious nature."

"He's standing right here," Giles grumbled. I glanced from Marcel to Giles, outwardly confused.

"Sorry, I don't understand French," I lied, so badly I was impressed at Marcel for not laughing.

Marcel's eyes drifted to Luke, who was watching the exchange from his post next to the fireplace. "You told me she was a good liar," he said in English, making it an accusation.

Luke said, "She is. She's sandbagging you."

I scowled at him. "Don't act like you know me."

I hoped I wasn't imagining the glimmer of approval in Luke's eyes as he frowned down at me. He crossed his arms but didn't respond.

Marcel said, "You should be nicer to my friend, Miss Bowman. It's his unexpectedly soft heart you have to thank for being alive today."

"Thanks, softie," I mumbled, not looking at either of them.

I already knew what Marcel meant. Luke had gone back to Marcel after leaving me in New Mexico back in July, and Marcel had asked him to kill me. Luke had refused. I assumed Marcel had hit pause on my contract murder, because there I sat, stubbornly alive and so confused I was forgetting to be mad or scared.

"Marcel," Giles said.

Marcel's gaze sharpened warily as he glanced at his brother. "What now?" he asked.

"I'm sick of her attitude. Just give me half an hour with her. Upstairs. I won't kill her, I promise."

Marcel shrugged. "If you must. I need to rest anyway. Bring her back here when you're done, please. Luke, we still need to talk."

Luke argued, "I'm not leaving her alone with Giles. You promised me she wouldn't get hurt."

"You tendered certain promises as well, if you recall."

Marcel's calm, even tone was deeply unsettling. I stared at Luke, silently begging him to drop it. Whatever was going on here, I could see Luke's position was nearly as precarious as my own. With my feet free, I was pretty sure I could handle Giles. Maybe I could even convince him to untie my hands. I'd take care of him, then come back down here and help Luke—

"I told you, I don't give a crap about her," Luke said, cutting across my conniving thoughts. "That FBI lackey she's working for does. You wanted her here, and she's here. Who cares about her attitude?"

Marcel weighed Luke's words for a long minute, gazing at me all the while. I tried not to look too hurt by Luke's assertion that he didn't give a crap about me, but it stung all the same.

"Giles, go feed the dogs," Marcel finally said. "Luke, get her something to eat."

2

Saturday, December 26, 2020
London

No one argued with Marcel's terse commands, but Giles was muttering to himself as he swept out of the parlor. Luke went silently, glancing back at me at the door. I halfway expected him to ask me what I wanted to eat, but he simply shook his head at me and stomped away.

"You brought me here to feed me?" I asked Marcel. "Seems like a lot of trouble."

"As Luke said, I brought you here, and now you're here. Are you expecting an explanation?"

"Is this about Jim? You think he's gonna come here himself to rescue me?"

"At the moment, Camposanto doesn't concern me. Neither, in fact, does your attitude. I can't imagine how Giles expects you to behave. Personally, I expected you to put up more of a fight."

"So what do you want? Where is Alice? Why did you attack

her?"

He sighed again. So exhausting, this woman, his expression said. He gave his attention to an iPad, poking away at it as he asked, "You have a large dog, don't you?" he asked.

"Yes."

"Luke told me about him. He's incredibly well trained."

"Dude's smart. A German Shepherd. I can't take credit."

"I prefer the Belgian Malinois. Quite a bit more agile, unbelievably high energy animals. I have eight of them."

He let the threat hang in the air: You might be fast, but you can't outrun a pack of trained dogs.

"Okay," I prompted.

"I would like to speak with you, but I suspect an empty stomach is making you unusually cranky. You can find Luke in the kitchen at the rear of the house."

I stood slowly, waiting for him to react or even look at me again. He was engrossed in his iPad and gave no notice as I walked to the door and slipped into the hallway. Though my eyes moved automatically to the front door to my right, Marcel's warning about the dogs proved effective. I turned left instead, the way Luke had gone, and meandered my way through a maze of hallways leading farther into the house.

The home was massive and "well appointed" as the British say, but cold and impersonal. I got the feeling Marcel and his brothers didn't live here full time, if they lived here at all. No framed photos or personal items were in evidence, and every door I passed on my way toward the back of the house was closed except for one leading to a small half-bath. Seeing it and realizing I didn't need it made my throat burn with sudden thirst, and I carried on with more purpose.

The kitchen was a cramped and chilly space separated from the rest of the house by a door and a drop of about a foot. I stepped down into it and felt an urge to wrap my arms around my torso against the cold, but my hands were still bound behind me. Luke was standing in an obviously defensive position, a large butcher block between him and the open doorway he faced. He was assembling two sandwiches and stopped mid-mustarding when he caught sight of me.

"You're alone?" he asked, frowning.

I took a slow breath in and out, finding it hard to decide what to say first. I settled on, "Take this thing off my wrists, *now*."

He picked up a knife next to the sandwiches and came toward me without a word. Against every instinct I turned, showing him my back, feigning boredom and impatience. He wasn't going to kill me. After everything that had happened, even his part in bringing me here, it didn't make any sense to stab me to death in his boss' pristine kitchen. I knew all that, but still I was as tense as a rattlesnake until Luke slipped the knife between my hands and sliced away the zip tie with one deft movement. He turned me back around by the shoulders.

Looking around to avoid looking at him, I saw ample evidence of modern retrofitting over the bones of a kitchen that might have been upwards of a century old. Labor-saving appliances had been shoehorned in where possible, but most of the far wall was taken up with a massive hearth oven. The inside was blackened with soot, but it didn't look like a fire had burned in it for quite some time. "It's an ice box in here," I concluded.

"You know I'm on your side, don't you?" he asked at a whisper. "I'd never hurt you. I won't let them hurt you, either."

I massaged my wrists, still refusing to look up at him. "What does Marcel want with me?"

"I don't know."

"What *do* you know? Did you find Alice like you said you would, or was that just a lie to get me to the museum?"

"I thought I was finding Alice! Marcel called me right after you left and said he needed help with something, and I figured it had to do with Alice. He didn't tell me the something was you until we were halfway to the museum. I made him promise not to hurt you. Told him Camposanto would make trouble for him if he did. What else could I do?"

"You told him you don't give a crap about me," I mumbled.

"Come on. You don't believe that, do you?" Luke wheedled. He tapped me under the chin, trying to get me to look at him. I took a step backward, out of his reach.

"Is Alice here?" I demanded.

"No."

"Well then where is she? At least tell me if she's okay!"

"Keep your voice down," he urged, stepping closer. He looked down at the knife in his hand and backtracked, placing it on the butcher block before approaching me more cautiously.

"Do not come any closer," I hissed as he edged a half-step toward me.

"Anna, I am so sorry."

"Shut up about it. I don't care if you're sorry."

"Are you actually afraid of me?"

The honest answer was that I didn't know. When I didn't reply, he took a few steps toward me again. He reached for me and I twitched away, giving up more ground as I backed out of arm's reach. We both knew I wouldn't retreat a third time.

"Anna, I know you're scared. I swear I'll figure out how to get you out of this."

"There's the door," I said, nodding behind him at a door that presumably opened onto the back yard. "Get me out of here already."

"Just take it easy, okay? He'll catch us, and then we're both dead. The last thing we need is for Marcel to figure out that you've got me wrapped around your little finger."

"Is that so."

"Look, Giles is a jerk and David is a little weird, but Marcel is the one you want to watch out for. He treats me like a brother, but if he thinks for one second that I'm not one hundred and ten percent behind him, he'll leave me in a ditch. Whatever he's got planned for you, it's not good."

"Sounds like a great friend to have."

"I'm not sure how I'm going to get you out of here, but I know you're going to have to trust me for it to work."

"I don't have much choice, do I?"

"I'm glad you recognize that."

"Why are you helping me?"

"You know why."

I crossed my arms, turning away to hide my reaction. A couple more steps brought him close enough to slide his hand onto my cheek. I batted it away just as the back door flew open to admit an openly disgruntled Giles. He stopped in his tracks, glaring first at me, then at Luke, then at the half-made sandwiches. His mouth twisted into a grin.

"Rolling out the red carpet?" he asked Luke, leering at me as he stressed the last two words.

"You know, disgusting isn't a personality," I told him. Giles moved toward me and I reacted in kind, eager for another round now that my hands were free, but Luke stepped between us.

"You don't give a crap about her, huh?" Giles asked, still addressing Luke as though I were a spectating house cat. "Why don't you prove it?"

Staring at Luke's broad back, I saw some change come over him that stiffened his posture and made him even taller.

"You're pretty dense, aren't you?" Luke quipped, a smile in his voice.

"Do explain," Giles invited.

"The dumb bimbo followed me all the way from the States like a little lost puppy, and I'm gonna make the best of it. She's *mine*. You don't lay your filthy hands on her. Don't even *look* at her. Got it?"

"Whatever," Giles snorted.

He didn't look at me as he whisked past us and disappeared through the kitchen door. I spotted a straight-backed wooden chair next to the hearth, settled into it, and stared expectantly at Luke. He shook his head, momentarily lost for words.

"Sorry," he forced. He returned to the butcher block.

"Part of the show?" I asked acidly.

"I'm not enjoying this any more than you are."

"Oh, I wouldn't be too hasty."

He finished the sandwiches, sliced them in half diagonally, stacked them on a paper towel, and set them on the hearth next to me. I ignored the offering.

"Aren't you hungry?" he asked.

I smiled. "No. I'm thirsty."

"Oh, okay, right," Luke said, grabbing one of the sandwich halves and eating it in one bite. With his mouth full, he went on, "So you're going to take that personally. Fine. Just pretend you don't understand the position I'm in."

"Good grief, swallow before you talk."

From down the hall, Giles called, "He wants her back in the parlor!"

I watched Luke open a cabinet, locate a pint glass, and fill it with water from the sink. I accepted it from him, trying to look grateful, and warned, "If I get half a chance to blow this pop stand…"

"I know. He'd expect nothing less."

"Does he think this is the first time we've seen each other since New Mexico?" I asked.

"As far as I know."

"He doesn't know I was at the office building and your house?"

"I'm not a mind-reader, Anna."

"But you haven't *told* him—"

"No, of course not. I told him everything that happened in

the States, and then I turned down the job in August. He thinks you're just some FBI red shirt I got weirdly attached to."

Some FBI red shirt. I repeated this in my head several times, wondering what Marcel might want with such a person. I drew a blank, guzzled the water, and sighed, "Okay. Well… I guess I'm ready to go talk to him."

"All right. I'm going to take you back to the front room, throw you down on the couch, and leave you there. Marcel might ask me to bind your hands and feet again. If Giles is in there, he'll probably say something disgusting. I really can't stress enough what a monumental jerk he can be. But I guess you've figured that much out."

"How did you get mixed up with these guys anyway?"

"Long story. Now's not the time."

3

Saturday, December 26, 2020
London

Luke led me back the way we'd come with just as much finesse as advertised. As I fell back down onto the sofa, propelled there by a churlish shove, I stared holes into the rug. By recalling how it felt to hear him call me a dumb bimbo, it wasn't difficult to act as frightened and confused as I needed to.

Thankfully, Giles wasn't there to complicate the issue by turning my fear into anger. Once Luke stalked out, it was just Marcel and me in the sitting room. The fire was crackling away merrily, filling the small room with warmth. I didn't realize how cold I'd been until the heat started thawing me out; the odd shiver here and there really helped sell my miserable, confused act.

"Do you know why you're here?" he asked, not unkindly. I shook my head. "You must have some idea."

"Something to do with Luke, I guess," I mumbled to the floor.

"Something, yes. When he told me what happened in Colorado, how you found him, who you were, I thought it best to dig a little deeper. Imagine my surprise when I discovered who you really are, and for whom you're working. At first I thought it best to simply get rid of you, but I couldn't find the right person for the job. Ordinarily Luke would take care of it for me, but for some reason he has an aversion to the idea of killing you."

"Great."

"I had to ask myself why, when he's never hesitated in the past to do what I ask. What's so special about you?"

"Nothing," I mumbled.

"Demonstrably untrue. In any case, I thought of a better use for you, and here you are to be put to it. I'm telling you this to try to put you at ease. I don't want you causing any trouble, trying to escape for instance. There's really no need for histrionics. If you settle into the right mindset, you might actually be content here."

"For how long?"

"That remains to be seen."

I glanced at an ornate carriage clock on the mantle: 80 more minutes until the check-in, 140 before Jim could take action. There didn't seem to be any imminent threat. Marcel didn't even seem in a hurry to get information out of me.

Just to make noise, I said, "Alice stabbed your brother."

"She did. David will be fine."

"She sent me a message. That's why I went to the museum. Where is she?"

"Elsewhere."

"Please, just tell me if she's okay…"

"She's alive." When I started to ask for more detail, he cut across me with, "I didn't bring you here to talk about your roommate. I want to know why you were dispatched to Colorado to find Luke."

"To find him? I ran into him by accident."

"The odds of that are astronomical. I know the story you told him, how you were hiding in fear from your ex-husband with political ties in Washington, DC. I know how you manipulated him, and I've tried to undo some of your dirty work by informing him that you are an undercover FBI Agent. I worry he's too infatuated with you to care all that much."

"I'm starting to think you've got me mixed up with someone else."

"You must be burning with curiosity about why I went to such lengths to get you here. If we can abandon this tiresome pretense, maybe you'll find out."

"Maybe I'm not that curious."

"No, maybe not," he sighed. "It doesn't matter, really."

He stood and walked to the door, and I couldn't help but notice a slight stiffness to his movement, a very minor favoring of the right leg. I wondered if this were an injury or something more permanent, and then I wondered how Luke could be so afraid of someone so wholly unintimidating. Marcel opened the door to reveal Luke leaning against the doorframe. He turned and looked searchingly at me, making no effort to disguise his interest in the conversation he'd missed.

"What do you want me to do with her?" Luke asked.

"Try to get her to stay in her room. I expect she's going to be difficult about every little thing."

"You're not wrong," Luke assented. "Anna, come on."

He held his arm out as though to usher me from the room. I stood my ground, glaring mistrustfully at him for all of two seconds before I decided that I was, in fact, exhausted. Staying in "my" room didn't sound half bad. I passed Marcel and offered no resistance to Luke gripping me by the arm. I reminded myself I was supposed to be afraid of him, and with a sick feeling I realized the reminder was unnecessary. There actually was a little knot of fear in my chest as I felt his massive hand encircling my arm. I still wasn't sure whether to trust him.

Luke escorted me up a staircase in the foyer. As soon as we were blocked from view of the parlor doorway, I twisted out of his grasp. I was still too lost in thought to offer any more resistance as I followed him into a medium-sized bedroom just off the second floor landing.

He shut the door behind us but remained rooted to the carpet by the door while I wandered over to a window overlooking the driveway. The van was still there, looking homely and out-of-place on its backdrop of manicured lawn and decidedly British statuary. As far as I was concerned, there was nothing more to be said, nothing to do but plot my escape while outwardly waiting for Luke to make good on his promises.

He crossed the room to stand behind me. "You still angry at me?"

"No," I intoned automatically, not sure if I was angry or not. His hand slid onto the small of my back, fingers closing tentatively around the trailing ends of my hair.

"I swear to you, I had no idea——"

"I don't want to talk about it anymore," I snapped. "I don't want to be here."

He whispered, "I'll figure out what he wants. What to do. You need to trust me. You do trust me, don't you?"

I took long enough to answer, staring fixedly through the window all the while, that eventually no answer was needed. His hand fell away.

"You need some space. Just don't go anywhere, okay? Try to get some rest."

When the door shut behind him and a silence descended over the bedroom to confirm I was really alone, I reached out and tested the window latch. It was crusted in white paint, the whole window painted shut by the look of it. I turned and scanned the room, seeing another door I hadn't noticed before. I walked over and twisted the doorknob enough to verify it would open, then turned away from the temptation and saw something I wanted even more than a too-easy escape: a fireplace.

It crossed my mind that I could burn the house down. Instead, I knelt in front of the cold fireplace, started building a fire, and cheered myself with a mental image of Jim: He would be drumming his fingers nervously on his desk, staring at his phone, wondering if I'd call 45 minutes late again or miss the scheduled check-in altogether. He'd be sending the cavalry soon, probably some grunt from MI5 or a CIA spook who was skulking around nearby, and somehow I realized it wouldn't be all that difficult to find me.

I had very limited time, then, to figure out why Marcel Marchand had wanted me dead and why he'd changed his mind.

▼

The fire had warmed the room, and I was lolling boredly on the bed, when Luke came back to check on me. Nearly three hours had passed. It was more than enough time to wander outside, try to flee, and get torn apart by dogs several times over. I was a little annoyed to have been forgotten about for so long, even though I'd spent most of that time catching up on sleep. Luke's slightly neater hair, change of clothes, and subtle hint of cologne gave him away the moment he opened the door without knocking.

"You got to shower?" I asked, climbing eagerly to my feet. "Can I?"

"Uh. Sure. Later." He paused in the doorway, confused by my attitude adjustment. "Kind of surprising that you didn't make a break for it."

"Is it really that surprising, though? There's obviously no immediate danger here, and I'm curious."

"I'm glad you feel that way." He opened the bedroom door wider, revealing a handful of large, plastic shopping bags. He tossed the lot of it onto the bed. I upended one bag onto the bedspread while Luke explained, "Marcel wouldn't tell me how much I needed to buy, so I went with a week's worth. I trust milady is pleased."

I sorted through the brand new t-shirts and athletic leggings with mingled relief and uneasiness. It would be nice to change clothes, but a week? I wondered if Alice were being treated to such luxuries.

The second bag was full of bulky sweaters, and the third with two pairs of jeans, a pack of socks, and some underwear. I hooked a pair of underwear with one finger and read the tag.

"Small? For real?" I asked, tossing it onto the bed with a sigh. "They're all yours. Nothing to sleep in?"

"Sorry, the lingerie section of Tesco was closed."

I ignored the sarcasm and crossed my arms, looking over the offering as a whole. "Lots of blue," I said, mostly to myself.

"It's your favorite color, isn't it?"

I turned to face him. "Yes. But I've never told you that."

"I made an educated guess."

"A week?"

"Uneducated guess."

"You must've raised some eyebrows at the store, buying all this at once," I fished.

"Please. Most people aren't that interested in what other people are doing. So will these work? I can go back if you need me to."

"It's all great, thank you."

"Don't mention it. I have to go. Marcel wanted my help with another small—uh—project. I might not be back until tomorrow morning." He paused, then added, "It would be best if you stayed in this room while I'm gone."

I scanned the tidy little room: no books, no TV, no computer, not so much as a deck of cards. "What am I supposed to do?

Can I at least have a scratching post?"

"Don't be like that."

"Ugh," I growled, plopping down on the bed amidst the piles of new clothes. "Are you really trying to find out what's going on, or are you just stalling me?"

"I'm trying. Will you please try to trust me? I'm sticking my neck out for you, you know."

"I know."

"I'll be back as soon as I can. Please stay out of trouble."

"Is this something to do with Alice?" I asked hopefully.

"I don't know. Maybe."

"Well if you see her, tell her I'm sorry."

He nodded stiffly and left. I sorted and re-folded all the clothes he'd bought, picked out something to wear, and opened the door I'd tested earlier. I'd hoped it was the bathroom, but it turned out to be a second bedroom door, opening into a different hallway. I followed the hall around to the right, away from the stairs, and found a bathroom. It had no shower, only a large, old fashioned claw-foot tub.

Hoping I was alone in the house, or at least that no one would come looking for me for the rest of the day, I drew a very hot bath and settled in to soak and muse for an hour or more. A tray set across the old tub was stocked with travel-sized bath products and a tiny vase of miniature, fake roses. Given the impersonal nature of everything else I'd seen in the house, it seemed pretty likely this was a vacation home, maybe a rental.

Where were Marcel's dogs hiding, then? Did the house come with a kennel or barn for them to hang out in? I pictured

Marcel sitting in front of a bank of security cameras, remote in hand, waiting to open the kennel door and release the hounds the moment he spotted something amiss. The idea was absurd on its face. Maybe he had fabricated the dogs, trusting to fear to keep me in line. He didn't seem like a dog person to me. Then I recalled him ordering Giles to feed the dogs. Unless that was a euphemism, I had to conclude the Malinois were out there somewhere.

For the first time in too long, I wondered what Dude was up to. My faithful German Shepherd, goodest boy, girl's best friend. I didn't feel like a complete person without him by my side, hearing danger coming before I could, sitting on my feet when he sensed I was feeling down, and being so smart and adorable that the world didn't seem like such a bad place. I knew he missed me, but did he have any sense of time passing? Did he wake up every morning and think to himself, "Another day, and still no Anna. I'll look around the yard for her one more time."

For a few fevered moments I wondered if I could find a computer, log on to the website that allowed me to track Dude's subcutaneous GPS transmitter, and gain a little reassurance by seeing that he was safe and sound with my parents in Manchester, Texas. But I dismissed the idea, realizing that tiny payoff wasn't worth the risk of getting caught with a computer.

Someday, my parents would delight in relating all of the ways he demonstrated that he knew I was gone and wanted me to come back. He'd perk up when a car drove past. He'd look at them if they said my name. He'd insist on sleeping in the bed I'd vacated.

My heart broke all at once, amusement crashing suddenly and painfully into abject, raw sadness. I couldn't fight it, but at least I was alone and had no reason in the world to hide or rein in the sobs that racked my body.

I had abandoned my dog, my best friend, to come here, not knowing if I'd ever make it back. And for what? Tommy was dead. Finding out why, or who was responsible, or what the big picture really was, wouldn't change that. Even if it would do some good in the long run, I wasn't likely to put the pieces together here. Luke's world was completely separate from mine until Jim forced us together on a hunch and sent me down the rabbit hole. All I'd accomplished was getting embroiled in whatever the Marchands were doing—and getting Alice dragged into it along with me.

There was a link, though. I couldn't deny that. Marcel had sent Luke to Houston to kill Francisco Lira, a top dog in the Tres Islas Cartel, for a reason. I didn't know what the reason was, but there was still a thin shred of hope that finding out more about Marcel and his nefarious Frères Enterprises would lead me to actionable information about the cartel, maybe even about how Philip, Tommy, and I fit into that elusive big picture.

Sadly, I'd never successfully trained myself to be a big picture kind of person. I was a detail-loving, behind-the-scenes, simple intelligence analyzer. I hadn't joined the FBI to solve sweeping mysteries all on my own. I wanted only the pleasure of doing the grunt work exceptionally well and letting other people worry about the glory and politics of bringing down a cartel, stopping an assassination, or finding a kidnapped child.

So it was impractical to believe I could put the pieces together myself, but not at all out of my wheelhouse to simply assemble them for someone else's later use. I recited the facts as they currently presented themselves to me:

Approximately one year ago, my old boss, Philip Levin, told Tommy that Jim was working for the Tres Islas Cartel, and that I was guilty by association.

Tommy believed Francisco Lira was an FBI asset, also on Philip's word.

Someone told the TIC who Tommy and I really were.

Marcel sent Luke to Houston to kill Francisco Lira.

Luke killed Lira. February 15.

Philip tried to kill me in Dallas. September 4.

Marcel tried to hire Luke to kill me, and Luke refused. August 31?

Frères Enterprises was into some as yet undefined illegal activity.

Luke had a new target, and he wasn't going to tell me who.

Marcel didn't seem to want me dead anymore. Not yet, anyway.

I sank into the rapidly cooling water, repeating these purported facts and dates over and over and willing them to show me something useful, something I could act on. I stayed underwater for as long as I could, depriving my brain of oxygen, boiling everything down to the most basic, urgent realities.

Marcel didn't want me dead yet.

Luke had a new target.

4

Saturday, December 26 to
Sunday, December 27, 2020
London

I dried off in a fugue, wrapping my hair in a towel and my body in a comfortable leggings, t-shirt, and sweater combo. Since I'd carefully avoided promising Luke that I would stay in that boring room, I felt no compunction about continuing to explore the house. I needed to move, to let my mind wander while my feet did the same. I had to talk myself out of the insane conclusion I'd just reached.

Because if the only reason I was alive was to make it easier for Luke to kill Jim, I needed to be absolutely sure.

There were so many reasons why it couldn't be true. One, though it had the appeal of a tantalizing mystery, it wasn't the simplest answer. It was more than my characteristically colossal intuitive leap; it was a spacewalk.

Strike one for my insane theory. Two, in the grand scheme of things, Jim was nobody. Sure, he seemed to be quite wealthy and had a powerful position within the FBI, but he was wrapped up in investigating Philip. He cared nothing for the Marchand brothers and their Frères Enterprises, at least not that I could tell. He might have looked into them to help me out, but it all came back to Philip. Jim didn't even seem too interested in the Tres Islas Cartel beyond Philip's connection to them.

I called that strike two, though it wasn't as clear-cut as the first. Any number of my suppositions could be wildly off the mark there, especially given Jim's infatuation with depriving me of information.

Three, most significantly: Jim, Luke, and I were all in the United States at the same time for most of the year. For a few hours, we were probably in the same city. Why have Luke come to the UK, only to have me follow him here? Jim wasn't personally coming here to get me. He would if he had to, though, if for instance Marcel were to surreptitiously inform Jim that I was being held here, and that he was going to kill me if Jim didn't show up. The exact same way Alice had been used to get to me. Even so, it made more sense to keep Luke in the States, not elaborately tempt Jim across the Pond.

All of that depended on a very particular succession of events, chiefly that Luke knew before he left the States that Jim was his target in lieu of me.

What if Luke hadn't found out until after he was over here?

What if this whole, circuitous plan was Luke's idea?

Logistically, murdering an FBI Agent on his home turf

would be pretty difficult, right? Why go to the trouble, when Luke knew I was almost certainly on the way to London? In an unfamiliar country, with limited resources, distracted by worrying about me, Jim was a much softer target. Maybe my strike three was more of a home run.

My feet had carried me around the perimeter of the second floor via a single corridor that gave access to the outer rooms on my right and the inner rooms on my left. Most of the doors I tried to open were locked, but just as I spectacularly failed to disprove my own theory, I found a perfect room in which to pass the time until Luke's return.

The room was, as far as I could tell, directly above the parlor where I'd formally met Marcel. One wall was solid books from floor to ceiling, which spelled hours of reading for me. It too offered a stellar view of the front lawn and driveway, where I assumed Luke or anyone else would appear before coming into the house. I selected a book from the wall, scooted an old wing-backed chair next to the closest window, and settled in to pass some more time.

I only got up twice, once to venture on tiptoe to my bedroom to hang up my towel and fetch a blanket and socks when my wet hair and bare feet became too uncomfortable to ignore, and again to slip down to the kitchen to raid the fridge. Halfway through *Wuthering Heights*, swaddled cozily in the blanket and warmed by the afternoon sun, I drifted off to sleep.

▼

A car door slammed, shattering my sleep. I sat up, confused, and the book on my lap slid to the floor with a loud *clunk*. Night had fallen, and the only light came from headlights in the driveway. While my eyes were adjusting, the headlights flicked off and plunged the room into total blackout.

I didn't have to know what time it was, or who had slammed the door, to know I needed to get back to my bedroom immediately. I bundled the blanket and book into my arms and crept toward the door, which I couldn't see. I misjudged the size of the room and bumped nose-first into the interior wall. Rubbing my sore nose, I shuffled sideways until my free hand nudged the doorknob. Once I was in the hallway, there was enough ambient light that I could flit across the banister overlooking the foyer and slip silently into my bedroom.

Over the faint rustling of me remaking the bed, I heard muted voices down in the foyer. They were all male. I had almost let myself hope that Luke was bringing Alice back to the house from wherever she was being held.

I pushed *Wuthering Heights* under the bed, turned off the bedside lamp, and burrowed under the covers just as the bedroom door opened. Feigning innocent slumber, I listened while Luke (I hoped) moved around doing who knew what.

He left the bedroom and returned about five minutes later, his identity confirmed when the bed shuddered beneath me and he breathed an emphatic curse. "Stupid bed."

As he started to slide in next to me, I dropped the act and sat up, inviting, "Want to tell me what you're doing?"

"Uh… going to bed."

Though it was dark, I could imagine his expression. The suppressed smile in his voice was all I'd needed to hear.

"It's a big house, Luke."

"It's a big bed. That's why I chose this room."

"Then I'll go find another."

As I started to climb to my feet, he caught the tail end of my shirt and pulled me back, pleading, "Hey, come on. I'm not an idiot. I just want to keep an eye on you."

"Did Marcel tell you to?"

"He told me someone would."

"Ah." Though I yanked my shirt out of his hand, I settled back into bed. "So you're protecting me from the consequences of your duplicity, is that it?"

"Yes, exactly—I mean, no. What duplicity?"

I sighed expansively. "Forget it. Just shush so I can go back to sleep."

With all the smugness of someone who'd just won an argument, Luke made himself comfortable in the bed next to me. I was grateful for the foot and a half of buffer space he left, but he ruined the gesture almost immediately.

"You'll warm up to me eventually," he said.

"Mmhm," I hummed, not caring enough to argue.

I rolled over and laid one hand on his chest, feeling it rise and fall. While I thought about how to ask what he'd been doing this afternoon, I faded away into a deep, dreamless sleep.

▼

It was still dark when I woke up, and I leaned carefully away from Luke, who was still sound asleep, to grab my watch off the nightstand. It was nearly 3:00 in the morning. Twelve hours had passed since I had failed to check in with Jim. Whatever he planned to do about it, I knew it was already well underway. For so many reasons, I wished that weren't true.

Knowing there was no chance I could get back to sleep, I considered switching on the lamp to read, but I didn't want to wake Luke up. Instead, I eased out of bed and peeked into the hallway. It was slightly brighter than the bedroom, illuminated by ambient starlight, which was enough to see the outline of a wall outlet very close to the door. I got dressed and took the lamp, my pillow, and my book and set up shop right there in the hallway. For a while I read in complete peace and isolation, confident I couldn't possibly be bothering anyone or breaking any rules by sitting in the hallway.

At first I thought I was imagining the soft footfalls and rapid snuffling down the hall, so wrapped up in the story that the walls between fiction and reality were becoming permeable; but after a while I was goaded into looking down the hall to see if there really was something there. My eyes slowly, agonizingly discerned two bright spots in the shadowy end of the corridor, about a foot and a half off the floor, frozen in space. A chill settled over me. Were the dogs in the house? Did Marcel's Malinois militia patrol the corridors at night?

I was on the verge of diving for the bedroom door when rational thought prevailed. It was probably a dog, but it wasn't showing any sign of aggression, and it seemed to be alone. I set my book on the floor with slow, smooth movements and whispered, "Hello?"

As it edged into the halo of light formed by my lamp, I could see it was a smallish Belgian Malinois, probably a female, and she was alone. Her posture was skeptical, neither friendly nor aggressive. She reminded me a bit of Marcel, actually. Wondering if this were really happening or if I was having a vivid dream, I held my hand out toward her. The initial shock of seeing her eyes scoping me out through the darkness had already faded, smothered by a natural attraction and admiration. I wasn't quite smart enough to be afraid of dogs, even those I knew to be dangerous.

I *was* smart enough to look behind me, at the other end of the hall, to see if I was being flanked. I couldn't see anything. When I turned back to the female, she had come close enough to sniff delicately at the tips of my outstretched fingers.

"Sitz," I said, faking some authority. She obeyed with enthusiasm, settling onto her haunches with rigid posture and awaiting my next command.

"Platz."

She shimmied to the ground, and her tail started to wag.

"Komm." She cocked an ear at me but didn't move, and I tried the more traditional, "Hier."

She got up, sat beside me, and then curled up next to me as though it were the most natural thing in the world. I let her lick my fingers a bit before risking a careful pat to the head, not wanting to startle her. I'd never been this close to a Malinois. She seemed to vibrate with energy, even as she stretched out along my leg and allowed me to rub her belly.

"Well, this is weird," I said.

I went back to my book with a bemused smile, still halfway convinced I was asleep in bed, dreaming. Her breathing became slow and shallow as she drifted to sleep. Gradually the darkness outside my lamplight began to dissipate as dawn broke, and I heard someone else stirring down the hall in the direction the dog had come. She perked up at the sound, her ears turning like satellites.

Her tail began to thump against the thick carpet just before Marcel came around the corner and said, "There you are, you silly creature."

She leapt up and trotted right to him, accepting a placid pat on the head.

"Some hellhound you've got there," I quipped.

"She is more of a pet than the others," he admitted. "I hope she didn't frighten you."

I laughed. "For about half a second."

"She has figured out how to open doors, much to my chagrin. Why are you sitting in the hallway?"

"I didn't want to wake Luke up."

"May I join you for a moment?"

"Uh… sure."

He eased to the floor with some difficulty, leaning against the opposite wall and assessing me with an unabashed stare. The dog lay down with her head on his bum leg and was soon asleep again.

Finally he said, "You and Luke seem to have resolved your differences."

"Thanks for noticing."

"Are you still determined to pretend as though you're not at all curious about why you're here?"

"All I want to know is where Alice is."

"If you help me with something this evening, I will let you talk to her."

"Help you?" I frowned. "How?"

"I'm having some guests over for a business meeting. They are all from Sardinia, and most speak only Italian. I need a translator."

"Oh, boy."

"You can do this, can't you?"

"Sure, I can do it. It's just… I mean, we're talking about mafiosos, right?"

"I suppose you could call them that."

"My organized crime dance card is full."

"You think you will overhear something you aren't meant to hear, and that it will endanger your life. Correct?"

"Duh."

"Then let me explain what I mean by 'translator.' We have agreed to conduct the meeting in English, because I lack the ability to speak or understand Italian. They will talk among themselves in Italian. I want to hear what they don't want me to hear. They will believe you understand French only."

Oy, this again. I saw the catch immediately and asked, "Then why will I even be there?"

"You will serve drinks and…" He paused to think, concluding, "Look nice."

"Ugh." I leaned back against the wall, bumping my head.

Marcel took that for a yes and said, "I apologize. I know I'm putting you in a demeaning position."

"You think?"

"I am not sorry enough to retract the request."

"Just tell me this isn't why you kidnapped Alice."

"It's merely a matter of convenient utility, I assure you."

I asked, "Do I have to wear a French maid costume?"

He came so close to laughing at this that I counted it. "I think normal attire will suffice. You will, however, have to mix drinks. Are you familiar with mixology?"

I snorted at the way he'd phrased the question. "I've studied it informally."

"Good. Please be ready and meet me in the foyer at nine o'clock. How you fill your time between now and then is of no concern to me," he concluded, his gaze flicking meaningfully to the wall I was leaning against, behind which Luke still slept. "I hope you will give Luke no reason to be concerned for your wellbeing."

I rolled my eyes and asked, "You mean no additional reasons?"

"Have it your own way," he said dismissively, climbing to his feet to go.

As he made for the stairs, the dog faithfully tagging along, I asked, "What's her name?"

"Penelope."

"Penelope the Bloodthirsty Maneater," I whispered to myself, trying it out. "Nope."

5

Sunday, December 27, 2020
London

I carried my lamp et cetera back to the bedroom to find Luke sitting up in bed, scrolling through his phone. Since he hadn't come to find me, I was surprised to find him awake at all.

"Have a good chat with Marcel?" he asked, answering my unspoken question.

"Define 'good'."

"What did he want?"

I sat down on the bed and rehashed the conversation pretty much word for word, concluding with, "I have to say, I didn't see that coming."

"You'll need something to wear. Guess I'm going shopping again."

"This is asinine," I complained.

"Marcel must think it's pretty important."

"Are you sure he doesn't understand Italian? He's not just…

testing me, or something?"

"Now *that* would be asinine."

Luke set out on this new mission right away, no doubt to continue to avoid an explanation of his activities yesterday. He left me with my book for entertainment but did not quiz me about where I'd gotten it or whether I had really kept to the bedroom the whole time he was gone yesterday. I left the bedroom door open, hoping for another visit from Penelope, and once again lost myself in the moors.

Three hours later, he found me exactly where he'd left me, working on a completely different book. I thought I detected a hint of irritation as he watched me bookmark my place in the Elizabeth George mystery and stack it on top of *Wuthering Heights*, but he made no comment. He pulled something inky black from one of the shopping bags he carried and unfurled it.

"How's this?"

"Oh, that's nice," I announced, grabbing it out of his hands. "You're a man of many talents."

He grinned. "Try it on for me."

Ignoring his true intention, I checked the tag and said, "It's the right size."

Luke slid the dress out of my hands. "What I meant was, I'd like to see you in it. I won't be there tonight, so…"

"What are you getting at, really?" I demanded. "I want you to say what you're really asking for so we can both hear how ludicrous it sounds."

"Hey, I—"

"I mean, what do you expect me to do? Your boss is holding

me here against my will. I don't even know if he plans to let me *live* and you're actually—"

"No, I'm not *actually* anything," he said hotly, tossing the dress on the bed. The slick fabric clung to the blanket for a moment before sliding down into a shiny, black pile at the foot of the bed. He stared at it, then turned to me and said more calmly, "I just—I know I'm not going to let anything happen to you. I'm glad you're here, and I want to make the most of it."

"Yeah, you seemed super happy to see me when I showed up," I shot back.

"I still thought Marcel wanted you dead, so excuse me for thinking it was more important to get you out of there than to talk about our feelings."

"Okay! Well. That… makes a lot of sense, so. I guess… I can be over it."

Unimpressed by my lukewarm forgiveness, he crossed his arms and waited for me to go on. I didn't have anything else to say, so I stepped closer to him, uncrossed his arms, and hugged him. His answering embrace was at once terrifying and reassuring, his sheer size making me feel tiny. Suddenly I knew he was telling the truth about at least one thing: He wasn't going to let anything happen to me.

Luke took a deep breath. I expected something profound to follow and almost laughed when he asked, "Do you like cars?"

I wriggled partway out of his arms to look up at him. "They have their moments. Why?"

"Marcel's got this hotrod he never drives, needs some work. Want to help?"

As odd as the request was, I still had several hours to kill before Marcel's sinister soiree and no idea how to kill them. I agreed, and Luke led me out of the house to a spacious, detached garage. Once inside, I was stunned to find myself looking at a cherry red, American muscle car—a Dodge Challenger. Luke patted it affectionately, smiling at my open-mouthed reaction.

"This is a Demon," I breathed, as though that were news to him.

"I know."

"Can I drive it?"

"What do you think?"

"I think I'm gonna steal this car," I whispered.

"Hey, whoa. Don't joke about that. This is Marcel's baby."

"A girl can dream."

"Girls dream about unicorns and cupcakes. You're not a girl, you're a wildcat."

"I think that's the nicest thing anyone's ever said to me." I walked along the Demon's body, fingers trailing over it, and stopped in front of it to take in the view. I said, "At least start it up."

"Anna, calm down. We're just changing the brakes."

I thought he was messing with me, until I found myself playing mechanic's assistant while Luke did just that. After two hours, one minor wound, all of the swear words, and lots of greasy fingerprints hastily wiped off the Demon's blazing paint job, we were finished. I realized I'd been so absorbed in the task I'd completely forgotten to quiz Luke about Alice. Before I could start in, Marcel appeared just as Luke was removing the last jack.

"Any issues?" Marcel asked, looking over the car. I saw a ghost of the first actual emotion Marcel had exhibited so far: pride.

"Nothing," Luke answered. "You up for seating them?"

"If I can take Anna with me," he answered. I was surprised, but Luke looked downright distressed.

"You want to take Anna?" he asked hesitantly, glancing at me. "Why?"

"To thank her for agreeing to help me tonight. Are you familiar with the procedure, Anna?"

I nodded, torn between sympathetic fear at Luke's reaction and a burning ache to get inside that car. I didn't, strictly speaking, know what seating meant, but from the context it obviously had something to do with the new brakes. I didn't care if Marcel drove us off a cliff, as long as he opened up the Demon before he did it.

"See, Luke, she wants to come. Go wash your hands."

I dashed back to the house to comply, groaning as the hot water tap took its sweet time heating up enough to wash away the grease. When I got back to the garage, Luke was putting away the tools we'd used, looking tense. I climbed into the passenger seat of the Demon and strapped in.

"Why doesn't he want me to go with you?" I asked Marcel, figuring there was no way to deny such an obvious reaction.

"Just between you and me, I don't think he considers me a very skilled driver."

My bland half-answer was completely drowned out by a dragon roar, deafening within the enclosed garage. I laughed with pure exuberance, and I couldn't even hear myself. Once he'd backed out of the garage and started down the gravel driveway, the roar faded enough that conversation was possible.

"We'll have to take it slow on this road, of course," Marcel explained. "The gravel is murder on the paint job."

"Mhm," I hummed, not sure how else to respond.

Marcel didn't require any more from me, at least until we made it to a paved, two-lane highway. He came to a stop, looked both directions, and confirmed there were no cars coming. He waited anyway, for what I had no idea.

He asked, "Why is it, do you think, that Luke is lying to me about you?"

Oh, no. I turned in my seat to face him, forcing myself to appear curious rather than defensive. "I don't know," I said, making it a little easier on myself by starting with the truth. I really had no idea why Luke was risking so much for me. "What is he lying to you about?"

"He wants me to believe that until yesterday, the last time he saw you was at some casino in Mexico."

"New Mexico. And unless I'm missing something, that is the last time we saw each other."

Marcel watched a semi-truck approaching from the left, asking quietly, "Are you certain of that?"

"Well, I don't know if he's seen me. But I haven't seen him."

He nodded, as though accepting my answer. Suddenly, when the truck was so close I could hear it over the roar of the engine, Marcel accelerated wildly into a right turn and put us directly in the path of the oncoming truck. The tires spun for an agonizing two seconds while the truck, horn blaring, barreled down on us; then with a gut-wrenching lurch, we shot forward. I watched the truck go from an imminent, deadly rear-end collision to a speck in the side view mirror.

"Luke was wrong," I said through a nervous laugh. "You're pretty good at this."

"I think we just got lucky," he replied, so boredly that I wondered if he were actually missing his adrenal glands.

After thirty seconds or so with the speedometer tickling 200 kilometers per hour, he slammed on the brakes. Unprepared for the sudden deceleration, I was flung forward so hard my forehead hit the dashboard. It wasn't a hard hit, but I got the message all the same.

"I'm not lying to you," I groaned, rubbing my forehead.

"So you didn't see him at my office building in London on Christmas Day?"

"Guess we missed each other," I said, flinching as the semi-truck caught up to us and blew past us on the right, horn still blaring. Marcel flipped him off.

"What were you doing there?" he asked.

"I was looking for Luke."

"How did you know he'd be there?"

"I didn't. I guessed."

"How?"

"Marcel, you already know I work for the FBI. We're pretty good at finding people."

He accelerated again, plateauing at a restrained 145 kilometers per hour. In very little time, we were stuck behind the truck, the driver of which probably thought Marcel was a madman. I had to agree.

His next question was, "Are you working for James Camposanto?"

He already knew I had some kind of connection to Jim. It was in the dossier Luke read to me at his house. The house where I was supposed to have never been.

"I can't answer that," I tried. "You know what classified information is, don't you?"

"Intimately. So I'm to believe that you came all the way to London just to pursue a man who, in his own words, doesn't give a crap about you?"

He had me there. I watched the speedometer tick up over 170 and tried to prepare myself a little better for the next brake check as we passed the semi.

I grumbled, "He's not the man I thought he was."

The tail end of my words was lost in a gasp as he slammed on the brakes again. We lurched to a stop just over the crest of a small hill, blocked from view by anyone coming over behind us. I watched the mirror anxiously.

Desperate to get moving again, I tried a new angle. "You already know I know James Camposanto. For your edification, he's been sexually harassing me for over a year. Even knowing what a scumbag Luke can be, I'd still come over here to get away from him."

"Do you know how to do a J-turn?" Marcel asked, from left field.

"In theory."

"Neither do I. Let's give it a try, shall we?"

He threw the Challenger in reverse, slammed on the gas, and got it up to a 100 before wrenching the wheel around. My heart jumped into my mouth as we spun, seemingly out of control. As soon as we were facing the other way, he shifted back into gear and hit the accelerator again. The whole car shook as the big rig blew past us once more, the driver gesticulating his anger through an open window. We shot back toward where we started, and I couldn't contain a whoop of elation.

"I'm sorry, I know you're trying to scare me," I said, grinning from ear to ear. "But this is way too much fun."

"You are a strange woman, Anna. Hold on, one more stop."

We ground to a halt, then started again at a perfectly reasonable speed. Marcel turned off onto the gravel road, looking pleased with himself.

"Luke is incredibly handy to have around," he said offhand as he pulled into the garage where the man in question was waiting. "He can figure out how to do anything."

What was that? Some kind of clue? The intelligence analyst in me couldn't keep from asking, "How long have you known him?"

"Long enough to know when he's hiding something from me," he dodged. He looked me over and added tonelessly, "It's very hurtful."

"I'm not going to figure it out for you," I said.

He sighed. "Well, I can't say I'm surprised. I find that women are irrationally eager to please him."

Now he was trying to make me jealous. I hid my contempt,

answering carelessly, "Yeah, he's a stud."

"Sure." He opened his door, started to climb out, and reminded me, "Nine o'clock, don't be late. And cover up that red mark on your forehead."

I touched my forehead gingerly, felt nothing, and flipped down the visor to look in the mirror. I saw a quarter-sized, red spot right in the center of my forehead that would probably fade in a couple of hours. I was gripped by an insane urge to jump into the driver's seat and take off. Marcel had dropped the key fob into one of the cupholders as though goading me to do it. I could do it.

I closed the visor and locked eyes with Luke, who was standing in front of the Demon with his arms crossed. He seemed to be reading my mind, and he shook his head. Heaving a sigh of regret, I got out of the car.

"What happened there?" he asked, his gaze focused just above my eyes.

"Just a little demon bite." I grinned. "I might have lied about knowing what 'seating' meant."

"What did he want? Did he ask you anything?"

"Oh, no," I held up both hands as though to stop an attack. "You two need couple's therapy. I'm not getting in the middle."

"This isn't a joke, Anna," he pled, lowering his voice. "You're obviously not afraid of him, because you don't know him. I need to know what he asked you about."

"If I tell you, you'll just be weird about it, and then he'll know I told you, and that will give legitimacy to his suspicion."

"That's some baloney."

"I'm telling you, if you're so concerned with provoking suspicion, the last thing we need to be doing is comparing notes."

He pointed a maledicting finger at my nose. "You're infuriating."

"So I've been told. What's for lunch?"

"… We just ate breakfast."

"True," I mused, wandering out of the garage toward the house. He followed, and I suggested, "Maybe we could work up an appetite."

"Oh yeah?"

"I do miss our training sessions. I wanted to take jujitsu classes when I was staying in Dallas, but Jim wouldn't let me."

"Why's that?" he asked with poorly feigned disinterest. He was leading me now, back into the house via the kitchen. I assumed he had some specific destination in mind.

"After Philip tried to whack me, he decided I should lay low. It was a grueling few months of boredom."

"And he was watching over you that whole time?"

"Like a hawk. When he wasn't busy trying to find you."

Luke fell silent, leading me up the stairs to the third floor, which I hadn't explored at all yet.

"This house is massive," I said, just to break the silence.

He stopped in front of a door with a brass nameplate affixed to it, reminiscent of an old hotel. The plate read 'Gymnasium'. Rather than opening the door, he leveled a probing glare at me.

"That dossier said you had a romantic relationship with Camposanto."

"Yes, I remember."

"Do you?"

"No."

"Did you?"

"It's crossed my mind. Obviously, I have a weakness for tall men who lie a lot. Why are you interrogating me about this all of a sudden?"

His serious expression disappeared in a careless shrug. "No particular reason."

He finally opened the door to reveal a huge, open room with floor-to-ceiling mirrors covering most of the walls. Mats covered the floor, and around the perimeter sat exercise machines, weight sets, and random fitness equipment that looked mostly unused. I slipped off my sweater, shoes, and socks and walked into the center of the room, rotating on the spot.

"This is grand," I breathed.

"I found it last night after you fell asleep."

I walked over to a shelf in the corner loaded with basic sparring equipment and began sorting through it. A yard-long, foam-padded stick caught my eye. I grabbed it and rounded on Luke.

"Let's see how much you remember," I challenged, twirling the stick threateningly.

He smirked, clearly unimpressed, and I slashed the stick horizontally, aiming for his right ribs. He blocked the blow but failed to capture the weapon.

"Simultaneous defense and offense," I reminded him.

I swung again, this time arcing overhead to bring the stick

down on his clavicle. He got one hand around the stick and tried to yank it away from me. I held on, using the momentum to crash into him, and twisted the stick out of his hand while he regained his balance. I whacked him on the thigh just to see if it would annoy him. He made a grab for the stick again, missed, and started bearing down on me. I jabbed at him with the stick, he batted it aside, and suddenly I found myself on the mat with him in my guard. The stick rolled away out of reach.

"Let's see how much *you* remember," he said.

In my defense, jujitsu is significantly more technical than Krav Maga, a true martial art against my 'rules are for dead losers' street fighting. I only recalled basic concepts, like keeping my elbows in and using my arms to maintain but not create distance. It wasn't enough to save myself from six submissions in a row, most of them accomplished in less than ten seconds.

Totally winded from the feeble and ineffective defenses I'd tried, I stayed down after the sixth defeat, sucking in air. Luke sat up next to me, flushed with victory.

"So, nothing," he concluded.

"I kicked Philip's narrow butt, remember?"

"True, that was a legitimate win. I'm afraid I can't confer a yellow belt on that basis alone, though."

"Bummer."

I lunged for the discarded stick, only to be pushed back down onto the mat. For once I saw what he was doing before he did it as he pushed my legs away and tried to lock in a side control. I shifted my hips so I was facing him again and planted my feet on his hips to push myself away from him. As he lunged on his knees toward me, I scrambled to my feet, got behind him, and latched onto his back. While I tried to remember what to do next, he flipped me over, pinning me to the mat with one hand twisted into my hair, preventing me from moving my head at all. I glared up at the ceiling, out of breath again.

"That was pretty good," he gasped. "You almost had me."

"Let go of my hair, that hurts," I snarled.

His hand loosened a bit, but not enough for me to move. He pressed his lips to my neck, and I buried my face in his hair. The smell of sweat, cologne, and automotive grease was maddening. I took two handfuls of his hair and pulled him off my neck so I could kiss him.

"You're just trying to keep me distracted," I accused against his lips. I felt him smile.

"Yep. It's way easier than I thought it'd be."

I groaned in reply, pulling him closer.

6

Sunday, December 27, 2020
London

A terse cough from the doorway brought us both back to reality. Luke looked up, and I craned my head backward to see Giles in the doorway. Even upside down, there was no mistaking his derision.

"If you could stop dumpster diving for five minutes, maybe you'd like to come see David. He just got back from the hospital."

He was speaking only to Luke, who answered by climbing to his feet. He held out one hand to help me up. I turned to give Giles a piece of my mind for interrupting us, but he had already left.

"I *hate* that guy," I mumbled.

"I think the feeling is mutual. You want to wait here?"

My eyes fell on a heavy bag hanging from a hook in one corner of the room. "Yeah."

Luke left, and I rooted around the gym to find hand

wraps and gloves. My search came up empty, so I decided to bare-knuckle it. What the heck. Giles' 'dumpster diving' comment had really gotten to me. My first warm-up strikes at the bag revealed it to be unusually hard, probably because it had hardly ever been used. Even though it hurt, I started wailing on the heavy bag with every ounce of pent up energy, anger, and anxiety in my body.

The heart-to-heart, the grease monkey routine, the sparring... Luke was deliberately keeping me busy and distracted. He wasn't even denying it. I knew why, and it made me see red. Would it really kill him to drop me some hint about Alice? Was he so afraid of Marcel he couldn't even tell me if she were alive or dead?

I worked up such a sweat that my t-shirt was clinging uncomfortably to my torso, my hair limp with sweat. After another fifteen minutes or so, I was so gassed that I had to stop. I clasped my hands together and rested them on top of my head, the better to breathe deeply, and realized I had a small audience.

Luke was leaning against the doorframe next to a vaguely familiar man who could only be David. I caught Luke's eye and he smiled, eyes glinting with unmistakable pride.

"You must be David," I said in French, when it was clear no one else was going to speak up.

"Yes, and despite the neck wound, I feel like a very lucky man suddenly."

"How's that?"

"You weren't home on Christmas Day."

"Ah, right," I grimaced, my gaze drawn to the gauze bandage on his neck. "Sorry about that. Alice was just defending herself."

"Very adeptly, too. No hard feelings. I must learn to be more careful."

"Your brother rang my bell pretty good for it. Twice."

"I'm told he also considered shooting you in the knee. Nonsensical behavior, when you are not the one who stabbed me in the neck."

I favored him with a smile. "I agree completely."

"I was going to go visit the dogs, if the two of you would like to join me," he offered. "I'm desperate for fresh air after that wretched English hospital."

A few minutes later, I was cooling down rapidly in the overcast, December afternoon as we passed the garage and followed David into the shade of the woods that surrounded the house on all sides. I did want to see the dogs, for several reasons, but I knew what this was: another distraction.

As we picked our way along the hint of a path through the loam, David explained, "This was of course not on the property when we acquired it. It had to be constructed hastily, since the dogs were all living in the house until they had an enclosure of their own. It was bedlam, as you can imagine."

I heard growls and barks ahead, and soon a towering, chicken-wire fence loomed up out of the forest in front of us.

"It has to be twelve feet high to contain them," David remarked. "Even so, one of them keeps getting out. They're such devilishly clever animals. Jax knows how to climb the fence."

I was reminded of a certain scene from *Jurassic Park*, suddenly feeling a little foolish for being out here unprotected. I couldn't see any dogs within the enclosure, though thick trees and bushes blocked most of it from view. David picked up on my uneasiness right away.

"Marcel has allowed you to believe these dogs are trained killers, hasn't he?"

"He heavily implied it."

"He's just trying to scare you. They're people-pleasers at heart." He whistled sharply, and seven Belgian Malinois materialized out of the trees to sit in a perfect row a yard from the fence.

"Looks like Jax got out," Luke said.

"No, he's there." David pointed to the large male on the far right. "Penelope is missing. She's probably still in the house. Do you want to go inside with them?"

I glanced at Luke, hoping his expression would give me some clue as to whether I were about to become dog food. He looked relaxed enough, so I nodded. "Lead the way."

We spent nearly an hour with the dogs while David put them all through their paces, half to show off and half to make up for some of the time he'd spent away. Apparently Marcel cared only for Penelope, and Giles didn't give a rat's fart about any of them, so they'd been pretty bored while David was in the hospital.

I felt bad for the beautiful dogs, hidden away back there with almost no human interaction, but they seemed happy enough. Two full acres were enclosed for their use, and they had a covered shelter, a massive water trough, and even an obstacle course to clown around on. They seemed to have settled on David as their alpha, but they were just as happy to take commands from Luke or me. I wondered if they'd remember they liked me when they stood between me and escape, if it came to that.

After the car repair, sparring, and tramp through the woods, I was feeling decidedly grimy when we arrived back at the house. Another hour-long bath took care of that, but I was so sleepy afterward that the hollow ache in my stomach wasn't enough to coax me down to the kitchen to eat dinner. I curled up in bed and asked Luke to wake me up at 7:30 so I could get ready for the Sardinians.

At 8:58 p.m., I was dutifully waiting in the foyer as instructed. Unfortunately, Marcel didn't show up until ten after nine, by which time I was sitting on the bottom stair, seriously regretting my choice of footwear. I stood up when I saw him, towering several inches over him in the stilettoes Luke had purchased to go with my dress.

"I apologize for my lateness," he said, eyes sweeping over me to rest on my hands, of all places. Sharply, he asked, "What've you done to your hands?"

"Oh, it's nothing," I dodged, clasping them behind my back to hide my raw, red knuckles. "I just went a little too hard on the heavy bag."

His eyes narrowed in annoyance. "Wait here a moment."

He disappeared back the way he'd come, returning a few minutes later with something black bundled into his left hand. He passed it to me. I unfolded a pair of soft, cotton gloves of the sort I imagined all the waiters wore on the *Titanic*.

"This seems… silly," I frowned, slipping the gloves on

nonetheless.

"You are supposed to be a disarming distraction, not an undercover UFC fighter," he groused.

"Sorry."

"There are five men coming. Presumably one or two will be unable to resist putting their hands on you. Please do not embarrass me."

"Consider me the cover girl for feminine submissiveness," I said, my clenched jaw somewhat undermining my words.

He narrowed his eyes at me again. I could tell I was making him question the wisdom of inviting me to join them in the first place. "I wouldn't go that far. Come with me. You need to familiarize yourself with the dining room before they get here."

He led me to a room off the foyer, where a long wooden table was gleaming beneath a horrifying, Rococo-style chandelier. Opposite the room from the entry doors, another pair of leaded glass doors opened onto a small courtyard. To the right of these stood an ornate dry bar stocked with a couple dozen liquor and wine bottles. I made a beeline for it and, without bothering to ask Marcel's leave, I poured myself a bourbon. I locked eyes with him over the rim as I took the first sip, enjoying his blatant disapproval.

"What?" I asked. "You expect me to do this stone cold sober?"

"How silly of me. At least pour me one, too."

Over the next ten minutes or so, Giles and David wandered in. The former smirked at me.

"Marcel, who is this?" he asked. "Hired entertainment for

the evening?"

Marcel ignored him, and I asked sweetly, "What do you want to drink? Bleach?"

At Marcel's request, we both found the fortitude to feign civility once the guests arrived, though it was a frosty sort of civility. David showed them in, and as they took seats around the table I caught a handful of glances ranging from appreciative to downright hostile. Marcel introduced his brothers in English, then explained why I was there while I pretended to ignore him.

Of the five guests assembled, the oldest, a compact little man in his mid-sixties with implausibly black, thinning hair, seemed to be in charge. He introduced his cadre, revealing his English to be markedly less proficient than Marcel's.

"We are not told this woman will be here," he said, studiously ignoring me. "I do not like."

"I can send her away if you like," Marcel said without interest. "But at least let her make you all a drink first."

"Let her stay, she's nice to look at," one of the younger men piped up, looking me up and down with frank enjoyment. The older man, Anthony, had introduced him as Anthony as well. I assumed they were father and son. I couldn't very well ignore his wolfish look, but I only smiled vaguely at him. "Doesn't she talk?" he demanded.

"She only speaks French," Marcel answered. Rigid postures around the table relaxed.

The younger Anthony waved me over and asked in very broken French, "How about a glass of merlot, cherie?"

"Yes, sir," I intoned. As I turned back to the dry bar, the

others began hurling drink orders at him to convey to me in French. I met Marcel's eyes again and tried to tell him, without words, not to worry; I wasn't thick enough to miss the signal that I shouldn't attempt any asides to him in French. He seemed to understand.

Two glasses of merlot, two vodka tonics, one straight gin, and a refill of bourbon for Giles later, I was out of things to do. The Italians showed every sign of being ready to get down to business, but it was clear their leader wasn't willing to talk shop with me hanging around. The younger Anthony waved me over again.

With a wink at the older man, he asked me a vile question that should have earned him two missing front teeth and a mouth full of blood. He'd asked it in Italian, and I turned en-quiringly to Marcel, who shrugged.

I shook my head slowly at Anthony. Sticking to French and a neutral tone, I said, "I'm sorry, I don't understand you. If you don't like the merlot, I can go to the cellar and find something else."

"I'd rather tie you up in the cellar and eat you alive," he shot back in English. David hissed quietly at him, but otherwise none of the Marchands voiced a word of protest.

The younger Anthony turned to his father and said, "See, she doesn't understand anything. Don't be such a stick in the mud." When the elder Anthony said nothing, the younger patted the arm of his chair and asked me in French, "Will you sit here and keep me company?"

At a terse nod from Marcel, I settled onto the arm of the chair and looked benignly down at Anthony, imagining how good it would feel to jam my thumbs up to the knuckle in his eye sockets. He grinned back at me and rested his left hand on my knee.

"Now this is a business meeting," he announced with delight.

"We can move on now?" the elder Anthony asked, addressing the question to Marcel.

"If everyone is happy, I believe we can," Marcel responded. He spared young Anthony a disdainful glance that didn't look at all affected and then proceeded to ignore him. The next words out of his mouth were such a shock that I might have toppled off the chair, if Anthony hadn't helpfully distracted me by sliding my dress up a couple inches.

"My contact told me you have a steady stream of unaccompanied women and children arriving from North Africa, as many as a dozen per week. Am I misinformed?"

"Is right," old Anthony replied casually, as though discussing the importation of nothing more controversial than Persian rugs. "The ones that are not being stopped at Sardinia or Malta do much come ashore between Marsala and Modica. I have men pick them up and bring to my facility in Palermo. To get them out of Italy is not easy, but if you think you can put them into the United States, I take the risk."

They bandied back and forth for well over two hours about logistics: numbers, division of labor, expectations, profits, risks, on and on while I periodically staved off Anthony's wandering hands. Thankfully, after the first thirty minutes, they all needed refills and I was able to get up. Once that was done, Marcel insisted that I perch on the arm of his chair instead. Marcel laid one arm across my legs and stared at Anthony as though begging him to argue about it; he wisely chose not to. I continued to get up every half hour or so, and each time I refilled their drinks it caused a break in the conversation in which the Sardinians consulted one another in their native tongue.

As Marcel no doubt hoped, they revealed far too much with these asides. They weren't as sure about the numbers as they claimed to be; their documents guy, someone either named Cagliari or living in Cagliari, was becoming unreliable; they expected a raid by the Guardia di Finanza or Guardia Costiera any day now, which would shut them down for several months at least. Several of them referred repeatedly to a man named Paolo Barbato as though he had unexpectedly missed this meeting, and his absence was being felt. Old Anthony looked sour every time the name came up.

When the meeting finally wrapped up with an agreement to meet again in a month, my feet were screaming in protest at those cursed stiletto heels. I began collecting empty glasses as the men filed out of the room, wondering how soon I could get away with taking off my shoes. A call from young Anthony interrupted my chore.

"Cherie, have you ever been inside a Lamborghini?"

He seemed incapable of letting Marcel have the last word. I shook my head, feeling eager despite my revulsion for him. "No, why?" I asked.

"Would you like to?" he cajoled, gesturing for me to follow him outside.

"Sure," I shrugged, trailing after him. At the front door, Marcel caught me by the arm and yanked me back into the foyer.

"Go clean up," he snapped. Turning to Anthony, he said in a low voice to the exclusion of the others, "Speak to her again, and you can explain to your father why we no longer have an arrangement."

Totally unabashed, Anthony retorted, "I'm doing you a favor. She's too much woman for you anyway. I'll make it an even trade: the Lambo for the lady."

I didn't hear the rest of the exchange as I returned to the dining room to finish tidying up. I was carefully piling all the glasses onto a tray to take to the kitchen when Marcel returned. The rumble of the supercar driving away made it clear I could speak freely now, but I just stared at him. Now that all the excitement had died down, I felt nothing but rage, rendering me temporarily incapable of speech.

Unimpressed by my livid expression, Marcel said quietly, "I have to admit, I really wanted that Lamborghini. Only deep affection for Luke and a perverse fondness for American-made cars convinced me to turn him down."

On its own accord, my right hand closed around an empty crystal tumbler. Marcel wouldn't be so smug with a gushing head wound. I knew I could throw it hard and accurately enough, but then what would happen? Could I dispose of Giles and David with nothing but my bare hands and raw fury and still have enough juice left to take on Luke, if he were so inclined? I let the tumbler clatter to the tray.

"You should've taken him up on it," I hissed, brushing past

him to carry the tray to the kitchen.

I knew now beyond the shadow of a doubt that I was not meant to survive this little episode. I knew more than I should, even discounting the minor detail of my employer being arguably the most powerful law enforcement agency in the world. This so-called affection for Luke wouldn't save me. I had to focus on getting out of there, with or without Luke's help.

David found me in the kitchen, where I was washing the used glasses just for something to occupy my hands. He presented me with a legal pad and pen.

"Marcel wants you to write down everything they said," he informed me. His expression softened as I met his eyes; sadly, I'd been unable to stop a few angry tears from falling into the sink. "I am sorry, Anna. I don't like it, either."

"You like it enough to let it happen," I snarled. "Just leave it on the table."

He complied without another word, leaving me alone in the kitchen. I took my sweet time with the crystal ware, my anger building rather than leveling out.

Human traffickers.

I repeated it to myself over and over, until I was sure steam must be coming out of my ears. Terrified women, hopeless teenagers, innocent children, all were getting scooped up in this opportunistic Italian mob's drag net, just when they thought they'd finally reached safety and freedom. The worst I'd imagined was drugs, maybe guns. Stolen antiquities. Exotic animals. State secrets. Anything but human beings.

Suddenly the wine glass I was washing exploded in my left

hand, sending large shards of crystal clattering into the sink. One remained stuck fast in my palm. I looked around for the source of some projectile before I realized I'd squeezed the glass too hard. I pulled the crystal fragment out slowly, grimacing as blood began to spill from my palm. I was watching my blood drip into the dishwater when I noticed Luke in my peripheral vision.

"Did you know?" I asked, not looking at him.

"Yes." He waited for me to say something, asking when it became clear that I had nothing else to say, "Did you do that on purpose?"

"No."

"Let me see," he started, reaching for my hand. I side-stepped out of his reach.

"Stay away from me."

"Please talk to me. At least let me get you something for that."

He stepped toward me again, and I snatched a random glass from the pink sink water and hurled it at his feet. He hopped backward, narrowly avoiding the shrapnel.

"Fine," he snapped. He left the kitchen, slamming the door behind him so hard that it popped back open.

The encounter had at least gotten me past the first stages of anger to more comfortable territory: numbness. I ran my left palm under the tap to dislodge any more fragments, then wrapped it in a clean tea towel. I sat down at the kitchen table, yanked off my shoes, pulled the legal pad toward me, and started to write.

7

Monday, December 28, 2020
London

I was wrenched from sleep several hours later by the most pedestrian of needs: food. I'd fallen asleep with the legal pad as a pillow, when my hand ached too much from the strain of writing. I sat up, back protesting, frozen to the bone, and pushed my hair out of my face. The pain in my left hand reminded me of the accidental, self-inflicted stab wound.

When I tried to unwind the tea towel from around my hand, it was only to find that my blood had dried and the cloth was stuck fast. I returned to the sink and turned on the hot water tap, letting first cold, then warm, then blisteringly hot water run over the bloody towel to loosen it up enough to pull away from my palm. It was agony. I cooled the water a bit and tried to rub away some of the dried blood, but it just started bleeding again. Pretending the pain didn't bother me, I pressed my right thumb to the wound and looked around the kitchen, wondering if I were lucky enough to be in the same room as a first aid kit.

My eyes fell on the table, where in addition to my legal pad and pen there sat a small box of adhesive bandages and a tube of antibacterial ointment. Someone had to have placed them there while I slept. I scooped them up eagerly, no longer feeling noble enough to abjure medical treatment.

Once I'd cleaned and dressed the wound as best as I could, I sat back down to read over what I'd written. I'd had neither the energy nor the motivation to lie, fabricate, or obfuscate. I had faithfully committed to paper every single thing the Sardinians had said, and in so doing I knew those same facts had been engraved on my brain. It wasn't much, but it was something.

The clock on the oven read 5:31 in the morning, a good three more hours of darkness ahead before the sun rose. I swept the detritus from my bandages into a trashcan and figured I might as well pocket a few more bandages just in case. As I looked into the box to see how many were left, I saw something black, out of place. I upended the box onto the table and peered inside it.

There, in bold, black letters, someone had written, "Demon. Trunk. Seven."

I closed the box at once, mind breaking into a nauseating sprint. It didn't take a genius to understand that I was supposed to get in the trunk of Marcel's Challenger by 7:00. The hard part was deciding who wrote the message and why.

My first thought was Luke. That was the simplest answer, a comforting belief.

What if it was Marcel, though? He had so carelessly dropped

the Demon's key fob into the cupholder earlier, and as I replayed the moment I felt certain he'd wanted me to see it. Following instructions from him, disguised as a friendly hand, would not end well for me.

It wasn't Giles.

Was it David? Had my sanctimonious jab last night really gotten to him?

I shook my head to clear it, gripped again by the intense hunger that had woken me up in the first place. I squished the box of bandages down, slipped it into the bodice of my dress, and almost walked barefoot over the broken crystal of the glass I'd thrown at Luke to get to the fridge. Rather than putting the stilettos back on, I went the long way around the table to avoid the shards.

After wolfing down a stack of cold cuts, a thick slice of bread, and a peach, I felt a little more clearheaded. Some forward-thinker had brewed coffee and left it in a pitcher to cool overnight. I downed most of that and really began to wake up.

I would certainly not stuff myself in the Demon's trunk just because a box of bandages told me to. I would wait in the garage to see who came at 7:00 to find me there.

My mind thus made up, I left the various brutalized crystalware for someone else to deal with, grabbed the legal pad, and left the kitchen in search of Marcel. I found him in the parlor, cozy next to a blazing fire as he scrolled through his iPad, the twenty-first century morning paper. I tossed the legal pad at his feet.

"There. That's everything. You're gonna eat it up."

Unflappable as ever, he picked it up and said, "Give me the short version."

"Their operation isn't as tight as they want you to think. They're having issues with some guy named Barbato."

His expression flickered at the name—a smile? He said, "I thought I heard that name last night. Did they say why he wasn't there?"

"No."

"Luke told me you slept at the kitchen table. Your little rebellion?"

"Yep, that's it, that's the whole rebellion," I spat, turning to go.

Marcel made no move to stop me, so I continued up the stairs toward the only bathroom I knew how to find. I locked myself in, cleaned myself up, and then filled the tub partway with hot water to thaw out my toes. Forcing myself to balance on the edge of the tub while feeling gradually returned to my toes had the helpful side effect of slowing my heart rate. I took several deep breaths, slowing it further.

Like it or not, I had to return to my bedroom to get a change of clothes. Luke was probably there, unless he'd succumbed to a reasonable fear of me harming him in his sleep. Still, I couldn't sashay around in a dress all day, so I couldn't prolong the run-in any longer. I crept to the bedroom, eased the door open, and saw Luke asleep in bed.

My clothes were stacked on a chair by the window, right where I'd left them. Trying not to make a sound, I whisked across the room and attempted in almost complete darkness to extract the right combination of garments. I dropped a sweater on the ground, bent automatically to pick it up, and winced as the flatted box of bandages fell out of my bodice and rattled across the floor.

I heard a low grunt, then, "Anna?"

I froze, sweater in hand, bent almost double, and waited for him to dismiss the sound and go back to sleep. Instead, he flicked on the bedside lamp.

"What are you doing?" he grumbled sleepily, peering at me in evident disorientation.

"What does it look like?" I shot back.

"Anna, come to bed. It's freezing."

"Clear out and I'll consider it."

He rubbed his face a little, waking up, and swung his legs out of bed. I actually thought for a second that he was going to leave like I asked, but instead he came toward me.

"No," I argued, edging toward the other door. "I told you to stay away from me."

"And I asked you to talk to me. If we take turns, we can both get what we want."

"Don't you talk down to me like that," I snapped. "I have nothing to say to you."

"Can you at least listen?"

"No!" I cried, aiming a kick at his groin as soon as he was in range.

He took the hit on his thigh instead and semi-gently pinned me to the wall by my shoulders. I grabbed his hands to twist them away, if I could, but only succeeded in causing a stab of pain as the cut on my palm reopened. It shouldn't have, but that took the fight out of me completely.

I stared up at Luke, shaking with a heady cocktail of cold, anger, and fear. "Fine. Talk."

"I thought you already knew."

"That's it? That's what you've been working on all night? Of course I didn't know! I wouldn't have gotten within ten miles of you if I'd known!"

"You knew I kill people for money! How is this so much worse?"

"*No,* I knew you killed *a* person for money and refused to kill me. I thought you only killed people who deserve it!"

"That's just foolish."

"Now I know why you won't tell me who your next target is. Because you know I won't like it."

"It's because you'll try to stop me."

"Who is it? Is it Jim?"

He appeared sincerely stunned by my accusation. "Camposanto? Your boss?"

"Tell me!"

"No, it's not him."

"I don't know why I should believe that."

"I don't either. But it's not him. It's some guy in Argentina, okay? A drug guy. That's okay with you, right?"

"I—that's—that's completely beside the point! Your boss, your *friend,* is a slaver! That's what they really are, Luke, they're modern day slave traders. And you help them."

He set his jaw, clearly unmoved by my words. "I have my

reasons. I don't have to explain them to you."

"Then what the heck are we talking about?"

"How about who your boss is, Anna? Please enlighten me as to how beneficent and blameless Uncle Sam is."

"Let's skip the needless comparison that has no bearing whatsoever on the reason I'm upset. Can we do that?"

"Fine. No pot shots at the U.S. government, or at Marcel. Let's talk about you and me."

I was furious at myself for letting him back me into such an obvious corner. Giving no response, I let him infer that I'd conceded the point.

Luke said, "I do what I have to do, and so do you. It's not always pretty, but it happens. I'm helping you, aren't I?" he asked.

"I guess so."

"You think you're the only person I've helped?"

That brought me up short. "Am I?"

"You're special, Anna, I won't deny that. But you're not that special."

"What have you done for Alice? Is she alive? Have you seen her?"

He stared at me, wanting to answer. Though I gave him a few seconds, I didn't even get a nod. With a sinking feeling, I finally admitted to myself that Luke might be sparing me from grim news.

I breathed, "Marcel is going to kill me. You get that, right? That meeting last night was the motherlode of insider information, and I heard it all, in three languages. I'm a dead woman."

"I'm working on it."

"I'm *scared.*"

"I know." He pressed his hand to my cheek. "I'm not going to let anything happen to you."

I closed my eyes, exhaled slowly, and said, "Look in the Band-Aid box."

"… Huh?"

"The box that fell on the floor." I pointed. "Look inside."

He gave me a concerned look and turned to follow my out-stretched finger. As he stooped to pick up the box, I slid down the wall to sit down, unspeakably exhausted.

"Demon, trunk, seven," he recited. "Where did this come from?"

"I was hoping you could tell me. Someone put it on the kitchen table while I was sleeping."

"I came to check on you at two o'clock, so it had to have been after that."

"My money's on Giles," I said.

He gave an unwilling laugh. "Whoever it was, the real question is, are you going to do it?"

"Yeah," I lied. "I have to take the chance."

"I don't like it."

"Me, neither." I paused, picturing Luke standing over my sleeping form early this morning. "Did you read my notes?"

"Sure I did," he confessed readily. "Knowledge is power, right?"

"Do you know who that Barbato guy is?"

"Barbato? No clue. Sounds Italian."

"Real helpful."

"Did you make a copy of the notes for yourself?"

I tapped my temple. "You bet. Unbeatable encryption."

He looked doubtful, but only for a moment. "Well. Better you than me. Look, I'm already committed to a job in the city for Marcel. I have to leave at six thirty. By the time I get back…"

"I know. I'll find you. You know I can."

"I'm not questioning your ability, I'm questioning your motivation."

"You'll just have to trust me."

Seven o'clock in the morning found me crouched behind a pair of toolboxes in the stately garage, watching the Demon's silhouette. Even dormant, the car looked vicious. Right on time, the garage door opened, admitting none other than Marcel. I suppressed a whoop of triumph, attributing another win to my gut. Giles walked into the garage right behind Marcel.

Unaware they had an audience, neither provided any helpful narration to let me know what they were up to. They climbed into the car, Marcel driving, and fired it up. Even knowing it was coming, the rush of sound made me jump. I crouched lower behind the toolboxes, then froze as Giles' eyes flicked toward my hiding place.

They backed out, and I remained in my hiding spot as the roar of the engine faded away. Right before the automatic garage door slid closed, I poked a toe in front of the safety sensor. It groaned back open and I left the garage, looking all around for some clue as to what to do next. I had watched Luke and David depart the house in the utility van half an hour ago. Now Marcel and Giles were gone. It seemed I had the place to myself. Inconveniently, it also seemed that I had no mode of conveyance other than my feet.

I thought of those seven magnificent dogs, all arrayed in a row, staring so fixedly at David that they might have been statues. Suddenly I wished I'd climbed into the trunk as instructed.

I returned to the house and found all of the exterior doors locked. I made a full loop of the house to try all the doors, then I realized any attempt to break into the house might trigger some kind of alarm. Shivering in the pre-dawn air and feeling increasingly foolish, I trudged back to the garage and sat down at a work bench. For a few listless minutes I fiddled with a multimeter, and then I heard the distinct rumble of a motorcycle engine outside.

With no idea what to expect, I crept out of the garage and used the cover of a massive oak tree to peer at the driveway. My jaw dropped: Sitting in the driveway astride a lurid green crotch rocket was a petite Black woman looking around as though the house and outbuildings were vaguely interesting to her. A jet black helmet was tucked under her arm, another strapped to the seat behind her.

"Anna Bowman?" she called, a thick British accent turning my first name into 'Annur'. "Helloooo?"

I emerged from the tree cover and approached her. She caught sight of me right away.

"Oh! If you're not Anna, I'm completely lost."

"Uh… you're not lost."

"Oh, good. Climb on, then, we're a bit pressed for time."

"Who… are you?"

"Absolutely nobody," she said, cramming the helmet onto her head and tossing me the other. "Go on, I haven't got all day. And I've heard there's dogs here. I'm not a big fan of dogs."

"Screw it." I jammed the too-big helmet over my head and climbed onto the bike behind her.

Her helmet moved up and down in an exaggerated nod. "That's the spirit," she approved, her voice coming through the helmet as clear as day. "Hold on tight."

8

Monday, December 28, 2020
London

I grabbed onto the woman just in time to stop myself being thrown from the bike as she opened the throttle, spinning on the spot and sending gravel flying behind us. We shot down the driveway and, slipping and sliding a bit on the loose gravel, made it to the paved road in very little time.

While we waited at the stop sign for a break in the Monday morning traffic, she asked, "What's happened to your hand?"

"I accidentally cut myself."

"You haven't been otherwise injured? You don't need a doctor or anything?"

"No, I'm fine."

"Wonderful. I'm Mary, by the way. Provincial, I know, but it's what I'm stuck with."

"Nice to meet you. Please tell me you're MI5."

"Since you asked, I certainly am."

"Who sent you? How did you find me?"

"Let's talk about this later," she hedged, accelerating to pass a truck that was going too slow up the next hill. "Driving this monster does require a certain amount of concentration."

"Sure, sure. Do your thing."

For the remainder of the trip back to London, I enjoyed the singular pleasure of zipping around traffic at speeds only attainable by a young person who thinks her youth and government credentials make her invincible. We entered the London metro area well before 8:00. Rather than heading toward the iconic MI5 building, to my disappointment, Mary maneuvered the bike into a sleepy, residential area on the west side of town and stopped in front of—

"A library?" I asked, perplexed, as she parked on the street.

"As instructed," she confirmed. "You'll want to head into the basement, as your contact is waiting for you there."

"My contact? Who?"

"No clue. Pleased to make your acquaintance, Anna," she said with a grin, zipping away on the bike before I could summon up a response.

As with my bizarre meeting with Penelope, I wondered whether I was really awake and experiencing this, or asleep and dreaming it. I hoped it was the latter, so if I encountered anything scary down in the library basement I could will myself awake.

The smell of old books and lemony air freshener hit me as soon as I walked through the doors. No one was in sight, so I wended my way toward the back of the library and soon enough found a door labeled Basement: Employee Access Only. It was unlocked.

I started down the staircase into murky darkness, almost laughing out loud at the absurdity of it all. Whoever was behind the note in the box of bandages must have known I'd wait in the garage rather than in the trunk. How else would MI5 Mary have known I was outside and unwittingly waiting for her? It was devious for deviousness' sake, bearing all the hallmarks of exactly one person. I was still unwilling to believe it in spite of all the evidence.

I reached the basement floor and looked around uneasily.

"Hello? Is anyone actually here?"

The voice that answered was colored by a familiar, patronizing tone.

"What did you do to your hand?"

I whirled on the spot to find myself face-to-face with Jim. A disbelieving laugh burst out of me. "Jim! How!" I threw my arms around his neck, too happy at the sight of a familiar face to temper my reaction at all. "How the world did you find me?"

"You'll be mad when I tell you," he answered, wrapping his arms around me with evident relish. He buried his face in my hair and breathed, "I was so worried about you."

"Why? I'm fine."

I pulled away to gauge his reaction, certain he'd be furious at me for missing the check-in and precipitating all this trouble. Instead he kissed me, uncertainly at first and then more insistently as he realized I wasn't objecting. His arms around me constricted, picking me up to deposit me on a worktable. Guessing we had a few minutes of free time, I pulled him closer, smiling against his lips.

"You're off the reservation," I whispered.

"You have no idea. That's offensive, by the way."

"Oops. Sorry." For a few more minutes he was content to kiss me, until I breathed, "We really can't do this right now."

"Why not?"

"It's just not—oh, crap," I gasped, staring wide-eyed at the base of the stairs where two figures had appeared. I couldn't quite believe what I was seeing. *"Alice?"*

"Please tell me that's not your uncle," she said.

All I could really take in was that she seemed perfectly okay: She was on her own two feet and sporting no obvious injuries. I wanted to laugh, cry, and scream at the same time. There she stood, cool as ever, smirking at me like I hadn't spent the last few days agonizing over her possible death. I hardly had time to process this emotional cocktail, let alone enjoy my relief at seeing her alive and well.

Next to Alice, looking especially enormous by comparison, Luke stood with his arms crossed, his expression stony. On the bright side, he didn't immediately whip out a gun and shoot Jim; maybe my theory about his next target was a little off after all.

"This is… awkward," Jim muttered.

"Yeah, get away from her," Luke shot back, arms swinging free in an unmistakable sign of aggression. Jim immediately and wisely took a step back from me, hands raised.

"Take it easy, big guy," Jim soothed, not looking nearly chagrinned enough.

Luke inhaled deeply and gritted out, "Anna, a word?"

"Yeah, yeah," I agreed hastily, hopping down off the table. As I started toward Luke, Jim's hand closed around my elbow.

"Take your hand off of her," Luke erupted, startling me as much as Jim. Half a second too late, Jim's hand fell away.

"It's fine," I assured him. Clearly unconvinced, he nevertheless allowed me to follow Luke up the stairs and back into the library.

As the door swung closed behind us, I heard Jim ask Alice, "What's this about her uncle?" Alice's answer was cut off by the closing door. Luke rounded on me as soon as it snapped shut, but his words weren't what I expected.

"Are you okay?"

"I—yeah, I'm fine. Are you?"

"Oh, no, I'm not fine," he assured me. "I just want to make sure you're not hurt before I ream you."

"I… not hurt."

"Good. What the—*what* was that?"

"Um. Secret FBI handshake?"

"Don't even try to laugh this off," he spat. "You told me there wasn't anything going on between you two."

"That's not exactly what I said…"

"I just burned my life down for you!"

"Well! Thank you," I said feebly, not sure how else to respond. He stared at me.

"I'm not accustomed to getting jerked around like this," he growled. "In fact it's an entirely novel experience for me."

"I'm sorry. I honestly didn't think the two of you would

ever cross paths."

"And that makes it okay?"

"Well, no! But also, kind of, yes?"

This bald honesty seemed to derail his anger. He blinked at me, bewildered. "You're actually serious."

"It would be pretty stupid to lie about that."

"You think you can have it your way all the time, don't you?" he asked, making it an accusation. "You greedy little—"

"Hey! Cool it. You're the one who told me you aren't trying to catch feelings…"

"Is that what you told *him?*" he demanded, waving a vague hand toward the basement.

I sighed impatiently. "This is stupid. This is a stupid conversation."

He backed off a little, taking another steadying breath. "Is it?"

"Yes. I like you both, and I'm not sorry about it, so can we move on?"

"I don't know, Anna. I don't like it."

I smiled sweetly at him. "I do."

"I'm sorry I almost called you a… well."

"I'm sorry you had to burn your life down to save me."

"I'm not." He ran a hand through his hair, clearly unhappy, and ventured, "So, you're like a sailor."

"Uh… am I?"

"Yeah. A girl in every port, right?"

"Oh."

"I can live with that."

I perked up, surprised. "You can?"

"Sure, I'm a twenty-first century man, you're a liberated woman. I can deal with it."

"Wow. I'm impressed."

"But just make sure *he* knows whose port this is," he said, tone sharpening. "Because I don't want to worry every time I walk through a door that I'm going to catch the woman I love wrapped around some other man."

I gazed dumbly at him, suddenly at a loss for words. He bit his lower lip as though embarrassed.

"Don't make it weird," he cautioned me.

"You love me?"

"Jeez, Anna. You are the dumbest genius I've ever met."

I raised my eyebrows.

"Yes," he groaned. "I love you. So," he added quickly, over my awkward response, "please try to understand that if I encounter *that* again," he pointed to the basement, "I will kill that guy. I'm not joking at all."

"Fine," I raised my hands. "Point taken. And I'm not a genius."

"Hm." His gaze flitted over me, appraising. "If you say so. How did you even get here?"

I turned and opened the basement door. "Let's regroup to talk about this. You've got some explaining to do, too."

We filed back into the basement to find Alice perched on the worktable I'd vacated, happily working her way through a protein bar, while Jim, his back to the stairs, was absorbed in a laptop open on the table next to her.

"They're back," she announced boredly.

Jim turned around, and I tensed. His expression warned of some situation-escalating sarcasm on the way, but he surprised me by asking, "Is everyone familiar with the concept of debriefing?"

I nodded, Luke grunted something that sounded like assent, and Alice raised her hand.

"You don't have to do that, Alice," Jim said.

"Oh." She lowered her hand sheepishly. "I've heard of it, but I'm not exactly sure what it is."

"Understandable. Anna, you first."

"Ugh, fine."

With clinical detachment, I related everything that had happened since my Christmas Day phone call with Jim had ended: Spotting Giles at the cathedral, bumping into Luke and going back to his house, learning of the hit he'd turned down, getting the voicemail from Alice telling me to go to the British Museum, getting kidnapped in the loading bay, being taken to Marcel's house, the meeting with the Sardinians, my escape this morning.

Alice listened to my story with increasingly evident disbelief, and I did my best to ignore her and the profoundly irritating noise of Jim taking notes on his laptop. Alice was the first to speak up when I'd finished.

"Should I be hearing all of this?" she asked warily. "It sounds awfully—er—sensitive."

"Don't worry, Alice," Jim answered, still typing as he spoke. "You're just going to have to sign a lot paperwork."

"Can't I just go home?" she pressed. "I'm really not cut out for all this spy business."

"We're not spies," Jim mumbled. Alice ignored him and looked inquiringly at me.

I said, "Alice, I'm sorry. For the time being, I think you're stuck with us. Marcel already knows he can get to me through you. What's to stop him doing it again?"

"*He* said," she pointed at Luke, "he was taking me home. Otherwise I wouldn't have gone with him!"

"He misspoke," Jim said.

"No, I lied," Luke shot back. He had the good grace to look sorry about it. "I didn't know how else to convince you."

Alice looked from Luke, to Jim, to me, then at the staircase. "So I couldn't just… walk out of here and call an Uber and go home?"

"I wouldn't," I answered, before Jim could speak. "But no one's going to stop you."

She pressed her lips together, musing, her gaze fixed on the staircase. She asked me, "You think those French ferrets would come after me again?"

"Almost certainly. You're the only person I know here."

"Couldn't I go to the police or something?"

"Sure, but what could they really do? They'd help you make a statement, and you'd leave the station just as vulnerable as you are now."

She took a bite out of her protein bar and said around it, "Well, great. I see your point."

The thoughtful silence following her concession was broken only by Jim's incessant typing. He finished abruptly, looked up at Luke, and said, "Jackson?'

"What?"

"He wants to debrief you," Alice answered, winking at me. I chuckled appreciatively.

"How far back do I have to go?" Luke asked, directing the question at me.

I glanced at Jim. "This morning?"

"If time were no object, I'd say February fifteenth," Jim said, invoking the date on which Luke's appearance on security cameras in Houston made him an official part of my life. "But, for now I just need to make sure it's safe to move so we can get out of here. This morning is fine."

"Whatever," Luke snapped. "After Anna told me about the note, I had to leave with David to take care of some business for Marcel. On the way into the city, he told me about Mary."

I stood up straighter, looking between Luke and Jim eagerly. The latter gave me a smug half-smile, hardly taking his eyes off Luke for a second.

"She came to visit him in the hospital and told him who she was working for, and he said she made him 'an offer he couldn't refuse'. He wouldn't tell me what it was. David left Anna the note on Mary's instructions, and he set up a meeting for Marcel and Giles in London to get them out of the house. He dropped me off at the house where they were keeping Alice, told me to bring her here, and left to take care of Marcel's thing by himself.

"She was locked in the attic. No guards. I told her I was there to take her home, but first we had to meet up with Anna, so we jumped in a cab and came here. That's it."

"Remarkably devoid of detail, thank you," Jim said.

"Well, what more do you want to know?" Luke asked.

"Did anyone see you take Alice out of the house? Do you have any reason to believe Marcel knows what David has done? How is he planning to explain your absence to Marcel when he returns to the house?"

"No, no, and if I understood his plan correctly, he's going to tell Marcel that I told him that Marcel told me to go to the house where Alice was and to take care of the job in London without me. Basically he's going to burn me and plead ignorance."

"What's the job in London?" I asked.

"Don't worry about it."

"Oh, yeah, okay," I replied with excessive sarcasm.

"That's not relevant at the moment," Jim said calmy. "Alice, you can skip this if you want to, but in your case, it might be cathartic."

"I'll just tell Teg—Anna later," she whispered, nearly invoking the name by which she'd known me—Tegan—until about half an hour ago. I could only imagine her befuddlement.

"Fair enough," Jim said. "Everyone ready to get out of here?"

"Depends on where we're going," Luke said.

"Berlin," Jim answered carelessly, focused on shutting down his laptop. Alice wriggled with excitement.

"Why?" Luke and I asked at the same time.

"Because she speaks German," Jim pointed at me, "And I had to make a deal of my own to get here. No one's making you tag along, Jackson."

"Do I have to be a honeypot again?" I asked.

Jim grimaced. "Do you really want me to answer that?"

"What's a honeypot?" Alice asked.

"The absolute outer limit of Jim's imagination," I snarled, starting up the stairs again and demanding, "Are we going, or not?"

Jim bundled us all into an SUV parked in front of the library. Waiting in the back seat was a familiar gray lump of canvas and MOLLE webbing.

"My backpack!" I exclaimed, ripping it open to make sure everything was there. "Where'd you get this?"

"Same place I got this," Jim answered, popping open the glove box and pulling out a small, maroon booklet, which he tossed to Luke. It was a French passport.

"You've been in my house," Luke said.

"Yep, and I had to go all the way to Maidstone to get this from your mother, Alice," Jim said, pulling out another passport, black instead of maroon, and passing it to her in the passenger seat. "She says hi, by the way. She is, in her words, 'quite thrilled you're not dead but annoyed you didn't come to see her yourself'."

Alice flipped through the stiff booklet and scoffed at her passport photo. "So I guess you knew all along I'd be baggage. I have always wanted to go to Germany, though. That's where my dad's family's from."

Jim smiled at her. "I admire your optimism. She was kind enough to pack a bag for you, and I picked up a few things for you too, Anna. It's a long drive to Berlin, and I'm going on about ninety minutes of sleep. Who's driving next?"

I volunteered for the next leg, starting in Brussels if Jim could make it that far. Luke agreed to take over in Hanover; and Alice assured us she could get us to Berlin, as long as we supplied her with a map and ample amounts of caffeine.

After less than ten minutes on the road, once we'd made it to a highway, Alice groaned, "Can we get some music on the radio or something?"

"The odds of finding music we can all enjoy are incalculable," Jim argued, "but feel free to try."

She gave it her best shot, but in the end we all agreed a different form of entertainment was needed. Jim surrendered his phone and let her find a podcast to play over the speakers using Bluetooth. A true crime series offered more than enough hours' worth of material, so she picked an episode at random and was lulled to sleep by it within minutes.

I tried to listen, but it didn't take long for the hum of the highway and the inherent boredom of a road trip to make my eyelids heavy. The short night's sleep on a table in an unheated kitchen had been the opposite of rest, and all the excitement before and after was finally catching up to me. I stretched out on the back seat with my head in Luke's lap and drifted to sleep while the city views gave way to countryside.

9

**Monday, December 28, 2020
Somewhere in Germany**

I was shaken awake just east of Brussels, which initiated a seat-shuffling procedure that left Luke and Alice in the back seat together. They were both snoozing within minutes, leaving me free to assault my passenger, Jim, with the questions that had been queuing up in my head.

I asked, "Want to explain why getting through the Chunnel was so easy? Isn't the Met looking for Alice?"

"No one calls it the Chunnel anymore," was Jim's disinterested non-answer.

"You've greased some wheels to make this easier, haven't you?"

"Sure. That's my job. Haven't you heard that luck favors the prepared?"

"Nope, hadn't heard that one."

"We didn't need that much luck, anyway. This is official U.S.

government business."

"How did you find me? You said I'd be mad when you told me."

"Are you so eager to be mad?"

"Just tell me," I sighed.

"There's a GPS tracking device in your passport. I had it specially made for you."

"What the heck, Jim!" I erupted. "Why would you do that and not tell me?"

"In the event that you ran, I didn't want to give you a reason to leave your passport behind."

"Ran? As in, AWOL, forget the FBI, I'm out?"

"Don't even tell me you didn't think about it."

I rolled my eyes. "Well, of course I thought about it."

"There you go."

"That only explains how you found my passport, not how you found me."

"I found it in a house belonging to the company you told me about—Frères Enterprises. Luke's house, I assume, since his passport was there. Mary, who you met, discovered that an eponymous frère was in the hospital recovering from a stab wound he received at the apartment of one Alice Murphy. Didn't take a genius to work it out. David told her where to find you."

"Why did you have to make a deal to get here?"

He smiled at me as though I'd said something stupid. "I have a boss, too. He wasn't a fan of me coming over here myself to get you. Officially, the operation to track down you-know-who—" he jerked his thumb into the backseat, toward Luke

"—is over; and now, as a matter of convenience, you and I are assisting the BKA with a small matter they've invited us to team up on. For your edification, my alias is Michael Mercer. Get it? Michael and Tegan Mercer? We had a lovely, intimate wedding in Aruba two years ago."

The BKA, the Bundeskriminalamt, was the German counterpart to the FBI. Assuming the 'us' to whom he referred was just Jim and me, I asked, "And Luke and Alice?"

"Luke's passport is probably a fake. I'm as sure as I can be he's a U.S. citizen by birth inside the United States. But Alice is—"

"I mean what's their role here, why are they getting dragged along?"

"They're obviously not safe as long as Marcel knows where they are. I haven't quite figured out what to do with them yet."

"Well…" I mumbled, mostly mollified. "At least you have a plan."

"I always have a plan," he assured me. "Don't you worry your pretty little head about it."

"Ugh."

▼

We shuffled again in Hanover so Luke could drive, and I was able catch up on sleep for about twenty minutes before Alice, riding shotgun, woke me up.

Disoriented, I sat up and tried to make sense of the darkness outside and the flashing blue and red lights. Thunder rolled in the distance, which at least explained why it was darker outside than it should be at that time of day.

"Wake up, Rosetta Stone," Luke was half-yelling, his voice tight with stress. I turned around to see a uniformed German state policeman approaching the driver's window, which was rolled down. Luke pointedly waited until the policeman was standing at the window to tell me, "This idiot is pretending not to understand French."

The idiot passed Luke back his passport and snapped in German, "Unless you can answer my questions, I will have to escort you to the nearest station to communicate through a translator."

Luke just shook his head and tried again in French, "Do you seriously only speak German?"

I rolled down my window and asked, "What's the problem?" in German. Clear relief passed over the officer's face.

"You speak German?" he asked.

"Yes. What's going on? Is this guy being difficult?"

"He was speeding, miss. I asked why he's in such a hurry, and he starts jabbering at me in French."

"He's been driving for a while," I explained. "He's a little cranky. How much was he speeding?"

"Twenty kilometers over."

I reached over the driver's seat and smacked Luke in the head.

"Frauline, please do not strike the driver."

"Sorry. Do you really want me to ask him why he was speeding? He'll probably just say he didn't think there was a speed limit."

"This is not the autobahn."

"Well, I know that. Can you give him a break? It's his first time in Germany. I'll take over driving from here."

"May I see your driver's license?"

I passed him my passport and Oklahoma driver's license, which identified me as Tegan Mercer. "This is all I have."

The sky chose that moment to unleash the rain it had been threatening at least since I woke up. The officer flinched, annoyed, and studied my license for about four seconds before passing it back to me.

"Please be sure to obey all traffic signs, Frau Mercer. Enjoy your stay in Germany."

He hustled back to his car, and I wordlessly traded seats with Luke. It took a while to find the windshield wipers, a thick silence prevailing in the SUV while I searched.

Finally, Alice whispered, "Germans are scary."

"All cops are scary when you act like a jerk," I retorted.

"What exactly was his problem?" Luke asked.

"He just wanted to ask the basic questions. You know you were speeding, right?"

"Huh."

I noticed Jim had been uncharacteristically quiet throughout this encounter and twisted in my seat to see that he was sound asleep, his jacket pressed between his face and the window as a makeshift pillow. Luke noticed at the same time I did.

"I say we push him out and keep driving," he suggested.

"I can't tell if he's joking," Alice said. "Is he joking?"

"I can't tell, either. I'm turning on the child safety locks, Luke."

"We gonna tell him about this?" Luke asked.

"What, the traffic stop?" I thought about it for a second, pictured Jim's reaction, and concluded, "Let's not."

With about three more hours left to drive, I pulled back out onto the highway and Alice hit play on the podcast. A chilling, true tale of three children killed in a house fire in Georgia in 1945 got us through the first two hours; and then Alice requested that we turn on the radio, since the only objections to pop music had come from Jim, who seemed unlikely to wake up anytime soon. After twenty minutes or so, I had converted to Jim's perspective on pop music, but I kept this to myself for Alice's sake.

An hour outside Berlin, Jim woke up in the middle of a particularly noxious song and asked the car at large, "What is that noise?"

I switched off the radio. "Ninety kilometers to Berlin," I read off a passing street sign. "I have no idea where I'm going."

Jim got his phone back from Alice and used it to guide me into the center of Berlin, stopping us in front of the Ritz-Carlton Hotel. I leaned over the steering wheel to look up at the building's façade as a valet materialized outside the driver's window.

"Seriously, Jim?" I asked.

"If you want to stay at a hostel, say the word."

"I want to stay here," Alice breathed in awe.

While Alice and Luke hovered near the hotel door next to a cart full of our luggage, looking deeply uncomfortable, I joined Jim at the front desk to check in. Not only did Jim have a reservation, but there was a package waiting for him, a thick white envelope with no writing on the outside. He slipped it into his jacket pocket, grinning slyly at me.

As we rejoined the others on the way to the elevators, I mumbled, "You shouldn't be smug about wantonly spending the taxpayers' money."

"Oh, I'm footing the bill for this."

"Show off."

Our room was a two-bedroom suite near the top of the hotel, which explained the deference Jim had received from the concierge despite our raggedy appearance. The first thing I did when we got in was check the inside of the door for the room rate, but I was disappointed to find it wasn't posted there.

Jim pulled my hand off the door and closed it. "Sorry, they don't do that here."

"Do what?" I asked lightly. "Is there a minibar?"

"Found it!" Alice cried from across the room. I smiled innocently at Jim as the clink of miniature liquor bottles announced her intention to enjoy this spontaneous vacation to the fullest.

"At least she's impressed," I said.

"I'm not trying to impress her."

"We should probably talk about that…"

"Hey, Anna," Luke called, poking his head around the doorway of the nearest bedroom. "You've got to see this room."

"… later," I finished.

"Please stick to the name on your passport," Jim chastised as I disappeared into the bedroom after Luke.

I paused in the doorway to take in the room as a whole: the

king-sized bed and cloud-white duvet, the Art Deco chandelier, the enormous flat-screen TV, and the view, good God the view. Night had fallen while we drove through the city, and now Berlin was lit up like a Christmas tree. In fact, a massive, 50-foot tall Christmas tree still stood in the square across the street from the hotel. A voice at my ear made me jump in surprise.

"Check this out."

Luke shepherded me into the bathroom and swept an arm toward the large, glass-walled shower. "How about that," he said. "Room for two."

"Two?" I echoed. "There's room for all four of us."

Catching the hem of my sweater, he said, "Let's just start with two."

"Let's start with one at a time," I countered, freeing my sweater. "You can go first."

He waved me off and left the bathroom, not bothering to disguise his irritation. I was dispirited for a moment, but I shook it off and happily availed myself of the luxurious shower. After winding my hair into a loose braid, I came out of the bathroom to find Luke already cocooned in the massive bed, watching the BBC.

"Anything interesting happening in the world?" I asked.

"Not really." He muted the TV and fixed me with a serious look. I was afraid he was about to start asking awkward questions, but he said, "I think you should go talk to Alice."

"Now? Why?"

"She's got to be really shaken up. You should talk to her about it."

"Yeah," I sighed. "You're right. Darn it… I'm no good at that sort of thing."

"It's not rocket science. Just get her talking, and listen."

I relented, grateful for an excuse to leave the bedroom. Most of the lights in the common room had been shut off, the light from a TV at low volume illuminating two large feet hanging over the arm of the couch. I spared Jim's slumbering form one pitying glance before creeping across the room to knock softly on the other bedroom door.

"'Ello?" Alice called from within.

"It's me. Can we talk?"

"Sure, sure."

She was sitting cross-legged in the center of the bed, playing solitaire. She flashed me a smile.

"I wasn't ready for bed, but Mister Camposanto insisted I take the bedroom. I think he wanted some peace and quiet."

"You can just call him Jim."

"I like saying 'Camposanto'," she replied. "Camposanto. Campo… santo… is that Italian?"

"Yes, it means holy ground, a graveyard."

"Yeesh, I like it better in Italian. Go on, sit down. D'you want to play gin?"

"As long as we can drink gin while we play it."

"Agreed."

We got through three rounds of the card game while I tried to think of a way to broach the topic we both knew needed to be discussed. It finally came to me while I was shuffling the deck.

"Did you really want to tell me about the last few days, or

did you just tell Jim that?" I asked.

"Mm." Her mouth twisted in consternation. "I dunno. I'd kind of like to pretend it never happened, you know?"

"That makes sense. Probably the worst thing that's ever happened to you."

"No," she said lightly. "Not really. And it's over now, anyway. No real harm done. Luke told it right enough. I was locked in an attic, and he came and got me."

"They didn't hurt you?"

"No. That beastly mop-headed creature, Giles, certainly wanted me to believe they would, but eventually I figured out that wasn't on the menu."

"Can you tell me what happened on Christmas?" I probed.

"Oh, it was awful," she said, needing no further prodding to dive into the story. "I was cleaning up the kitchen after making a mess with Christmas pudding—which didn't turn out very well, unfortunately—and they knocked on the door. It was Giles and the other one from the pub, looked like his brother. I was just going to crack the door you know, to see who it was, but they pushed through and knocked me onto the floor. I'd carried a knife from the kitchen with me, and the brother got down on the floor with me and tried to gag me, and I took a swipe at him with the knife. It's a good thing the knife wasn't sharper, or I might've killed him. I don't think I could live with that..."

"Why'd you arm yourself, then?"

"Arm myself? I did no such thing. I just forgot I was holding the knife when I went to the door. I got him pretty good though, and it scared me and I dropped the knife, and Giles got me from behind. He gagged me and tied my hands up, and went to help his brother. They were talking to each other in French, so I don't know what they said, but then Giles asked me in English where you were—only I didn't know your real name at the time, so I shook my head meaning I had no idea. He went through the whole apartment as if he was going to find you hiding under a bed or something. Anyway, the brother was looking pretty white by then, so Giles took his coat and hat and threw it on me, and he just left him there. He marched me down the stairs and out to the curb, threw me in a van, and brought me here."

"Why didn't you run?"

"He had that knife up against my ribs, didn't he!"

"Did he say anything to you?"

"Only that he'd cut my throat if his brother ended up dying. Once we got to that house, they made me send you that voice-mail, then they stuffed me in the attic and ignored me except for bringing me meals and letting me use the loo. It was deadly boring. Luke brought me a deck of cards, at least."

"So this morning wasn't the first time you saw Luke?"

"Oh, no. He was my prison guard so to speak the second day. I wouldn't have gone with him at all, knowing he was with the likes of Giles, but he doesn't seem so bad, especially now."

I raised my eyebrows, suppressing a smile.

"I'm not saying I'm moving to Stockholm," she laughed. "I just think he's got a nice face."

"You should taste his enchiladas."

She snorted. "Is that one of your Americanisms? I don't get it."

"No, I mean he literally—Gin!"

We ran out of gin about the same time our enthusiasm for the game waned, turning our attention to the hilarious spectacle of *Pride & Prejudice* overdubbed in German on TV. I fell asleep to the confusing yet oddly comforting sound of Mister Darcy proclaiming his love for Elizabeth in a thick Bavarian accent.

10

Tuesday, December 29, 2020
Berlin

Something even stranger than German Jane Austen was happening on TV when I woke up. I sat up, shaking the sleep away, and peered at the screen. It appeared to be a reality talent show, and the current contestant was playing a vuvuzela. I turned off the TV, but it was too late. I was awake. A peek through the blackout curtains Alice had drawn across the window confirmed the sky was beginning to brighten with the dawn.

I returned to the common room and found Jim pretty much right where I'd left him, except that he was sitting up and drinking a cup of coffee. I brewed myself a cup and sat down next to him. Wordlessly, he picked up a shooter of whiskey from the coffee table and tipped some into my cup.

"Uh… thanks."

He pointedly waited for me to take a drink, stirring his own coffee with one finger. Though I cooperatively tried it, I made no attempt to hide my disapproval or my disgust at the combination of coffee and liquor.

"Really, Jim?"

"Really what?" he asked, taking a slow, defiant drink.

"A grouchy, lone wolf FBI Agent with an alcohol problem? Don't you think that's a little hackneyed?"

"I'm not trying to break new ground here, kiddo."

"Ugh."

"I'm not trying to be a lone wolf, either," he added, leaning back to drape his arm over the couch behind me.

"So you're just sitting out here, feeling sorry for yourself?"

"It's my fifteen thousand dollar per night hotel room, I can cry if I want to."

I choked on my coffee, sputtering, "Fifteen thousand dollars a night?"

"I might have gone a little overboard, considering I've been relegated to sleeping on the couch."

"How long are we staying here?"

"Two more nights," he took another draught of Irish coffee, adding, "They gave me a fifty percent discount on the third night, if it makes you feel any better."

"Not even slightly."

"Don't worry, I can afford it."

"Jim, have you ever heard the term 'unexplained affluence'?"

"Every five years since Y2K."

"So?"

"Obviously, it's not unexplained, or I'd be short one security clearance. I just don't feel like explaining it to you."

"Well, you can cool your jets. I'm not impressed by money."
I looked around the suite and added, "Though it does have its advantages."

His voice dropped to a whisper, his hand sliding onto my shoulder. "What are you impressed by?"

I turned to face him, giving the question serious thought while he twisted a lock of my hair around his finger. "I don't know. Those plaid pajama pants kind of do it for me."

"Anything else?"

"I really don't know," I admitted. It seemed like a good enough segue into, "Luke said I'm like a sailor. He said I have a girl in every port. You know, figuratively."

"And he's okay with that?"

"He said… as long as he doesn't catch us together, he can live with it."

"How generous. And if he does catch us together?"

"You're dead, Jim."

He laughed, unimpressed. "Tell me you didn't agree to this."

"Uh…" I stammered. It hadn't occurred to me to argue.

Jim sighed dramatically. "You're kind of a pushover, Anna."

"He told me he loves me."

"Of course he does."

"I'd rather not mess around behind his back. It just doesn't seem right…"

"Ah. Now we get around to why you brought this up in the first place."

"He said this is his port."

"When?"

I frowned. "At the library."

"Well he should have been more specific. Did he mean England? Europe? The Eastern Hemisphere? Public libraries?"

"What's your point?"

"I have no idea. I was just hoping you came out here to knock boots."

I scooted closer to him, almost without thinking about it, and asked coyly, "Is it worth your life?"

"I'm going to have to say no," he said, giving my hair one last little tug before letting go, "but only because I fully believe Jackson will kill me."

"Yeah, he totally will," I agreed, sitting back and attempting, again, to take a drink of coffee. I grimaced, spat it back into the mug, and walked to the coffee maker to brew a new cup, asking, "So what's the job the BKA needs help with?"

"I didn't get many details before I agreed to it. Basically we need to wine and dine some low-level criminal so we can get a bug into his car and phone. And by we, I mean you."

"Seriously? That's it? Why can't someone in the BKA do it? They've got to have hotties galore."

"They wouldn't tell me that. And I would've gone with pussy galore."

"Aw, crap. That would've been way better."

"We're meeting with the BKA guy running the op tonight. He'll fill us in."

"And until then?"

"Berlin is your playground."

With this is mind, I found myself impatient for Alice to

wake up. I was eager to ditch the two men in the hotel and run off with her to shop and explore the sights. As the only German-speaker in the group, I wasn't thrilled at the prospect of acting as tour guide, even given the assumption that many Berliners spoke English or French as well. Much more appealing was the picture of Luke and Jim stuck in the hotel room together. Sure, boredom would probably goad them outside to communicate as best they could, but Jim might still insist they stick together for safety. It would be good for them.

I ordered room service at Jim's urging, and the siren smell of bacon and eggs undid my plan: Luke was coaxed out of the bedroom to get some, and Alice slept blissfully through. As soon as one bedroom was free, Jim grabbed a small bag and ducked into it.

"What's his problem?" Luke asked, helping himself to a piece of toast.

"He slept on the couch, you know."

"So?"

"So maybe you could work out some kind of human time share arrangement with him. Like civilized gentlemen."

"Um, no. You're joking, right?"

I rolled my eyes. "Yes. Sure."

"So where did you sleep last night?"

"With Alice," I said, smiling archly at his reaction. "What?"

"I... have no further questions about that."

"What!" I pointed a piece of bacon at him. "Don't try to make it sound dirty. You don't care if I spend the night with another woman, but I can't even have feelings for Jim?"

"Can we not talk about this again?"

"Fine," I snarled. "Save some breakfast for Alice."

I dragged my butt back to Alice's room to see if there was anything I could actually use in the suitcase Jim had packed for me. A quick rifling through its contents revealed Jim hadn't taken much care in packing it, but I wasn't too aggrieved. How he'd even had time to do this was beyond me. I picked out a too-small, mercifully stretchy pair of jeans and a sweater, and I made a mental note to buy some boots to cover up the four inches of bare leg between my jeans and my socks.

A good two hours after I was ready to go, Alice finally made an appearance. An hour after that, we were at last making our way out of the hotel and into light foot traffic headed north toward the Brandenburg Gate. Alice sportingly endured the historic sightseeing and my educational monolog until after lunch, and then we hoofed it to the Berlin mall to supplement our meager wardrobes as best as we could with the five hundred euros Jim had pressed upon me and the money I still carried in my backpack.

In exchange for the cash, I had a small shopping list from Jim that included burner phones for Alice and me, something for me to wear to the meeting tonight, and an intriguingly vague request to "take a ton of pictures." Fortunately, I'd read through the list before leaving, and we'd picked up the phones right away from a street vendor at the first major intersection we'd passed. We dutifully filled up the cheap phones with lousy, low-resolution pictures, blew the entire wad of cash and some of my reserves, and rushed back to the hotel to meet the 5:00 p.m. deadline Jim had imposed.

▼

At half-past seven I was leaving the hotel on foot again, this time with Jim, on the way to meet our BKA contact. Even bundled up in coat, hat, scarf, and gloves, I was shivering within seconds of hitting the sidewalk. Jim put an arm around my shoulders to help stave off hypothermia. It helped a little.

"Where are we meeting him?" I asked, teeth chattering.

"A little French restaurant, Le Petit Royal. His selection."

"How far away is it?"

"About five kilometers that way," he said, pointing behind us.

I stopped in the middle of the sidewalk. "So where are we going?"

"You'll see," he dodged, pulling me forward again. "It's very close. You'll warm up if you walk faster."

Aside from a mumbled insult in German and a slightly increased pace, I gave no response. Fifteen minutes later we arrived at our destination: a humble little guard shack incongruously situated in the middle of a busy street, modern high-rises towering on either side. A hand-painted sign over the empty shack read 'US ARMY CHECKPOINT'.

"Checkpoint Charlie?" I asked.

"Yep. Pretty cool, huh?"

"I don't know," I mused, gazing around in puzzlement. Behind the guard shack was a McDonald's across the street from a museum dedicated to the Berlin Wall. Turning, I saw another sign warning us in English, Russian, French, and German that we were leaving the American Sector. "This is… eerie."

"Oh. I thought you'd like it."

"I do."

"Good." He pulled me in for a kiss, and though I turned my head at the last second, it was hardly less thrilling to feel a rush of warm air against my neck as he vented a sigh of frustration. He kissed my neck a couple of times and breathed, "Just you wait 'til I get you back to the States. That's definitely *my* port."

Some cheeky passerby whistled suggestively, prompting us to break apart. I glared after the comedian, whose unsteady gait hinted at mild to moderate inebriation.

"Schweinehund!" I called after him. He didn't appear to notice.

"Tegan, my delicate flower, please don't start a street brawl."

"Why?"

"It might make us late for dinner."

We took the U-Bahn to the restaurant and arrived a few minutes late. As we squeezed into the cozy, deliciously warm space, I asked, "How are we supposed to find this guy?"

"Blue shirt, gray jacket, blonde hair," Jim recited, scanning the restaurant. "I don't think he's here yet."

I spotted a willow-thin, distinguished sort of woman halfway concealed in an alcove far from the door. Most of her face was blocked by a large, paper menu. She matched Jim's description, mostly.

I asked, "Are you sure he's a he?"

"His name is Klaus."

"Text him."

Jim complied with poor grace, clearly believing I was wasting his time. We both saw the woman's phone light up on the table in front of her about a minute later. She lowered her menu, saw us, and waved us over.

"Ha, nailed it," I gloated, leading the way through the crowded tables.

"You're Klaus Jaeger?" Jim asked, not bothering to hide his disbelief as she courteously stood up to shake both our hands.

"No, Klaus had to make an unforeseen trip to Hamburg. He asked me to fill in for him," she explained in a very thick, but attractive, standard German accent. "I'm Ingrid Breker, no relation to the artist."

Jim threw me a curious look, but I shook my head. It was way too early to start talking about Nazis. We hadn't even ordered drinks yet. He let it go and introduced us, then cut right to the chase.

"Klaus hasn't given me much in the way of details. It sounds like a pretty simple job, which begs the question: Why us?"

Ingrid had an open, friendly face, at least until Jim finished his question. Her gaze fell to the table and she said, almost to herself, "He left this for me to explain. Wunderbar." She turned her icy blue eyes on me and asked, "May we switch to German? I would be more comfortable."

"Of course. I'll fill Jim in later."

"Thank you." As Jim leaned back, arms crossed in undisguised disgruntlement, she said, "The target is a member of the NPD. Do you know what that is?"

"No, sorry."

"It's a political party. I would rather not go into the politics, but it is considered by many to be the modern successor of the Nazi party."

She clammed up, and a moment later the waiter appeared to take our drink orders. Once he was again out of earshot, she continued, her voice noticeably quieter than before.

"Even for this group, he is considered quite extreme and generally repulsive. Already four agents have attempted to get close to him in order to do what we're asking you to do, but they have been unsuccessful."

"Why?"

"These are young, liberal-minded, in some cases rather naïve female agents. To put it bluntly, they simply can't stomach him. The last agent who tried, six months ago, threw her drink in his face. We thought an older agent, with a stronger stomach, may be able to do it, so I gave it try. He did not even take a second look at me. I fear if we continue to make attempts, he may realize these attempts are connected. The consensus is that we should only try once more."

I made a face, disliking the direction she was going. "So your theory is that an American might get along better with a Nazi? That's insulting."

"Please do not misunderstand me. I don't think it's quite possible for an American, especially one so young, to grasp how sensitive we are as a nation about the entire subject of national socialism. And you do not have to live in this city after being seen with this man."

"It's a big city."

"He's a vile person."

I took a deep breath, giving myself time to think, and looked at Jim.

He was perusing the menu, not even trying to follow the conversation, but he glanced up when he felt my gaze and asked, "What?"

"I'm not sure about this."

"The deal's made, you don't have a choice."

Though I glared at him, I knew there was no point in arguing. And Ingrid was right: After this dirty job was complete, I had the luxury of leaving. When I turned back to her, she could tell by my defeated expression that she'd won.

"I have brought you a file containing all the necessary details. In order for me to turn it over to you, you must complete some paperwork. It has all been translated into English so James may look over it as well."

Jim heard his own name and looked up, snatching away the small stack of papers Ingrid was passing to me. "What's this?"

I explained as briefly as I could while he read through the briefings and ubiquitous NDA. The waiter brought us our drinks, took our food orders, and conveniently disappeared for a solid half hour. This gave me plenty of time to read the paperwork, sign it, ask a few more questions, and finally get a peek at the file.

I found a dossier on our Nazi and opened it eagerly, dying to know if he was as ugly on the outside as he was purported to be on the inside. The wallet-sized photo paperclipped to the first page of the dossier gave me my first good surprise so far. It featured a man not much older than me, with strong but attractive features, a thick mop of blonde hair, green eyes, and a rakish smile. According to the identifiers on the page it was clipped to, he was six feet, four inches tall and weighed two hundred pounds.

"Yowza," I muttered, passing the folder to Jim.

"Yowza?" Ingrid repeated. "What does this mean?"

"He's pretty easy on the eyes," I explained. "I'm surprised your girls had so much trouble."

"Wait until he opens his mouth."

I shrugged off her warning. "I think you've prepared me pretty well for that. It's a lot easier to pull this sort of thing off when the target is actually attractive."

"All right," Jim snapped. "We get it."

"Did you see his dimples?" I prodded, tapping on the photo.

He closed the dossier and slid it back into the file, which was sitting on the booth between us. "Please forgive Anna's juvenile behavior. She does it to annoy me."

Ingrid suppressed a smile. "I understand."

The rest of the meeting was indistinguishable from an everyday dinner among friends, Ingrid charming us on behalf of the BKA and Jim becoming slightly less grumpy as the waiter refilled our wine glasses. I watched them interact, mostly ignored, with increasing amusement. As Jim opened up, Ingrid began telegraphing subtle signals: touching her hair, toying with her wine glass, taking exaggeratedly small bites of food until her meal was ignored altogether. By nine o'clock, I was nodding off and the restaurant was closing, so the festivities had to end.

As we filed out into the icy night, Ingrid pulled a business card from her purse and handed it to Jim. "Klaus has been passing your messages to me, but now that we've officially met, we may communicate directly. I will keep Klaus apprised, as necessary."

We parted ways, Jim and I toward the U-Bahn station and Ingrid to a BMW parked on the street next to the restaurant. I grinned at Jim as we walked until he finally looked at me.

"What, Anna?"

"She likes you," I taunted, nudging him in the ribs with my elbow. "You charming devil, you."

"You think?" he asked, uninterested.

"She was cute. Maybe Klaus tagged her in to butter you up."

He shook his head, sighing, "You are so crude sometimes."

"*I'm* crude?" I laughed, poking him in the chest "You called me a gold-digger on our first quote-unquote date!"

He pressed his lips together and didn't respond, and I understood that he'd reached the end of his exceptionally long patience.

11

Tuesday, December 29 to
Wednesday, December 30, 2020
Berlin

As Jim and I walked past the darkened, recessed doorway of an apartment building, he yanked me inside and pushed me against the wall, not hard enough to hurt but plenty hard enough to catch my attention. He grabbed the collar of my coat.

"Why are you doing this to me?" he demanded, his face an inch from mine.

I froze, so surprised by the sudden change in demeanor that I couldn't decide what to say before he stopped waiting for an answer.

"It's not enough that I have to sleep on the couch with you and Jackson in the next room, now I have to hear about how hunky your Nazi friend is and how Ingrid's cute and on and on! Do you think I want to hear that?"

I just stared up at him, wide-eyed. So this was what lay hidden at the end of his seemingly never-ending patience. He shook me.

"Answer me, Anna."

I opened my mouth, still couldn't put any words together, and kissed him once, whispering against his lips, "So do something about it."

He pulled away, letting cold air rush around me again, and snapped, "No. We have work to do, and I expect you to take it seriously."

After a moment of bafflement, I recombobulated myself and hurried after him, catching up as he started down the stairs to the U-Bahn station.

"You should know better than to come at me like that," I chastised. "I might've freaked out completely."

"I'm sorry," he said flatly, leaving it at that.

I grabbed his hand, pulled him to a stop, and forced myself to ask, "What exactly do you think Luke and I have been doing?"

Looking over my head, he asked, "Was that a rhetorical question?"

"Was *that?*" His only answer was a quick, humorless laugh. I said, "Honestly, I'm pretty much sick of both of you at this point. Slamming me against a wall to lecture me about professionalism… ironic."

He had the decency to look upset by this. He asked, "Did I hurt you?"

"No."

"Has he?"

"No," I lied, so easily I almost believed it. "Never."

▼

My suppressed disgust and exasperation with the whole affair manifested itself overnight in a bizarre, chaotic dream which left such an impression that I remembered it even after I got out of bed, used the restroom, and snuggled back under the covers next to a gently snoring Alice.

The dream had begun simply and rationally enough, with me waiting under a bridge in New York's Central Park to meet my blonde-haired, green-eyed, probable Nazi mark for a midnight picnic dinner. While we sipped wine and swapped recipes, the sun rose and a pack of Central Park Rangers, who were also velociraptors, descended on us to hustle us out of the park. We ran, they gave chase, and suddenly I wasn't running next to blondie anymore; I was barreling down a steep mountainside in Hesperus, Colorado, following Dude, while behind us two tall, dark figures slowly gained on us. I reached the cabin, Dude locked the door behind us (I didn't even think to question how), and the scene shifted again. I was standing in the open door of an airborne plane, looking down at the Amazon rainforest thousands of feet below. Alice, identifiable only as an open parachute below me, was screaming at me to jump, but I was clipped in to the fuselage and unable to free myself. The plane went into a sharp nosedive, and I woke up with my stomach clenched by the freefall.

As my dreams went, it was a little heavy-handed. I got a couple more hours of sleep, and then I couldn't keep my eyes closed any longer. I stayed in bed anyway, afraid of what I might do if I went into the common room and found Jim out there, alone.

Our ride back to the hotel last night had been undertaken in uncomfortable silence. We'd hardly acknowledged one another's existence after Jim paid for my fare. I should have pushed back harder on his hypocritical nonsense, but I'd let the moment pass. He plainly thought I was sleeping with Luke. The assumption made me angrier than I cared to admit to Jim. I was a little embarrassed too, which only added to the anger. What had I ever done to make him think so little of me?

Alice gave a more emphatic snore, an impressive sound for such a small person, and I realized this was a conversation I needed to have with another woman. Talking to myself about it wasn't getting me anywhere. As soon as Alice began to show signs of wakefulness, I pounced. Though she was bemused by my sudden enthusiasm for girl talk, she didn't complain.

After we'd conferred in whispers for nearly an hour, she concluded, "You ought to be proud of the way you've comported yourself. Don't let them get you down. They'll have to sort themselves out, won't they?"

Though I appreciated Alice's birds-eye view of the situation, her advice was easier given than followed.

She and I wandered out a while later in search of coffee and food, and I found my homework assignment lying on the coffee table. Ingrid had instructed me to read through the whole file and familiarize myself with its contents, chiefly the three thumbnail-sized bugs that I was going to plant in the target's car, phone, and his apartment. Ingrid had conveniently left that last part out.

And then there was the target himself: Fredrich Hammel, who of course went by Fritz.

According to the dossier, he had a definite type: tall, blonde, and under 40. That was hardly surprising. He liked to hang out at a dive bar on the north side of town that was abjured by tourists due to bad online reviews and favored by—ironically—a mostly anarchist crowd. He liked to argue with people there, and the owner didn't care enough to swat him away.

He was twice-divorced and supporting three children who lived with their mothers, two in Berlin and one in Amsterdam. He had a menial job as a furniture assembler for IKEA, lived alone in an apartment that was stumbling distance from his favorite bar, and had no pets. He had only been arrested once, for assaulting a meter-reader at his parents' house near Dresden five years ago. He paid his taxes, did his job, and spent every spare minute either stumping for his political views, drinking at the bar, or both.

Though Fritz eschewed social media, the better to avoid losing his job at IKEA due to venting his distasteful views, the BKA had laid eyes on enough text messages and emails from other subjects of surveillance to Fritz to suspect he was in the early stages of involvement with a nascent domestic terrorist group. To the BKA, he was the ideal, low-hanging fruit.

Fredrich Hammel was not someone I relished spending an evening with, but I had no doubt about the outcome. The file included photos of the four agents who'd attempted this before me, along with reports they'd written that showed where they all went wrong. The first had taken a classic approach: Buy him a drink, get him talking, and see where the night went. Fritz had left the bar while she was in the restroom. The second tried skulking in a corner looking like a snack, and though she did manage to catch his eye, her shy act caused him to lose interest the moment another woman drifted fecklessly into the bar.

The third agent had foolishly allowed herself to get drawn into a political debate, and, as Ingrid had already divulged, that ended with warm beer dripping down poor Fritz' face and the agent, Natalie Borden, reconsidering her desire to work under-cover. The fourth attempt, if it could even be called that, was by Ingrid herself. Her dry and well-written report gave no indica-tion that her feelings had been hurt by his dismissal. She must have been hoping she wouldn't have to flirt with him.

I'd work out the details with Jim later, but I knew already how my approach would differ from the others. No way would I be making contact with Fritz at his bar. I was willing to bet the farm that if one more blonde bombshell slinked into that cramped, smoky sausage-fest, even the dullest-witted person would start to get suspicious.

12

Wednesday, December 30, 2020
Berlin

Shivering once more in the sub-freezing night air, I huddled in the insufficient shelter provided by the awning over an apartment building's main entryway. A light, nearly frozen rain had started to fall about ten minutes ago, and I wasn't prepared for it.

I jammed my thumb into a random intercom button, the third I'd tried so far. This time I was rewarded by a raspy, possibly female voice demanding, "What? What do you want?"

"I'm looking for Fredrich Hammel," I gasped, trying to sound both polite and loud enough to be heard through the dated intercom system. "Please, can you tell me which apartment is his?"

"If you press my button again, I will call the police!" she shouted back, so fiercely that I took a step back from the intercom and got a handful of frozen rain down the back of my jacket.

Glancing along the street, I saw a tall figure walking slowly toward the apartment, arms stuffed into coat pockets. Steam rose in plumes from his face, bent forward against the slanting rain. Finally. I'd seen Fritz leave the bar over fifteen minutes ago, and it wasn't a long walk. I looked over the bank of intercom buttons, wondering which one to try next. Closing my eyes, I jabbed one at random. Unfortunately, it ended up being the one I'd just pressed.

A beat later, "I am calling the police!"

As Fritz stepped around me to enter the building, I pleaded, "Please, I really need to find Fredrich Hammel. I am desperate—I will pay you—"

"Go away!"

I gave a sob of frustration and rested my forehead against the freezing metal frame of the intercom buttons.

"Excuse me? Miss?"

I jerked upright and turned to face him. He had taken a respectful step back, as far as he could go without leaving the shelter of the awning.

I narrowed my eyes at him, shrinking away, and said, "I am not breaking any law…"

"Why are you looking for Fredrich Hammel?"

"I—I can't tell you. Please, can you let me inside? I need to find which apartment is—"

"You've found him," he said, "Though I don't see why I'd let you inside. I don't know you."

"Oh!" I cried, brightening immediately. "You're Fredrich? You are the Fredrich Hammel who lives here in this building?"

He smirked. "Why are you looking for me? Do I owe you money…?"

"No, no, no, nothing like that." I reached into my backpack and started to extract a manilla envelope, but he reacted badly.

Throwing out one hand, he shouted, "Whoa, take it easy! I don't want any trouble."

I froze, one hand in my backpack. "It's just—"

"Show me what you've got in there."

"Sure, sure." I ripped open the backpack, letting him see inside the main pocket. "You can take it—wait!" I yanked the backpack away as he reached for the envelope. "How do I know you're really him?"

I watched the indecision play across his face, loving every minute of it. He had no idea who I was or what was in the envelope, but he wanted it. He wasn't that drunk though, at least sober enough to fix me with a fairly careful stare.

"An impertinent question, when I have no idea who you are."

"I'm nobody."

"Come up, it's freezing out here. I'll show you my passport," he laughed, probably realizing how absurd this sounded. "Will that be good enough?"

I glared up at the sky, hesitating.

"Unless you think you can find a different Fredrich to give that to," he cajoled.

"All right—but only for a moment. The trains will stop running soon…"

He smirked again, to great effect, and opened the door. "After you, please."

I slipped inside, exaggeratedly maneuvering to keep him in my line of sight. He led the way to the elevator, and I hesitated again before stepping inside.

"This is not what I agreed to," I muttered under my breath.

"Me neither," he answered. "The weather report said no precipitation."

I forced a laugh. "You must think you're talking to a crazy person."

"I'm just curious," he said vaguely.

The elevator doors opened onto a dimly-lit hallway, and he opened the first door on the right. The apartment he ushered me into was messy but not overly so, the furnishings obviously secondhand; odd, I thought, for someone who probably got a hefty employee discount at IKEA.

He opened a desk drawer and extracted a German passport, tossing it to me. "There, see for yourself."

I squinted at him, opened the passport, and held it up to compare the photo to the man. Acting mollified, I tossed the passport back to him.

"All right, so you're him. Here you go." I handed him the envelope. "Thank you for coming along when you did. I was freezing my butt off."

I turned to go, paper rustling behind me as he tore open the envelope. My hand on the doorknob, he arrested me with a sharp, "What is this?"

"I don't know," I groaned, rotating on the spot. "I did not look inside. I just agreed to bring it to you. The weirdo who gave it to me didn't even tell me your apartment number."

He held the contents of the envelope at arm's length, turning it this way and that. I forced back a smile. It was the cover of a vapid, pop culture magazine, tiny rectangles carefully cut away to form something that resembled a colorful, first-generation scantron test key. Alice had been so kind as to take Exact-O Knife to cardstock for us, armed with the latest copy of an NPD brochure Ingrid had helpfully included in the case file. Outwardly indifferent, I watched him examine it.

"I wish I could help you," I sighed. "But I believe my job here is done. Have a good night, Mister Hammel."

I had my hand on the doorknob again when he sucked in a breath and asked, "Do you know what this is?"

"I already said I don't…"

"This is a Cardan grille. Who gave this to you?"

I leaned on the door, crossing my arms. "I have no idea what that means. And I cannot tell you who he was, because he didn't tell me. He just gave me fifty euros and told me your name, and address, and that you needed it. Okay?"

"What did he look like?"

I thew up my hands, exuding impatience to leave. "Like a person, I don't know! This is not worth fifty euros." I checked my watch and groaned. "And I have now missed the last train home. Wonderful. Perfect."

"I'll drive you home," he said, distracted as he continued to study the magazine cover. "Please, sit down."

"Why?"

"You must remember something useful to me. Please, I

won't take up too much of your time. Would another fifty euros turn your head?"

I watched him move a small stack of books off the couch, deliberating. At length, after he'd sat down as though to demonstrate how it was done, I sighed, "I suppose."

"Great. Would you like something to drink?"

"Sure, whatever you've got." I settled onto the couch and watched him disappear into the kitchen. My hand slipped under the coffee table: One down, two to go.

He brought me a beer and resumed his seat before cracking open his own beer. Leaning eagerly over the grille, which he'd laid on the coffee table, he asked, "Can you tell me anything about this man? Where did he meet you, and did he say anything else to you? Do you remember anything at all?"

I took a long draught of my beer before answering, "Sure, I remember a little bit." Well aware that he was hanging on my every word, I slid off the hat I'd stuffed my hair into and let it tumble free. "I was just sitting at a café, reading, and he sat down next to me and put that envelope and the money right in front of me. I told him to beat it, there were plenty of open tables, but he said he needed my help and that he'd pay me.

"I started to leave—I mean, it was pretty weird and I didn't exactly feel safe, you know—but he said all I had to do was deliver this envelope. I eventually agreed, and he left. Of course first he told me where to find you. Mostly."

"Can you describe him?"

"Uh… not very tall, a little bit fat. Brown hair. Glasses. He dressed well. I thought he might be a banker or something. I guess he had kind of a foreign accent, but I don't know for sure. Is that enough? Do you know him?"

He shook his head. "He didn't tell you anything else?"

"No."

"What were you reading?"

"A brochure someone handed me on Bornholmerstrasse. I was bored, my phone died."

"Do you still have it?"

"My phone?"

With very slight impatience, he corrected, "No, the brochure you were reading."

"Oh, sure," I said flippantly.

I pulled a crumpled up roll of paper from a side pocket of my backpack and handed it to him. After Alice had finished making the grille, she'd spent several minutes abusing the brochure so that it didn't look brand new.

"You can have it, if you think it's important," I offered.

He unrolled the brochure and flattened it out on the coffee table. "This has to be it. Why else choose you in particular? He must have seen you reading it."

"Sure, lots of people did. One woman even tried to take it from me, if you can believe that. People are so sensitive."

For a few minutes I was content to observe as he laid the grille over various pages of the brochure at every possible angle. Alice had been clever about it: There was no message to find, but it would take him ages to figure that out.

I finished my beer and sighed pointedly, checking my watch again. "It's getting pretty late. Were you serious about driving me home?"

"What? Oh, yeah, sure. But I have to sober up a bit first."

"Now you tell me," I snipped, glaring at his half-full beer bottle. "How long am I stuck here, then? I might just walk home."

"About an hour. Aren't you curious at all?" he demanded, waving one hand over the coffee table. "There is a message here, there must be. I just can't find it…"

"Well obviously I'm not supposed to know. Otherwise he would've just told me instead of making this grille thing."

"Right…" He left off staring at the encoded message to smile at me. "You know, you're smarter than you look."

"I know," I shrugged. "I practically have to be, right?"

He chuckled. "Great, you know how pretty you are. A dangerous girl. You never told me your name…?"

"No, I didn't."

"Well, that's not very fair. You know my name, and where I live."

"True. You can have my first name only. Ilse."

"Nice to meet you, Ilse."

He turned back to the message and started to take another swig of beer. I snatched the bottle from his hands.

"No, this will not help you sober up. You are trying to keep me here."

"Of course I am, look at you," he grinned.

I stood up, saying with forced calm, "Mister Hammel—"

"Fritz, please."

"Fritz then. Please do not take this the wrong way, but I am very uncomfortable and would like to leave now."

"Fine, fine," he grumbled. "At least let me drink some coffee first."

I waited by the door while he brewed a cup of coffee and threw it back as quickly as he could. He led me back down to an aging Volkswagen parked on the street about half a block from the door of the building and gallantly opened the passenger door for me.

While he walked around the car, my hand found its way between the seat and the center console: One more to go. My job was nearly done, but I still had to bug his phone. I hadn't even seen it yet.

While we waited for the car to warm up enough to melt the accumulated ice on the windshield, he asked, "Where do you live?" I gave him the address of another apartment building. He put the address in his phone, which had been hiding in his coat pocket, and set it in the change tray under the radio. "All right, then. Let's hope I don't get pulled over."

"Are you really that drunk? Do you want me to drive?"

"I'm not drunk at all. I just didn't want you to leave so soon."

An unwelcome twinge of pity caught me off guard. He seemed sincere. Ingrid's dire warnings about unpalatable political ramblings seemed to have been wasted, too. He hadn't even asked me what I thought of the brochure.

Softening a bit, I answered, "I guess I should take that as a sort of compliment."

"Please do. I'm a little rusty with women."

"You? I find that hard to believe."

Slightly appeased, he proceeded to chat me up all the way to the apartment building I supposedly lived in. I could tell he was resisting an urge to bring up politics: Maybe BKA Natalie's snub six months ago had taught him a lesson. He seemed to be building up to asking me for my phone number, but we arrived at the building and he walked me to the door without mentioning it.

I was about to go to plan B and simply offer it, but as I started to go inside, he said, "Give me your phone number."

I turned, giving him a disapproving look instead.

"I mean, may I have your phone number?"

Still saying nothing, I walked back to him and held out my hand. I didn't even have to ask for it: He unlocked his phone and handed it to me. I entered a random number, saved it, and dropped the phone on the ground.

"Ah, no," I groaned, stooping down to recover it. The battery cover had popped off perfectly, leaving the screen undamaged with just a little scratch on one corner. "I'm so sorry, my fingers are frozen. I will buy you a new one—"

"It's okay," he dismissed. "I've dropped it a hundred times."

I snapped the battery cover back on with quiet triumph: Three bugs planted, easy as pie.

"Still, sorry," I said. "Thanks for the ride."

"No problem at all—oh," he started, reaching into his pocket. "I almost forgot." He handed me a fifty-euro note.

"Uh—you keep it," I said reluctantly. "You can buy me a lot of drinks with that."

"Sounds like a plan," he smiled. "Good night, Ilse."

"Good night. And good luck with your puzzle."

13

Wednesday, December 30, 2020 to
Friday, January 1, 2021
Berlin

As Fritz drove away, leaving me practically dancing with smugness, I ducked into the apartment building and waited. About three minutes later, the headlights flashed on an SUV parked across the street. I crossed the street and climbed into the passenger seat. Jim was behind the wheel, staring at me with unflattering disbelief.

"I did not think that would work."

"I know, you made that abundantly clear," I sniffed. "Maybe next time you won't argue with me so much."

"Did you… um…?"

"What? Talk politics?" I glanced sidelong at Jim, searching his profile for a reaction as I said, "For all the interest he showed in the NPD, Ingrid's file on him might have been completely made up. It was weird." When he only gave a disinterested shrug, I added, "I planted all three bugs, and I don't think he noticed."

"Great. I am beyond impressed, Anna." He moved to turn on the car, pausing with his finger on the start button. I read his mind easily enough.

"Don't even start," I warned.

"We don't have to head back right away," he said. "Maybe we should talk about last—"

I cut across him, snapping, "Maybe you should just drive."

He started the car with an expansive sigh and let the matter drop—hopefully for good.

We arrived back at the hotel room well into the early morning hours of New Year's Eve. Alice was asleep on the couch, an arrangement that looked significantly more comfortable for her than it had for Jim. He went to wake her up anyway and instead came back to me with a piece of hotel stationary in his hand, looking amused.

"This was on the table."

"'Don't be a bloody hero, just take the bed,'" I read, shaking with quiet laughter. "That's awfully nice of her."

I turned toward the other bedroom, where Luke was presumably asleep, and Jim asked, "So that's how it is, then?"

"Jim, I'm exhausted. Give me a break, please."

"Fine. But only because I'm exhausted, too."

"We're checking out tomorrow, right?" I asked. He nodded. "So, where are we going?"

My simple question seemed to trouble him. He dithered for

a moment, then said, "Let's talk about that tomorrow."

▼

Whether out of mercy for the long night, or because my presence for the morning's discussion was not wanted, I slept in past 10:00 a.m., less than an hour before we had to check out. I listened to Alice, Jim, and Luke talking in the common room, trying not to be curious about why their voices were raised, their muffled words crisscrossing like fencing blades. I gave up after a few minutes when it became clear that Alice was genuinely distressed. They fell silent when I exited the bedroom.

"What's all the bickering about?" I asked, not bothering to hide my irritation anymore.

"Anna!" Alice cried. "Please talk some sense into this man. He's saying I've got to go back to DC with you. I want to go home!"

"You can't make her come with us," I said at once, frowning at Jim. I struggled to guess why he'd even want to. "Once Marcel knows I'm back in the States, he'll leave her alone."

Jim shot Luke a look of triumph. Luke protested, "So you're not even questioning it, you're going back to DC?"

"Well… yeah. I want to go home, too, Luke."

"What about me? What am I supposed to do?"

"Come with us?" I suggested.

"I'd love to, but I can't."

"Why?"

"Ask him!"

I rounded on Jim, who didn't look even a little sorry. He said coldly, "The FBI doesn't have any current openings for a hitman."

"So you're kidnapping Alice and ditching Luke here to fend for himself," I summarized. "Nice, Jim."

"Obviously, I can't force Alice to come with us," he relented, ignoring the second half of my summary. "I was hoping you could convince her that for now, it's the safest option for her."

"Don't you talk about me like I'm not sitting right here," Alice spat.

"What about Mary?" I asked eagerly. "Couldn't she look after Alice until we're sure the heat's off? I mean, you've got to leave something for the Brits to do."

Jim started to argue on reflex, then shut his mouth and gave my suggestion serious thought.

"Would that be okay with you?" he asked Alice.

"Yes, sure, whatever."

"And I am not going back to the States without Luke," I declared.

Jim looked from Alice, to me, to Luke, fuming. His gaze settled back on me, and he asked, "You really do always get your way, don't you?"

"You say that like I should be sorry."

"Brat," he snarled. "Go pack. Everyone else is ready to go."

I retreated gratefully to the bedroom to do just that, seething less at being called a brat (which was true) and more that I was staring down the barrel of a full day of air travel without being given the chance to take a shower first. I decided halfway through packing that I would just make time for a shower. What were they going to do, leave without me?

An hour later we were all back in the car, a frosty silence prevailing. I had insisted on sitting in the back with Alice, since we would be parting at the airport soon, most likely forever. Fifteen minutes into the ride, she finally loosened up enough to tear her eyes away from the city flashing past her window. She turned to me.

"I'm sorry I don't want to stick with you and all," she said awkwardly.

"I'm surprised you stuck it out this long. You don't have to apologize. I'm the one who lied to you and got you mixed up in all this."

"It's honestly been a total riot. Even with the little kidnapping bit, I think I'd do it again. It's just too bad I can't ever tell anyone what happened."

"You've got ice in your veins, Murphy. You should ask Mary about joining MI5."

She laughed. "Yeah, maybe I will."

Though we arrived at the airport well before noon, the flight Jim had booked for us didn't leave until 4:15. Jim, making no bones about his displeasure with the whole arrangement, set about getting Alice's ticket changed to London and securing a flight for Luke. The latter task was accomplished with extraordinary pettiness: Jim and I had first class seats, and Luke was relegated to the very back of the airplane in coach. At least he was on the same flight.

Alice left just after two, a parting that nearly brought me to tears. I had stupidly let myself become attached to her, knowing full well how brief our acquaintance would ultimately be. With a request to say hi to Cat and our other cohorts at the pub, and an empty promise to visit London if my life ever stopped being a complete goat rope, I watched her board the flight to London and then wandered despondently back to my gate.

It wasn't a full flight, and it didn't leave for two hours, so the seating area was almost empty. Luke and Jim had posted up at opposite ends.

"Stupid babies," I whispered to myself, drawing a stern look from a young mother sitting nearby with her infant. I stared at her, gasping, "Oh, no, sorry. I didn't mean you."

She turned away, either not understanding or not caring. I plopped down in a seat equidistant from both men, making sure they saw me. Whether from pride or because they were tired of my lousy attitude too, neither one got up to sit with me. Good. I jammed a wildly overpriced pair of earbuds into my head and sat back to find another podcast to listen to.

I found the series Alice had gotten us started on and began scrolling through a mile-long list of episodes. The date December 7, 1945 in one description caught my eye. It seemed like an interesting place to start, so I clicked on the episode. Five minutes in, my jaw popped open in surprise.

Dante Barbato was born in Italy in 1901, on the island of Sardinia...

I backed up, listening more closely, wondering if I'd misheard. I hadn't.

Was Barbato a common name? I'd never heard it until the

meeting at Marcel's house. I certainly hadn't expected to hear it again so soon. With the podcast carrying on, halfway ignored, I began digging through the internet for more details about this Dante character who shared a last name with Paolo Barbato, the missing man who was of such interest to Marcel Marchand and his five Sardinian friends a few short days ago.

I told myself it was just something to do, a meaningless distraction from the present. It was a noteworthy coincidence, no more and no less. The full story was heartbreaking: A family of seven children had been slashed to four when a house fire consumed their home in Georgia on a cold December night in 1945. The father, Dante Barbato, had changed his name to Donald Barber when he moved to the United States in 1938. He'd been a vocal opponent of Mussolini and the Italian Fascist regime but otherwise tight-lipped about his life prior to immigrating to America. Conspiracy theories therefore abounded about the cause of the fire that killed three of his children on the fourth anniversary of the attack on Pearl Harbor.

I got sucked into the story and nearly missed my boarding call. After grudgingly pausing my podcast, I joined Jim in the short queue of first-class passengers waiting to board. Once comfortably ensconced in my spacious window seat, I went right back to the program. Jim yanked one earbud out of my ear to get my attention.

"Are you going to ignore me for the whole flight?" he asked.

"If you'll let me," I shot back churlishly.

"No, I don't think I will. What are you listening to?"

"A bossy jerk."

"On your phone."

"No, sitting next to me."

"Anna…"

"It's just that crime podcast. I've got to pass the time somehow!"

Without asking, he put my earbud in his own ear and listened. For some reason, his face darkened; but as soon as I noticed it, the expression was gone.

"Interesting choice," he said, giving me back the earbud. He got his own pair from a flight attendant, picked a movie to watch, and kindly ignored me.

Several hours in, when I'd tired of murder and mayhem and switched to music, my attention was arrested by Jim pushing a half-full glass of champagne into my hand.

I pulled out the earbuds and asked, "What the heck is this for?"

He pointed up, toward the overhead speakers. Apparently I'd missed something. A couple seconds later, the captain's voice counted down from ten and then wished us a happy new year with supreme disinterest. Glasses clinked all around the first class cabin.

"Happy new year, you little monster," Jim said, a smile in his voice somewhat reducing the sting of the insult. He nudged my champagne glass with his and downed it in one big gulp.

I studied my glass and asked it, "Are the peasants getting champagne, too?"

"What do you think?"

"I think it's good to be the king."

"That's the spirit. Drink up."

I complied happily, then leaned across the armrest to plant one on his lips. "For good luck," I explained.

▼

According to my stomach, it was time for breakfast when we touched down in Miami around midnight to catch our connecting flight to Washington, DC. Immediately after landing, the captain wished us a happy new year again, to general laughter. We deplaned, met up with Luke after he'd worked his way through customs, and shared a quiet breakfast at a coffee shop. Luke wasn't nearly as grumpy as I would've been after fourteen hours in coach.

"By the way, Jim," he said cheerfully, breaking the silence, "I forgot to thank you for the ticket. Must've cost you."

Jim shot back, "My pleasure."

"Hope you're not thinking of sending me a bill, because I'm currently between jobs. What's the plan, by the way?"

"For starters, I thought I might arrest you for murder and for entering the United States with a phony passport."

I perked up, roused out of my desire to tune them both out. "Say what?"

"Don't worry, kiddo. We'll make a deal, he'll hardly spend any time in prison."

"You know what, old man?" Luke fired back. "I'm not too worried about it."

"Oh, spare me," I sighed, standing up so quickly I made

myself lightheaded. "Can you two grow up? You're driving me bananas."

Neither cared to answer, leaving me free to drag my suitcase and backpack over to a quiet bench and try to get some shuteye. Sweet sleep closed over me almost instantly, as I'd hardly slept a wink on the plane. When I snapped out of it, the sky beyond the huge terminal windows was still black, the airport only slightly busier. I realized what had woken me when I felt a tug on the strap of my backpack, which I was both wearing and using as a pillow.

"Anna, come on, we're about to miss our flight," Jim was saying, his voice soft as though trying not to fully wake me.

I stood up and followed him, groggy and unsteady on my feet. After a second I asked, "Wo ist Luke?"

"Luke? He already boarded. I didn't realize you'd be so hard to find. What are you, trying to get left behind?"

"Nein. Ah, mein koffer," I mumbled, starting to turn back.

Jim caught me and dragged me along with him. "Are you looking for your suitcase? I've got it. Just walk. And if you want me to understand you, stop speaking German."

I searched my brain for the right words and sighed, "Man, I'm tired."

I allowed Jim to lead me to a tiny gate at the farthest end of the terminal, where instead of tunneling through a skybridge to board our plane, we walked right outside onto the tarmac and headed for a tiny Cessna. The infamous Florida humidity only amplified my bleary state, but I finally realized something was strange when I was climbing up the staircase ahead of Jim.

I stopped and asked, "We're taking a private plane to DC?"

"Sure, didn't I mention that earlier?"

"I must've been ignoring you. Is this yours?"

"I don't own a private jet, Anna. Move it, we need to take off very soon."

It didn't take a detective to discern Luke's absence inside the little jet. I glanced at the bathroom, but it wasn't in use. The last tendrils of sleep vanished, and suddenly I was wide awake.

"Jim, where is Luke?"

"I really couldn't care less. Sit down."

"No," I growled, trying to push past him. He blocked the narrow aisle, gripping the seats to either side for extra stopping power as I insisted, "Get out of the way, I mean it!"

Without warning he shoved me backward, and I dropped into the nearest seat. As I started to pop back up, he drew a pistol from his belt and pointed it at me. I froze.

"Sit down, shut up, and buckle your seat belt."

14

Friday, January 1, 2021
Miami

I stared at the gun in Jim's hand, trying to make it make sense. Shock had completely taken my breath away, along with any impulse to fight. My hands shook as I fastened the seatbelt, my eyes never leaving the gun. As soon as the seatbelt clicked into place, he holstered the weapon.

"Jim…"

"What part of shut up don't you understand?"

While I tried to wrap my head around this turn of events, an achingly familiar, keening whine hit my ears. I sat up ramrod straight, staring at the still-open door through which the sound was coming. Through the door, half-dragging an airport employee, bounded a massive German Shepherd.

Dude.

He saw me, ripped the leash out of the man's hand, and thundered down the aisle to lick my face in greeting. I wrapped my arms around him and held on, too baffled at this point to ask why, how, or when. I heard Jim apologizing to the man for the trouble and thanking him for bringing Dude.

Not content with my calm reunion, Dude jumped half in my lap and tried to lick my face while I struggled to hold onto 100-plus pounds of squirming German Shepherd. The last time I'd seen my faithful dog was the morning of September fourth. He'd been sitting inside my parents' fence, shrinking in my rear-view mirror as he watched me drive away. I hadn't known then that I was saying goodbye for four months.

Dude.

One sob racked my body, but I refused to fall apart with Jim only yards away, probably congratulating himself for arranging this. Burying my face in Dude's neck scruff, I hid long enough to compose myself and then let him go. He licked my face one more time, then turned to Jim and would have lunged toward him for another reunion if I hadn't wrapped my hand around his collar to hold him back.

The door closed, and we began to taxi. Dude disliked it, showing his distress by jumping into the seat next to me and resting his head on my shoulder. I decided to buckle him in too, to which he consented with an uncharacteristically mild manner.

I sat back, Dude's big face brushing against mine, and stared at Jim.

He'd chosen the long seat facing the door and was sitting with his elbows on his knees, his face in his hands. He was as still as a statue. Not until we began our ascent did he straighten up and put on a seat belt himself. He met my eyes and turned away in the same second, his expression unfathomable.

Thanks to Dude being much worse at flying than I was, I was able to ignore my own fear and confusion in favor of consoling his. He was okay once we leveled off, and then I was rewarded for my efforts by being trapped underneath him while he snoozed. It wasn't such a bad way to pass the time, and I was glad I could be there for him. However he'd gotten to Miami, it probably hadn't been his idea of fun. Helped along by every variety of exhaustion and a 110-pound heated blanket, I slipped into a light doze.

▼

I woke up to a completely different cabin. All the shades were down, and sunlight pierced the hairline gaps around them, filling the interior with a soft glow. At some point my seat had been leaned back and I'd been covered by a blanket, and now I was alone in the cabin. For a while I just lay there, listening fecklessly to the hum of air around the plane.

Suddenly the hum stopped and I sat up in terror, expecting to start plummeting to earth. Several loud bumps followed, and then voices outside near the wing caused a gut-wrenching reorientation of reality: We were on the ground.

I opened the nearest shade and looked outside, thinking foolishly of Dulles or Hobby or DFW; but this was no airport. It was a long, dirt field surrounded by green and yellow pastures, with steely gray mountains far in the distance. For the first time in my life, I couldn't narrow my location down to anything more specific than planet earth, and the effect was not what I'd have guessed. Far from being afraid or despondent, I found myself oddly excited. And furious at Jim, of course.

Movement outside the window caught my eye. Looking down closer to the airplane's nose, I saw Dude sniffing along the ground and Jim following, holding a slackened leash. I decided Dude's license to sniff out bad guys was officially revoked, and then I got up and headed for the lavatory with my trusty backpack.

I fished out a change of clothes and my toothbrush. With dulled surprise I noted the absence of my laptop and quickly ascertained that my phone and passport had been taken as well. While searching all the pockets just in case, I dislodged a scrap of blue paper which floated down to rest on the floor. I picked it up and stuffed it back in the much-abused backpack without really looking at it, then realized that there was no blue paper in my backpack; or there shouldn't have been.

I pulled the paper back out and stared at it around the toothbrush poking out of my mouth. Nothing but a very sloppy, unfamiliar phone number. I committed the number to memory, flushed the paper down the toilet, and carried on brushing my teeth. Refreshed by my change of clothes and by the thought that someone, most likely Luke, was leaving me helpful clues, I returned to the cabin. The main door opened at the same time, and Dude bounded inside with Jim on his tail.

They looked more or less equally glad to see me. Wishing to discourage one of them, I asked coldly, "Where are we?"

"Colombia. Just a quick stop for fuel. Are you hungry?"

"Where in Colombia?"

He locked the door, held up one finger, and said, "Hold on a sec—" before disappearing into the cockpit. When he came out a minute later, we were bumping along the makeshift runway and gaining speed for another take off.

"We're in Plato," Jim said.

"Where's that?"

"You tell me, smarty pants."

"Don't try to get cute with me. Where are we going?"

"What difference does it make to you?"

My mouth popped open in surprise. "Seriously?"

"Yes, seriously. You were going to come back with me to Washington, and now you're coming with me somewhere else. Just go with it."

"Screw that!"

My continued bad attitude had the desired effect. Scoffing, Jim took his seat and gave his phone his undivided attention.

As the hours ticked by, I sat and watched the clouds with detached fascination. Sometimes we were above them, sometimes in them, and every now and then we'd drop down under the clouds so I could see the earth far below. I couldn't deny that the view was killer. Though I was still drifting in and out of sleep as though my body simply couldn't get enough of it, it seemed like the perfect time to start wrapping my head around what was happening.

I had seen my boarding pass for the second flight, and it definitely said Miami to Washington, DC. Clearly we were headed in the opposite direction, and I knew our final destination would be Argentina. That was the location, according to Luke, of his next target; and I just didn't believe in coincidences anymore.

What Jim was up to now, and why I had to be strong-armed along with my dog, wasn't something I could guess at that point. Obviously, he wanted to separate me from Luke. That was a no-brainer, but this seemed like an awful lot of effort to accomplish that. I wanted answers so badly I stooped to the only available means of finding out. I got out of my seat and held up my hands in a sign of surrender when Jim caught sight of me.

"I'm not trying to start anything," I reassured him.

"I didn't tell you you could get up."

I shrugged. "If you keep being so mean to me, I'm gonna get really mad, and you know I'll get that gun away from you."

He glared at me, furious, and then his expression relaxed into defeat. "What do you want?"

I sat down next to him and asked, "What do *you* want with me and Dude? Why are you doing this?"

"My hands are tied. I'm sorry."

"That answer contained no information. Come on," I dug, scooting a little closer to him. "I'm gonna find out sooner or later. I'm dying of suspense, here."

He stared straight ahead, immune to my wheedling.

I asked, "If I guess, will you tell me?"

"No, but I'm interested to hear you guess anyway."

"Okay… Obviously, we both need a vacation. Are we going dove hunting?"

"No."

"Are you taking me to a secret bunker to ravish me and keep me locked up as a sex slave?"

He laughed, almost in spite of himself. "Good idea, but no. One more guess."

"Are we going to Argentina?"

He turned to me, half surprised. "Yes. How did you guess?"

"There's only so much south of Colombia. You don't seem like a Paraguay sort of guy."

"Uh huh. Any other reason?"

"Luke's next target is in Argentina. Even though I assume he's not pursuing that anymore… You know, because he uprooted his entire life to save mine… let's just say I'm already at my coincidence threshold."

"You give him far too much credit."

"That, explain that," I said eagerly, scooting still closer.

"Nah."

"Okay, then… What's in Argentina?"

"Lots of things."

He was plainly done answering questions. I was wearing him out. I leaned my head against the window just as the plane rolled into a gentle turn, and I could see straight down when we dipped below the clouds again. Leagues of dark green stretched out all around us, but in the distance ahead I saw snow-capped mountains. I returned to my seat, stymied for the moment.

We followed the Andes south for a few hours. As the sun was sinking, we turned straight east.

"This view is unreal." I said.

When I received no answer, I turned to see Jim stretched

out on the seat, fast asleep. One arm had fallen to the floor, but the other lay over his chest. In his hand, pressed between his palm and his shirt, was his phone.

Without making a sound I stood, slipped the phone out of his grasp, used his thumb to unlock it, and slinked to the lavatory. I'd dialed the number from the piece of blue paper and had one finger poised over the Call button when second thoughts, those insidious enemies of the most dedicated impulse-follower, stayed my hand. Talking to whoever was at the other end would make noise. Noise would get me caught. I had no idea how Jim would react to me taking his phone, not after he'd pointed a gun after me.

Instead of calling, I opened the web browser and looked up the number. The results were meaningless. It was a cell phone registered in Lyon, France. The internet would surrender no further details for free. Ten more seconds to delete the browser history and attempt to snoop through Jim's text messages (there were none), and I'd done all I could. I locked the phone and rubbed my fingerprints off the screen, then slipped the phone into my pocket. I was reaching for the door when it began to shake under a barrage of impatient knocks.

"Anna—open the door."

"Can't a girl use the bathroom in peace?" I demanded, searching the tiny room for some place to hide the phone. The doorknob rattled loudly. "Jim! Seriously?"

"Open the door."

There wasn't anywhere to hide his phone that wouldn't be completely obvious. Feeling a little spiteful, I flushed the toilet and used the sound to mask the *plop* of his phone dropping into a half-full water bowl that I'd placed on the floor for Dude.

I opened the door to find a very perturbed man blocking the hallway. I couldn't blame him, but I pretended to.

"What is your problem?" I hissed.

"Where's my phone?"

"Do I look like your personal assistant?"

"It was in my hand when I fell asleep, and now it's gone. Are you suggesting someone else took it?"

He couldn't have set me up better. Fighting a smile, I said innocently, "Dude's been known to chew on expensive electronics. Why don't you ask him?"

His gaze fell, and I knew without following it what he was looking at when he said, "Great."

"What—oh, no! Naughty dog."

As he stooped down to retrieve the dripping phone, he muttered, "If you think I'm buying that innocent act you can think again."

"Is it ruined? You should put it in rice to dry it out."

"You think you can get away with murder, don't you?" he snarled. It would have made me laugh—I probably could—if he hadn't reached behind him and slammed the door shut as he said it. I pressed against the wall opposite the sink, trying to get some breathing room, but it was a wasted effort. He grabbed me by the chin and forced me to look up at him.

"We'll be landing in about three and a half hours," he said with forced calm. "It's two more by car to my cousin's estate. That gives you five hours and thirty minutes to get the rest of these theatrics out of your system."

"So I can impress your cousin, whoever that's supposed to be?"

"Look, all I'm asking is that you hide your total contempt for me, if you don't mind. Around him, at least. In private you just be as ornery as you want."

"You don't know what you're asking for," I warned.

A thumb raced across my lips, and he breathed, "We both know you'll forgive me."

"I will hurt you, Jim."

"What's stopping you?"

I looked up at him, rolled my eyes, and said, "I'd like to leave the bathroom now."

He nodded. Reaching behind himself to grab his phone off the counter, he gave it an experimental shake. It sloshed audibly.

"Rice, huh?"

"That's what they say."

"And you're blaming Dude for this?"

"He's a monster."

"Yeah…" He spun the phone around a few times between his fingers but made no move toward the door. "You know, maybe you can get away with murder. But I still need to know. Did you call anyone?"

I shook my head.

"Text?"

"No."

"Anything?"

"No, Jim. I couldn't get past the lock screen. I didn't even put it in the bowl on purpose. I dropped it. Some spy I am."

"It's for the best, I guess." He sighed, finally opening the door and letting us both out.

We took our accustomed seats and stared at each other for a second. I didn't know what to make of him now. He was definitely not the person I thought he was, but somehow he was still, at least partially, my Jim.

"What do you want to do for the next three and a half hours?" he asked.

"Eat. Continuously."

"I was wondering when you'd notice you hadn't eaten all day."

In a couple minutes he'd assembled quite a feast of supplies from the plane's stores: fancy crackers, goat cheese, dehydrated fruit, little pieces of chocolate, and two tiny bottles of wine. I worked my way through the food without any help from Jim. He claimed to have eaten while I dozed, but I suspected he'd been sustaining himself with liquid calories for a while.

We touched down in a city called Alto Río Senguer at a bona-fide airport, no more strips of dirt in the mountains. It was clear from the moment we deplaned, descending the staircase straight into a waiting SUV, that someone with clout was pulling the strings. There weren't even any customs and immigration people waiting to check our passports et cetera. Behind the wheel, Jim required neither escort nor directions to find his way out of the airport and onto a southbound highway.

The promised two-hour drive started around sunset. We drove south for a while, then turned west toward a roiling bank of dark orange clouds in front of the sinking sun, beneath which the land rose to meet the Andes. As night fell a thunderstorm was unleashed, periodically brightening the way ahead with flashes of lighting.

I guessed we were closer to the Chilean border than any Argentine city by the time we stopped at a monumental gate at the end of a gravel road. We hadn't made any turns for at least half an hour. The whole road seemed to be someone's driveway. After several seconds, the gate groaned open on its own power and admitted us.

About two kilometers later a sprawling, palatial, Spanish-style home appeared, framed against the angry sky and blurred by torrents of rain. We pulled into a wide portico over the driveway, and an eerie quiet fell around us. Dude barked once from the back seat as two young men hurried out of the house toward the car. Jim got out and beckoned for me to follow. I let Dude out and kept a death grip on his leash.

One of the men greeted me politely in Spanish and asked for Dude's leash.

I shook my head. "He stays with me."

"What does he want?" Jim asked.

I gaped at him, floored. "All this and you don't understand Spanish? You lazy American."

"I'm working on it. What does he want?"

"Dude."

"Oh. It's okay, There's an enclosure for him behind the kitchen. Apparently they used to have a pet jaguar... He'll be fine."

I scoffed. "He'll be fine because he'll be with me."

"Ask him if you can take him back there yourself. I'm sure it'll be perfectly cozy."

I complied, and the man led Jim, Dude, and me through a dizzyingly grand house to a small courtyard behind the kitchen. The exterior lights had been retrofitted, their wires stapled to the plaster and painted white along with the exterior of the house. Within the halo of visibility provided by these lights was a tiny herb garden, a compost heap, a shed, and, at the end farthest from the door, something that looked like it belonged in a zoo.

A neat border of gravel surrounded the enclosure, its base composed of concrete. The metal bars enclosed an enormous volume—I estimated eight feet tall, ten feet wide, maybe twelve feet long—as well as an oversized doghouse, some toys, and a set of food and water bowls that some Argentine princess had probably eaten out of a hundred years ago. I relinquished Dude's leash to our guide and watched as he cooed lovingly at my dog and coaxed him unresisting into the enclosure. He even went inside with him and showed him around as though Dude were a four-legged diplomat.

"Okay, I'm convinced," I said. "This isn't happening. I'm still asleep on a bench in the Miami airport."

"If it helps you deal with this, then sure," Jim said quietly. "Come on, I want you to meet Fernando."

15

Friday, January 1, 2021
Argentina

I wasn't that eager to meet Fernando, presumably this cousin Jim had mentioned, but I trailed along behind Jim as he found his way to a pair of closed doors on the second floor. He was obviously familiar with the house.

He knocked twice and turned to me while we waited for an answer. "Please be nice."

"I'm always nice," I hissed back. "Remember how *nice* I was when I didn't take your gun and shoot you with it?"

The doors were thrown open from the inside to reveal a man who looked so much like Jim that I could only stare dumbly at him. He was shorter, darker, and younger; but any doubts I had about there being a real, blood relation vanished at first sight. He looked about as grumpy, too, at least until he saw Jim.

"Oh, it's you!" My question about how Jim sustained this relationship without speaking Spanish was thus answered: Fernando's English was flawless. "Sorry, I thought it was Marisol again. Come in, please. How was your trip?"

We entered a cave-like study of luxurious proportions, our footsteps muffled as we crossed from bare terra cotta tiles onto a thick, room-sized carpet.

"Anna made it needlessly difficult."

"As anticipated," Fernando agreed with a smile at me. "James has told me so much about you. Where is el perrísimo?"

"Dude?" I asked. Fernando nodded, and I said tersely, "He's in a cage."

He stopped in front of an enormous desk, resting the tips of his fingers on it and regarding me with interest. "I see."

I studied him, taking in the fine clothes, clean-shaven face, and rigid posture with vague detachment. Finally his supercilious expression broke through my stupor, and I remembered Jim's instruction to be nice. I said, "Sorry, I didn't mean for that to sound so rude."

"Think nothing of it," he dismissed with a wave of his hand. "You must be confused and tired. Wine?"

"Yes, please."

While Fernando poured three generous glasses of wine of such a dark purple hue that it was nearly black, he said in rapid Spanish, "I take it from your dumbfounded expression that James hasn't told you anything that would explain why you've been brought here."

"No, he hasn't," I said to the exclusion of Jim, who soon wore a familiar look of annoyance at being shut out of the conversation.

"I apologize on his behalf. He might have believed he wasn't supposed to. I'm sure he will be very forthcoming once I assure him that there's no reason to keep you in the dark."

"Okay. Thank you."

"What are you telling her?" Jim interjected.

Fernando *tsked* sadly. "James, you really need to learn Spanish. It's not right to have to converse in this ugly way."

"I've been a little busy. We don't all have Anna's gift for languages."

"Too bad. Please, sit down," he said, gesturing at a sofa in the center of the room. We obeyed, and he passed us each a wine glass before settling into an armchair. "I'm sure you're both ready for bed, but I wanted to ask a few questions before…" He trailed off, focusing on the open door, and asked, "Yes, Mari?"

I turned to see a woman in her late teens standing in the doorway, arms akimbo, regarding the three of us with regal disdain. "They're doing it again," she hurled at Fernando. "If you don't make them stop, I will!"

He shook his head, looked up at the ceiling as though praying for patience, and rose to his feet. My hopes of learning who "they" were and what they were doing were squashed as Fernando sighed, "Never mind. We'll talk in the morning. James, take any room you want, but I'm afraid I'll have to be rude and ask you to see yourselves there. Feel free to take the wine with you."

He departed, two pairs of footsteps and one shrill voice fading away down the hall. I took a drink of wine, not sure what else to do.

"This is really good," I said.

"It's older than you," Jim answered. "So, try to savor it."

"Fernando told me it's okay for you to tell me what's going on."

"Did he now?"

I nodded. "Yes, just now. He seems to be el jefe. So… are you going to tell me anything?"

He stood up, waiting until I did the same before answering, "I don't really feel like it right now. Let's go find a place to sleep."

I let him lead me from the room. Out in the hall, Mari's voice was once more audible: farther away, but louder. We turned away from the sound and climbed to the third floor, where Jim found a large bedroom that met with my approval. He showed me inside, and I made a beeline for the bathroom, announcing, "I'm going to take a shower, please leave me alone!"

"Fine. I'll go get our luggage."

"You mean *my* luggage?" I asked, but he was already gone.

Ignoring the cool, gray-and-white finery of the bathroom, I locked the door, stripped naked, and fired up a very hot shower. Soon the bathroom was opaque with steam, and I stood under the tap and let the heat burn away everything it could.

When I opened my eyes, I could almost believe I was standing on a rock in the center of a lake, dense fog erasing all visual detail, impossibly hot rain drumming against my bare skin in an exhilarating tug-of-war between pain and pleasure. If I took a step in any direction, I'd plunge into the water, never to be seen or heard from again.

The fantasy withdrew as the rain became warm, then tepid, then downright cold. The steam began to dissipate as well, revealing the walls of the shower, the glass door, and the empty bathroom beyond. I was alone in the bathroom. It didn't really matter. Any effort to avoid Jim would be wasted, even if I could commit to it. Until he brought my luggage, I had no clothes to change into, so I wrapped myself in a cashmere-soft purple towel and crept out into the bedroom.

My spirits sank at the sight of the empty room. I was fully prepared to tell Jim to get the heck out of my sight, so why was I disappointed that he already was? Probably, I just wanted the satisfaction of yelling at him.

Now that I was a little calmer, I looked around appreciatively. The floor, ceiling, and furniture were all dark teak, and everything else was white or yellow, with splashes of turquoise and red here and there. The effect was soothing, an impression helped along by the high ceiling and open double doors across the room from the main door. One would be hard pressed to feel trapped in such a setting, even if one were, in point of fact, not free to leave.

At least I was free to pepper Jim with questions, which I planned to do the moment I was dressed. I stepped through the open doors onto a small, semi-circular balcony and felt my spirits lift again. The balcony faced the courtyard behind the kitchen, and I could see Dude curled up in his gilded cage far below. If he was relaxed, I could relax.

Turning back to the room, I belatedly noticed a few things that were definitely not there when I'd entered the bathroom. Next to my mostly-full glass of wine on the dresser, someone had placed an unopened bottle. A '59 Malbec, no less. No corkscrew.

My suitcase had already been delivered and left next to the bed, and lying on the foot of the bed was something I took for a bright blue, silk scarf. I was more interested in the hair dryer I'd stolen from the Ritz-Carlton in Berlin. I gave the scarf one last curious look as I walked away, and I stopped mid-step. It wasn't a scarf, it was a negligée. I snatched it off the bed, examining it in disbelief.

That man had some nerve. I stalked over to the trashcan by the door and was about to hurl it in when I stopped myself again. It wasn't the negligée's fault Jim was being a jerk. And it was an absolutely flawless shade of bright, royal blue—my favorite color. I checked the tag, wondering if I could determine where, and thus when, he'd bought it. It was in German.

"Fine," I whispered to the garment. "I accept this inappropriate, wildly optimistic, and stupidly expensive gift, but I'm not wearing it."

Savoring the warm, dry air, I dried my hair, brushed my teeth, threw on a t-shirt and shorts, and returned to the bedroom. This time, nothing had changed. I took my glass of wine back out to the balcony and gazed down at Dude, halfway wishing I could curl up next to him. I considered calling to him, just to let him know I was okay; but they say to let sleeping dogs lie.

I finished off my wine and padded across the thick carpet to the dresser, pondering how best to uncork the new bottle without the necessary equipment. A knock at the door cut through my thoughts.

"Unless you have a corkscrew, go away," I called cheerfully.

The door opened and Jim let himself in, responding to my

sharp look by holding up a corkscrew.

"Oh. Fine."

In open retreat, I returned to the balcony while Jim uncorked the wine and poured two glasses. He followed me out, pressing one glass into my hand and standing behind me to sip quietly at his own. After a few minutes of almost comfortable silence, Jim swept my hair over my shoulder and pressed his lips to my neck.

"I had no idea how else to get you here," he breathed. "I didn't have time to argue. I couldn't fight you if I wanted to. I'm sorry."

The halfway decent apology only solidified my anger, and I asked tonelessly, "What's the first rule of gun safety, Jim?"

"Um… keep it pointed in a safe direction."

"Don't point it at anything you're not willing to kill or destroy," I corrected, using the more colorful version my dad had taught me. "I guess I know what that makes me."

"It wasn't loaded."

"… What's the second rule of gun safety, Jim?"

"All right, I get it. It was a horrible thing to do. You think I don't know that?"

"You're terrible at apologizing."

"Hey, it's no picnic trying to apologize to you. You're terrible at accepting it."

For half a heartbeat I was so incensed I couldn't even see, but the bald truth in his words got through. I laughed. "Fair enough."

His hand slid down my back. Through a sigh, he asked,

"Will you at least look at me?"

I rotated, took a slow drink of wine as I looked him over, and concluded, "This is uncomfortable. If you're going to make me do this, sit down so I don't break my neck."

He suppressed a smile and walked over to sit on the bed. I followed. Standing in front of Jim, I was able to enjoy the novelty of looking down at him while I gathered my thoughts.

At length I said, "I do not forgive you, or trust you, or believe anything that comes off that evil, lying, silver tongue of yours, got it?"

He nodded.

"Good. That said, I'm willing to see how this plays out. I mean, what are the odds it goes as badly for me as your last diabolical plan?"

"Fifty-fifty," he said.

I took his wine glass and mine, found a table to set them on, and came back to him. He didn't object when I pressed my hands to his face, or when I slid them into his hair.

I whispered, "Every time I try to kiss you, you practically run screaming from me. Why?"

"Why do you keep trying?"

He had my number, and he knew it. My fingers twitched, giving his hair a not-so-gentle tug. I wasn't sure whether I wanted to kiss him or tear him up into little pieces, and he didn't seem to care which way I was leaning. I tried a kiss, and for once I pulled away before he could.

Looking around the room, I saw my luggage where he'd left it. His luggage was nowhere in sight. Though he'd grabbed me by the waist and pulled me closer, he'd already let go and folded his hands together. I noticed he was still wearing shoes. He hadn't even asked me about the stupid negligée he'd left out for me.

Something clicked, and I asked, "You're making a point, aren't you?"

"Is it working?"

I kissed him again. "Yes. It's actually kind of sweet. You can stay and talk though, if you want. I have a lot of questions."

"Tempting, but I need to sleep. We'll talk in the morning, okay?"

"Fine."

I backed up so he could stand, and he grabbed his wine glass from the table. He topped it off, then gave me a quick kiss on the cheek before heading for the door.

I finished my wine, rinsed out the glass, and turned off all the lights. After a few more minutes on the balcony, gazing down at Dude while my thoughts refused to take any discernable form, I crawled into bed. I tossed and turned and failed to fall asleep before the clock radio next to the bed confirmed the longest New Year's Day I'd ever lived through had finally come to an end.

16
Saturday, January 2, 2021
Argentina

Jim woke me up midmorning by inviting himself into my room and announcing it was time to talk. I would rather have skipped it in favor of more sleep, but he was in an indulgent mood, so I took full advantage. Sitting up in bed with the cup of coffee he'd brought me, I waited while he made himself comfortable in a nearby armchair.

"So, what do you want to know?" he asked, when I was still thinking over how to start prodding him for answers.

"Everything," I said eagerly.

"Can you point me to the starting line?"

"Hm," I mused, distracted by my study of his hair. I spotted a few hints of silver in his otherwise black hair and said, "Hey, you've got grays."

"I didn't when I met you."

"Har, har."

"Don't you want to know why I brought you here?"

"I want to know who Fernando is. You only told me he's your cousin."

"He's my second cousin, actually. Fernando and Marisol's grandmother, my grandmother's sister, changed her last name when she married their grandfather. Even if she hadn't, she was supposed to have died in the house fire in nineteen forty-five. My uncle still has the death certificate."

My next question caught in my throat, my mind suddenly racing so fast I couldn't do anything but try to keep up with it. "Nineteen forty-five?" I repeated.

"I can tell you're skipping ahead. That stupid true crime podcast…"

"I wasn't even sure that was the same Barbato."

"Well, the damage was done. I had to tell Fernando you were putting it together. I'm sorry, Anna. He convinced me to bring you here."

"I'm glad he didn't convince you to punt me out of the plane over the Gulf of Mexico. What exactly was I putting to-gether?"

"My grandmother, Bettina, was one of the seven children, one of the four who made it out. She married a Camposanto. You'd have gotten to the Barbato-Barber connection in a day at most, if you were curious enough."

"So I listened to a popular podcast episode and might have figured out your great grandfather was Donald Barber? The FBI already knows that. How does that lead to Fernando?"

"Paolo Barbato. Marcel shoehorned you into that meeting

with the Italians, and you heard the name Barbato not a week later, drawing a line right back to the Barbers and their descendants. You would've told someone at the FBI about the connection, and they would've done the rest."

"I didn't even know Fernando existed until you dragged me here! Is Barbato even his last name?"

"It's Serna."

"So you've explained nothing!"

"The FBI has closed the Barber case. The presumption is that if any of the missing kids survived, they'd have surfaced by now. The FBI isn't looking for them anymore, let alone their descendants. That's what Paolo Barbato and Fernando have in common. The existence of one allows for the existence of the other, and Fernando's and Marisol's survival depends on no one making that connection."

Doggedly, I argued, "How in the world was I ever going to find out Paolo descended from one of the survivors? I know nothing about him, except that Marcel was interested in him for some reason."

A blank look crossed his face, and he focused on thin air behind me. "I thought Marcel told you. Isn't that why you were listening to the podcast on the plane?"

"No! Alice had picked it out earlier, I was just finishing it because I was bored! You're telling me this is all because of a stupid misunderstanding?"

"You're asking me to believe in an impossible coincidence."

"I'm not asking. You pompous, paranoid—oh my God! I can't even wrap my head around this."

"I don't know what to say, Anna. I'm sorry."

"Here's a little script for next time you think you know why I'm doing something: 'Hey, buddy, I'm about to traumatically derail your life for a hot minute, but before I point a gun at your face, let me ask *one flipping question first!*'"

He grinned at me. "You're so cute when you're mad."

"Let me show you how cute I am when I'm kicking your narrow butt."

His expression held none of the fear I sought to provoke, so I climbed out of bed with every intention of slapping the smile off his face. My anger had already faded to sarcastic amusement when I reached him, and I perched on the arm of his chair instead.

Tucking my feet in between him and the other arm, I said, "It's no big deal, right? I'll explain to Fernando that there's been a misunderstanding, you'll pitch in and assure him I wasn't snooping around in his background and have zero interest in exposing his existence to anyone, and Dude and I will be on our way back to DC by this time tomorrow."

"Sounds like a good plan," he said.

I wove my fingers through his hair, taking a closer look at the strands of gray I'd seen. Engrossed in one another, we chose to ignore the polite knock at the door. The next knock was louder, followed by a call through the door.

"Sir, ma'am? Fernando wants to see you. He asked me to bring you."

"What's he saying?" Jim asked.

"Fernando wants us."

He turned to check the clock. "It's barely even morning anymore. I guess we should spend some time with our host."

"We'll be right out!" I called in response to a third knock.

Once I'd spruced myself up as best as I could on short notice, we left the room to find a young man waiting outside. He smiled in greeting and said, "Good morning. I'm sorry to have woken you."

He led us back down to the first floor, through a maze of twists and turns, and finally out into a large courtyard dominated by a swimming pool at the center. Around the perimeter were shuttered doors and windows, and directly across from the door by which we'd exited the house was an open archway, beyond which stretched a manicured lawn.

In the distance, transparent-looking in the clear, late morning light, lay the spine of the Andes mountains. While I admired the view, another young man dashed past the archway on the lawn. Right on his heels came Dude, tail wagging madly.

"Dude!" I called, starting automatically toward the opposite side of the courtyard.

Dude stopped, framed magnificently in the center of the archway, ears at full alert as he stared at me. He started toward me but stopped short at the edge of the grass and turned back, galloping back to his playmate.

"He really is a beautiful animal," mused a voice over my left shoulder.

I started and turned around, realizing I'd walked right past Fernando seated at a table left of the door. Jim had already taken a seat next to him and was smiling patiently at me.

"Oh—Good morning," I said awkwardly, casting one more look through the archway at Dude, but he was too busy playing with his new friend. "He seems happy."

"Mario is likewise thrilled to have him for company. The boy enjoys dogs more than most people."

I hovered a few paces from the table, unsure what to do. "I could go show Mario the basic commands, and some of Dude's tricks…" I ventured.

"Please, sit down," Fernando said. "You missed breakfast, so I'm afraid you'll have to make do with this until lunch."

Sliding into a seat across from Jim, I looked over the fruit, cheese, bread, and coffee arranged in the center of the table.

"I think I'll survive," I concluded.

"Good. Please help yourself."

He seemed unwilling to move on until I'd done just that. Feeling rather foolish with two pairs of eyes on me, I slowly filled a plate with cheese and bread and poured a cup of coffee.

"I'm not a big fan of fruit," I explained in response to Fernando's raised eyebrows.

"Perhaps the so-called fruit in the United States has left something to be desired."

He again fell silent until I obediently piled an assortment of fruit onto my plate.

"Excellent," he said. "Now, what can you tell me about Marcel Marchand and his Frères Enterprises?"

I paused in the act of conveying my coffee cup to my lips. "Say what?"

I locked eyes with Jim, letting my expression ask the question.

"I told him," Jim explained.

Shrugging off the news, I told Fernando, "They're an import-export company based in London."

"According to their website, yes."

"They're also human traffickers."

"Ah."

I felt no compunction whatsoever about telling Fernando everything I knew, from the breadcrumbs I'd used to locate Luke, to the office front in London, to Luke killing Francisco Lira on Marcel's orders, to the meeting with the Italians. "And he's got eight dogs and a cherry red Dodge Challenger SRT Demon with brand new brakes," I finished.

Both men had time to polish off two cups of coffee apiece as I spoke, while I'd barely made it halfway through my first. I took the opportunity while Fernando was processing everything to chug my coffee, stuff some cheese and bread in my mouth, and refill my cup.

At length, Fernando asked, "And you never found out the purpose for which Marcel brought you alive to the house outside London, rather than killing you as he originally intended?"

"Nope."

"You must have conceived of some theories," he prodded.

"Well, one. I thought maybe Luke was planning to kill Jim."

Jim sat up a little straighter. "You did?"

"It was the only thing I could think of." I shrugged. "Obviously, I was wrong. He never did tell me who it really was," I lied on impulse. The "drug guy" in Argentina he'd mentioned could refer to anyone, really. "What I want to know," I asked, following a separate impulse, "is how you got Dude to Miami in time to fly here with us. Don't get me wrong, I'm thrilled he's here, but how?"

"That was James' idea. His demand, I should say. He asked me to make room for a last minute passenger, and I already had a jet in Dallas that could bring him to Miami. He said it was necessary, for you to be happy."

This frank admission brought a wave of affection for Jim crashing over me, followed immediately by vague panic. "For me to be happy? Why do I need to be happy?"

Rather than answering, Fernando turned to Jim and said softly, "I think this will be easier if you aren't here. You understand."

"Sure," Jim muttered, avoiding my gaze. He took his coffee and drifted away to the other end of the courtyard.

"Anna, I can't have you telling anyone else what you know, and what you suspect. I'm sorry."

"But I don't know anything. This is all just a big misunderstanding. It's Jim's fault."

"My sister and I have been hunted all our lives. We are safe here, as long as we are hidden. Not only our location, but our very existence, must be a secret—especially to your FBI."

"What are you saying?"

"I'm sorry," he repeated, and he seemed to mean it. "You can't leave here. James I can trust. I made the mistake of seeking him out, but since then he has proven his fidelity many times over. But you... I am nothing to you, my sister's life and my life are nothing to you. I can't silence you, because I care for my cousin and he cares for you. We are left with the one option."

I stared at the oily surface of my coffee, processing his words much too slowly. "I can't... leave?"

"No."

"Ever?"

"Perhaps a better way to look at it is, this is your home now."

As if on cue, Marisol burst out of a door midway down the courtyard and slammed it behind her. I watched listlessly as she stalked barefoot toward the table, sheer sundress flapping over a white swimsuit.

"What is it now, Mari?" Fernando sighed.

"Are you going to be done soon? I want to go swimming."

"No one is stopping you from using the pool."

"I want privacy."

"We'll pretend you're not here," he countered, nodding at me. "We'll all be happy that way."

"I don't like it when you talk to me like that!" she cried, whipping off the wide, floppy hat she wore and twisting it cruelly. "This is the only swimming pool, and there are tables all over the house! You could talk in your study."

"We're done talking anyway," he said, standing up. "At least for now. Anna, I hope you'll discuss this further with James rather than doing anything rash."

"I never do anything rash," I mumbled. I looked up to see Jim standing in the archway, watching us. "I'll discuss it with Jim."

Fernando said something in answer, but I didn't really hear it. Giving Marisol a wide berth, I walked around the swimming pool until I was toe-to-toe with Jim. He said nothing, watching me warily.

"He said I can't leave," I whispered, hoping beyond hope to see some glimmer of surprise on his face. There was none.

"It was that, or kill you. What did you expect me to do?"

I took a moment to marvel at this, the way he'd framed the whole decision as though *I'd* backed *him* into a corner. I slapped him as hard as I could and walked away, out onto the lawn where Mario and Dude were still gamboling.

When Dude caught sight of me, he broke off a game of tug-of-war with Mario and trotted over to me, perfectly happy. The sight of him eased the vise around my lungs enough that I could suck in a few deep, calming breaths. I turned to look at the house, thinking there was no possible way Fernando and Jim could be serious.

Jim had disappeared from the archway, and Fernando was no longer in sight. There was a brief flash of brown and white as Marisol cannonballed into the swimming pool, creating an impossibly small splash. I laughed, surprised someone so insufferable could be capable of anything as whimsical as a cannonball. Maybe she was just glad she'd finally gotten her way and had the pool all to herself. The thought made me leery of returning inside through the courtyard. She seemed the type to hurl a flip-flop at me.

Seeing that I was distracted, Dude loped back over to his new friend and rejoined the tug-of-war. I sat down in the lush grass and watched them for a while, until automated sprinklers kicked on and forced all three of us to flee. Though Mario hadn't said a word to me, I could tell from his shifty glances through the archway that he didn't want to get within screaming distance of Marisol, either. He went around to a side door further south, waving me along to follow him.

He let us into the courtyard where Dude's cage sat, explaining awkwardly, "I am told he can't come inside the house. I have to help get lunch ready. Will you put him in the cage when you're finished playing with him?"

His gaze was directed at Dude the whole time he spoke, as though I were the dog and Dude were the person. Fighting back a laugh, I said, "Sure, of course."

I found a stick and engaged Dude in a game of fetch, played according to his rules: I threw the stick once, he caught it, and then I chased him around the small courtyard grabbing for it while he darted just out of reach and growled at me if I managed to touch the stick. Winded after several minutes of this, I let him into his cage and decided on impulse to follow him inside. I leaned against the bars of the cage and stared up at the rectangle of bright, blue sky above, letting it all sink in.

That I'd elected to pass the time in a literal cage was not lost on me, even though I'd done it just to stay close to Dude in the absence of anywhere else in the house I wanted to be. My wrath at Jim didn't wane, either. The longer I sat there, the more I devolved into a seething mass of indignance, disbelief, and even a little bit of hatred.

Why the heck would Marcel have told me anything about Paolo Barbato, let alone given me a glimpse into his murky family history? What a stupid assumption, all the more infuriating for being out of character for Jim. I had to work through a substantial amount of anger before arriving at the conclusion that turned everything on its head.

Jim was lying again.

17

Saturday, January 2, 2021
Argentina

When Jim found me, I had more than a handful of verbal darts ready to sling. Since my back was to the kitchen door, I heard him before I saw him.

"Anna, what are you doing in there?"

I let a few thick seconds tick by before turning my head to ask, "Should I not be?"

"Is this where I ask why you'd rather sit in a cage instead of the house, and you pretend like you thought you were supposed to stay in the cage now, or something like that?"

I pressed my lips together and turned away, even madder than I was a moment ago. He couldn't even let me have that one.

"How long have you been waiting out here to say that?" he asked.

"Not as long as you've been lying to me."

"Ah, the cage metaphor was way better."

I rose to my feet, stiff after prolonged sitting on the concrete, and grasped the bars of the cage to look out at him. With the added height of the cage's foundation, I found myself eye-to-eye with Jim. I decided to keep it simple.

"Go away, and leave me alone."

He leaned forward until our noses were nearly touching and whispered, "You're going to feel very silly about this when you find out what's really going on here."

"I've found out what's 'really' going on more times than I can count. It wears thin."

Undaunted, he said even more quietly, "If you ever trusted me, even the slightest bit, just pretend like you've accepted this. It's important."

"Fine, on one condition: Tell me everything."

"I will."

"When?"

"Soon."

I shook my head. "Not good enough."

"Then figure it out for yourself. That's more satisfying anyway, isn't it?" When I didn't answer, he said at a normal volume, "Why don't you let me show you around the house? It's getting hot out here."

Still letting my disgust with Jim show as much as possible, I ushered Dude out of the cage and the two of us followed him on a tour of the house. He dragged me into every single unlocked space, from billiards room to home theater to library to kitchen number two. We skipped over Marisol's and Fernando's rooms, and the tour moved upstairs. I couldn't tell if Jim was trying to show off or had some ulterior motive, at least until we arrived at a windowless room on the second floor that I decided had to be the reason for this whole home tour charade.

It was an art gallery, a vast, mostly empty space dotted with sculptures and lined with paintings, tapestries, and display cases. As Jim flipped on a row of light switches next to the door, more and more artwork appeared until the far end of the room was illuminated to reveal an entire wall dedicated to a single, not especially large painting in an elaborate gold-and-black frame. I walked toward it, not daring to believe what my eyes were telling me.

I stopped a yard from the painting and studied it in subdued silence. It depicted an effeminate Italian boy in a floppy black beret, puffy white shirt covered by some kind of animal fur cloak, sitting next to a window overlooking a city far in the distance. On its face the painting wasn't remarkable. Certainly to the untrained eye, it didn't merit the place of honor it had been given. To the trained eye, like mine, it was earth-shattering. It was heart-stopping. It wasn't possible.

Jim let me examine the painting in peace for about five minutes, then came to stand next to me. I realized my cheeks were wet and wiped them hastily, trying to hide my reaction. I knew he wouldn't understand, and I didn't want to explain it. I didn't think I could.

"A reproduction, obviously," I said thickly.

"No," he breathed, his tone almost reverent. He did understand, at least in part.

I turned to him, every ounce of ill will gone without a trace.

I couldn't keep my eyes off the painting long enough to force out, "You know what this is?"

"Of course I do." Gripping me lightly by the chin, he turned my face toward him again. His voice dropped to a whisper, and again I sensed his intention to exclude eavesdropping ears. "This is why you're here."

"My chest feels hollow," I gasped, thinking for some reason that I needed to try to articulate what was happening to me. "It's like I can breathe out, but I can't breathe in."

"I've heard that can happen. I've never felt it myself, but I'm not really an art guy."

I gave up on my legs, which were getting pretty shaky anyway, and sat down cross-legged on the tiled floor. I asked, "Can I stay here with him for a while?"

"Sure, Anna." He knelt down next to me, kissed me on the temple, and said, "Just don't get saltwater on it."

Never one to pass up a good snuggle, Dude curled up next to me and rested his head in my lap after Jim walked away. For as long as my neck could bear the strain, I stared up at the painting. Then, when I thought my head was about to snap off, I stretched out on the floor with Dude as a pillow and carried on devouring the painting with my eyes until I could hardly keep them open.

Figure it out for yourself, Jim had said. Well, if all I had to start with was Raphael's *Portrait of a Young Man*, stolen from Krakow, Poland by Hitler's art thieves in World War II and missing for well over 70 years, figuring it out was going to take a long time.

▼

My head struck the tile floor as Dude jumped up. As his claws clicked away toward the door at the far end of the room, I rubbed my head ruefully and checked my watch to find I'd been in the art gallery for over four hours.

I labored to my feet, distracted from the pain in my head, shoulders, back, and hips by the vague smile of the boy in the painting—the artist himself, many believed. I felt a strong, foolish urge to get closer, to touch it, to look at the back of the painting, even to smell it. To fight the temptation, I turned away to see what had caught Dude's attention.

One of Fernando's housekeepers had found us. It wasn't Mario or the young man from this morning, or the other of the two who'd greeted us on our first arrival. That made at least four men who took care of the house and its occupants, seemingly full time. I wondered if they weren't allowed to leave, either.

This man was quite a bit older than the others, and he had a lot more personality. I could see it on his face as he looked at Dude, then at me, then at the Raphael, then back at me.

"Why have you brought a dog in here?" he demanded.

"He hasn't messed anything up," I defended. While his eyes roved the walls and floor, no doubt trying to prove me wrong, I decided to test the waters on a little intelligence gathering. I pointed at the Raphael and asked, "Why is that one on a wall all by itself?"

His eyes darted to the painting, then away, as though afraid the very way he looked at it might give away too much information. "It was Mrs. Serna's favorite."

Yeah, I bet it was. "Someone she knew?" I asked stupidly.

"Uh, no. Please." He edged into the room so that Dude and I were between him and the door. Dude's tail wagged slowly as the man moved, not quite sure what to make of him. "I need to clean this room. Please leave."

"Sure. I won't bring the dog back. Sorry for upsetting you."

Dude fell into step next to me as we carried on with the tour Jim had left half done. It couldn't have been plainer to me that the Raphael was the whole point of the silly home tour, but what escaped me was the meaning he seemed to give it.

The stolen Raphael was the reason I was there? That didn't make any sense.

I could identify the painting, sure, but no more than that. I didn't even have the technical expertise to take an educated guess as to its authenticity. Given its provenance, or lack thereof, Jim's belief that it was the actual, original, five-hundred-plus-year-old masterwork felt overly confident. Maybe he'd seen some paperwork related to its provenance. That, much more than the painting itself, would have been of interest… if proving the Serna family held one of the most sought-after lost paintings in the world were the point of all this. So, maybe it wasn't.

While I pondered, I wandered down the corridor, testing handles on doors. Most were locked, and the ones that weren't were far less interesting than the art gallery. Storage closets full of cobwebs, bathrooms, a spare room, nothing struck me as desperately in need of exploration. I found the stairs to the third floor and returned to my room to get cleaned up.

I was a little bit more bedraggled than expected, my clothes wrinkled and scuffed with dirt and grass and my hair a tangled jungle. I combed and braided my hair, then began digging in my luggage for something to wear. As comfortable as they were, I was getting sick and tired of t-shirts and leggings. They were the most tangible trappings of what my life had become: getting dragged around from one unfamiliar place to another, always leaving things behind and starting over from scratch, never really home. It was a minor miracle that my trusty watch and I had managed to stick together.

The more I thought about it, the sadder I got. I was leaving crap everywhere: Houston, Dallas, DC, London… If it wasn't physically on my body nearly one hundred percent of the time, like my watch, I could hardly count it as mine. Anything could be taken from me at any moment, like my passport, laptop, and phone. Like Dude. I stared at him, curled up on the cool tiles of the bathroom floor, perfectly at ease. A thrill of sick fear shot through me at the thought of something happening to him. How quickly and irreparably that would destroy me.

I shook my head, flinging the thought away like a nuisance fly. As I pawed through the contents of my suitcase, I felt paper brush my hand. Thinking of that mysterious scrap of blue paper, I snatched it up and scanned it eagerly. It was a pale yellow sticky note bearing Jim's familiar handwriting.

"Got my hands on some real clothes for you. Check the closet," I read. I dropped the note back into the suitcase. "Yeah, what do you consider 'real clothes'?" I asked the empty room, heading toward the closet.

Inside was an assortment of insubstantial garments, all light-colored, mostly dresses and skirts.

"Do you even know me?" I snarled as I flipped through them. The clothes were obviously Marisol's cast offs, which meant they were bound to be too small for me as the young woman was nearly as tiny as Alice. Still, I grabbed a couple of possibilities and decided to give them a shot, if only to show my gratitude to Jim for taking the trouble.

He found me planted in front of a long mirror in the corner, turning this way and that as I tried to decide if the dress into which I'd squeezed myself was too small to get away with. One glance at Jim's reflection told me which way he would've voted. I watched in the mirror as a hand rose behind me, carefully brushed my braid over my shoulder, and slid out of sight down my back. I watched him lean over me, and even with all that warning I jumped as he pressed his lips to my neck.

"Cut it out," I whispered.

"Why?"

"Do you really think you're forgiven just because you brought me a bunch of stupid clothes?"

"You don't like the clothes?" he asked, disappointed.

"They're fine, they're just too small."

"Oh… Sorry, I'm not great at that."

"I'm great at picking out my own clothes," I sighed, turning from the reflection to the real man to see a wary look on his face. "When can I look forward to doing that again?"

"Can't say," he mused, sliding his hands around my waist as he looked me over. "Once I get you back to the States, I'm going to lock you in my basement, probably forever."

"I really can't tell if you're being serious."

"I'm dead serious. I'm never letting you out of my sight again." Unimpressed by my glare, he added, "You know, once all this back-and-forth is over."

"Back-and-forth?" I echoed. "What does that mean?"

His hands fell away and he drifted over to the balcony doors, looking guilty and uncomfortable.

I pursued him, asking again, "What do you mean, Jim?"

"I have to go back to DC. I'm leaving tomorrow morning."

"You're leaving me here alone?" I demanded, flaring up at once. "You're kidding me!" A groan and telltale shuffle from the bathroom told me Dude's rest had been broken by my raised voice. He trotted out to sit on my feet, gazing quizzically at Jim.

"You won't be alone. You'll have Dude."

"How long will you be gone?"

"I don't know."

"What am I supposed to do?"

"Just pretend you're on vacation," he snapped, finally rising to his own defense. "It's not like I'm leaving you in a Turkish prison."

I crossed my arms, pouting, refusing to concede the point. Jim pulled me closer and kissed me a few times, using the closeness to tell me in a nearly inaudible whisper, "You've seen the painting. Figure it out."

"Figure *what* out?"

"The reason you're here. Both of you."

I glanced down at Dude, who looked up to lock eyes with

me, almost as though he'd heard Jim's words and was as perplexed by them as I was. I looked back up at Jim. "I don't know what you mean. Can't you be any clearer?"

"I can't."

"You are driving me *crazy,*" I breathed, actually clenching my hands in the air in a pantomime of throttling him. I turned to leave and he caught me around the waist, pulling me against him.

"Look who's talking," he breathed right into my ear. "I was just about to say the same—*ow*—why, Dude?"

I had looked down at Dude just in time to see him bottlenose Jim in the thigh, hard. As Dude's attack profiles went, it was pretty benign. Jim let go of me, rubbing the spot with one hand.

"Why'd he do that?"

"You attacked me," I answered, brimming with pride at Dude's immediate and effective action.

"I did not."

"That's what it looked like to him."

"Ow."

"Oh, don't be such a baby. He obviously likes you, otherwise he would've bitten you."

"Gee, thanks," he said ruefully, directing this at Dude.

I pulled Jim against me to finish the thought Dude had so rudely interrupted, but I couldn't keep my mind on the kiss for more than a couple seconds. I was ravenous, faint with hunger. Jim informed me dinner time around here was still several hours away, and since I'd missed lunch I was again limited to snack food until then.

We ventured down to the kitchen, snagged some food, and carried it to a spot outside of the grounds that afforded a decent amount of privacy. So much privacy, in fact, that as soon as we sat down Jim astonished me by volunteering, "Regina Barber, one of the kids who disappeared that night, is Francisco Lira's mother. Was, I should say."

18

Saturday, January 2, 2021
Argentina

I nearly choked on an almond, asking, "The Francisco Lira Luke killed in Houston? His mother is Fernando's… great aunt?"

"Yes. I'm sorry I couldn't tell you more this morning, but I worry about being overheard in the house. All those servants tiptoeing around, and Fernando getting more paranoid almost by the day…"

"Why?"

"It's not unfounded. It's easiest to start at the beginning, the night of the fire."

"Is this going to be a long story?"

"If you're up for it."

I stared at Dude while I considered my response. Rather than exploring the nearby area as he normally would, he'd chosen to post up at my feet, one eye on the scenery and one on Jim. He clearly had misgivings about letting us out of his sight.

"Will it be true?" I asked.

"Of course. Why wouldn't it be?"

"You lied to me this morning, when you told me you thought Marcel had tipped me off about Paolo and that's why I was listening to the podcast about the Barber children. Intuitive leaps are my thing, remember? You're the tortoise, I'm the hare."

"I was kind of hoping it would take you longer to figure that out," he admitted. "But I was telling the truth about the painting. You recognized it. You understand what it is."

"If you lie to me again, I'll crack you like an egg."

"I believe you. Just listen, okay?"

He paused, giving me a chance to interrupt. I scooped up a handful of almonds and popped them all into my mouth to demonstrate my compliance.

"Great. So. In nineteen forty-five in Georgia, three of Donald Barber's—Dante Barbato's—children were supposedly killed in a house fire. You listened to the podcast, so I assume you're aware of the suspicious circumstances and the fact that none of their bodies were ever found, as well as speculation that Barbato had fled to the United States to get away from Mussolini's thugs.

"The three children were Etta, Emilio, and Regina. They were all young, ages twelve to six, so we can assume whatever happened that night, someone else was involved. Let's start with Etta, Fernando's grandmother; and Regina, Francisco's mother.

"They ended up in Colombia three years after the fire. They'd gone through Florida to Central America and finally stopped in Barranquilla for a while. They got separated in nineteen fifty, when Etta met a man from Argentina, married him, and moved back here with him. That was Fernando's grandfather, Victor Serna. I'm sure I don't need to tell you he made his fortune under the table."

I could hold it in no longer and asked, "Why?"

"Consider the decade, the people who stole the Raphael in the first place. What do you know about Argentina's German expat population?"

"Wait… Serna was a Nazi?"

"No, but he had them to thank for everything he had, just about. They were business partners."

"Gross."

"I know. Anyway, after nineteen fifty Etta never saw Regina again, but they stayed in touch for a while. As far as I can tell, they're the only two who maintained a relationship after the fire. Regina ended up in a similar situation. She married a Colombian man, Alejandro Lira. Unaware he was reinforcing a negative stereotype about Colombians, he made his fortune in the illegal drug trade. That's all Fernando's been able or willing to tell me about Regina. He's never met her, but I believe they began to correspond after Etta cut herself off. But I'm skipping ahead. Obviously Regina had Francisco at some point, and he was running the show in Houston until Luke killed him."

"Why?"

"I'll get to that. First, Emilio Barber. Emilio got to Italy somehow, and he found his uncle in Sardinia and posed as his son. He changed his name to Barbato. I'm not sure why, but I know Donald Barber was looking for his missing children. It makes me think Emilio didn't want to be found. As for Etta and

Regina, I suspect they would've gone home if they could, at least at first. Emilio had Paolo in the late fifties, and they're both still in Sardinia as far as I know."

"Didn't anyone think to look for Emilio with his family in Italy?" I interrupted.

"At first, no. Weeks passed before Donald Barber even admitted he *had* family in Italy. The local LEOs didn't have the resources to send someone to Italy to look for him, so they did the only thing they could think of: They called. Trouble was, they needed a translator. While they looked for one, Barber kept insisting he'd never told any of his children about the Barbatos in Italy. Eventually the police found someone who was willing to translate for them, and they called the state police in Cagliari. No dice."

"Just like that?"

"All they could do was ask. The Italian State Police spent about a week checking for signs of Emilio in Italy, then called back and said he wasn't there. It took the cold case guys years to track down the translator's name, because no one back then thought to write it down. He was a close friend of the Barbers. If the GBI investigators tried to communicate through an English-speaking translator on the Italian side, they didn't note their attempts. From what I can tell, they believed Barber that Emilio wouldn't have had any way of knowing, let alone getting to, the Barbatos.

"Either the Italians didn't look hard enough, or Emilio wasn't there yet when the GBI called. Either way, that suspicion went cold along with the rest of the case, and by the time I came in, it was taken for granted that Emilio couldn't have gone to Italy.

"My grandmother, Bettina, and her other siblings all believed the three of them died in the house fire, and they never had any reason to suspect otherwise. Neither did I. Of course I knew about the fire, and it was one of the reasons I became interested in law enforcement. What I'm about to tell you is pieced together from Fernando and Paolo as best as I can. It could also get us both killed, so keep it to yourself, okay?"

"You mean you *know* Paolo?" I cried.

"Yes, I'll get there. Before Paolo was born, Emilio was introduced to the family business. I don't know why, given what we can assume about how Donald Barber felt, but that's what happened. Emilio found out his uncle and another Sardinian family had taken advantage of the post-World War Two confusion in the Mediterranean and were involved in smuggling on a massive scale by then—first weapons and possessions stolen from Europe's Jews, then drugs, and eventually people starting in the early sixties.

"Emilio went along, but from what Paolo tells me it never sat well with him. He toyed with the idea of tipping off Interpol or the Italian government, but he'd seen what happened to snitches and he didn't want to risk it. Eventually he grew to hate the entire family, he deeply regretted going to Italy in the first place, and so Emilio started looking for somewhere to run.

"He knew Etta and Regina made it out, too, but he had no idea where they were or if they were still alive. It took him years, and Paolo won't even tell me how he did it, but he managed to track Etta down, and Emilio actually went to Buenos Aires to see Etta and meet her family. By then she had a son just a little older than Paolo.

"While Emilio was there, he also met some of Victor Serna's business associates and learned organized crime ran in the family. Etta's husband was a legitimate businessman, mostly, but he was underwritten by some very unsavory but wealthy Germans who had arrived in Argentina in the early forties. Victor was likely interested in joining forces with the old guard back in Italy. Etta told Emilio about Regina and Alejandro Lira, too. That just made it worse. Emilio never went to see Regina, never sought out or revealed his existence to the siblings living in the States. He just came home.

"Emilio decided Etta and Regina were dead to him. Paolo's a little more proactive about it. He thinks the family tree needs to be pruned. Best I can figure, Paolo took it pretty personally that the family his father had hoped to escape to—Etta's—turned out to be just as shady as his relatives in Italy. Paolo thinks his grandfather's anti-fascist sentiments are what started all this, and I think the Sernas' connection to the Nazis in Argentina might have pushed him over the edge. I'm just guessing there.

"Etta's husband died of a heart attack in the eighties. In two thousand nine, Fernando and Mari's parents—Etta's son and daughter-in-law—were killed, run off the road. The people who did it were never caught, but their car was riddled with bullet holes, so it was no accident. Etta was convinced it was a group of vigilante Nazi hunters who decided her family was too mixed up with a group of expats from Germany. She was probably right about that, but I don't think she knew her nephew, our buddy Paolo Barbato, was the one who tipped them off."

"Okay, time out," I begged. "This is disorienting. You go from telling me jack squat to all this and expect my head not to explode?"

"Did I lose you?"

"I don't know. Etta and Regina got mixed up in some bad stuff, and Paolo wants them and their descendants dead, so he offed Fernando's parents. Does that about sum it up?"

"More or less. Do you want me to go on?"

"Yes. Slowly."

"At the time, Etta lived in Buenos Aires. After her son and daughter-in-law were killed, she grabbed Fernando and Marisol and disappeared. She cut off ties with everyone, even Regina. After slinking around from place to place for about a year, she was able to get her hands on this place. They've been in hiding since then. Fernando was in his early twenties, and Mari was just a kid, so they didn't acclimate very well. Fernando ended up running away almost immediately.

"Like I said, my family name makes the Barber connection very easy to figure out. Fernando virtually tracked down a number of his relatives in the States and decided to seek me out. It wasn't easy for him getting all the way from southern Argentina to northern Virginia. It took the better part of two years. He showed up at my house in the middle of the night on March fifth, twenty-twelve, a total mess. His English wasn't as good back then, so it was difficult to understand what he wanted. Eventually it got through that he was my cousin and he wanted to seek asylum in the United States. I could see the resemblance, otherwise I probably would've sent him packing then and there.

"Once he got some rest and calmed down, he managed to make me understand he'd been living in Argentina with his grandmother and sister and ran away because she was basically keeping them prisoner. To keep them safe, she said. Even though he'd located several other relatives in the States, and some much closer than me, he'd decided to come all the way to Arlington because he'd been told along the way to get as far as he could from the southern border. He had no idea I worked for the FBI. At least that was his story.

"He told me about the siblings that didn't really die in the fire. He had it all from his grandmother…." Jim trailed off, looking expectantly at me.

"His grandmother, Etta?" I finished.

"Yes. Good. He didn't go to Regina because he thought she'd send him back to Argentina, and he didn't think he could get to Italy even though he knew Emilio had settled there. The other kids, the official survivors, had all settled way farther south: Texas, California, Florida. So that left yours truly. I got him settled and went to work. I took a water bottle he'd used, hoping for some DNA.

"I had to report the contact to my boss. I felt bad about it, knowing the kid was going to get deported, but I didn't want to lose my job. I met with my boss first thing the morning after Fernando showed up, and we sent the bottle to get tested.

"When I got home from work, I told Fernando who I worked for, and he freaked out. He wanted to leave, but the fact was, they'd decided above my pay grade that Fernando had opened up a golden opportunity to solve the Barber case once and for all. The cold case guys were doing cartwheels over it. I had to get Fernando to take me back to Argentina to meet Etta.

"So, I told him I'd quietly looked into the possibility of him getting asylum and determined that he wouldn't get it if he applied, and that'd he get kicked out of the country. I told him his best bet was to go home and that I could help him get there safely. It took a week to get the DNA back, and that proved we were related.

"Fernando didn't know I'd had the test done. As far as he knows, I never told my boss about him and have instead been doing everything in my power to make sure he and Marisol stay hidden. It's partially true. I have been able to keep his exact location hidden from everyone but my boss. You can't even find this house on satellite images, not if you type in the exact coordinates.

"Unfortunately, Etta died while Fernando was on his way back here with me. I never got the chance to speak with her. He's had to raise Marisol pretty much by himself, which as you can see hasn't turned out that great."

"No idea what you mean. She's delightful."

"She's a beast. Anyway, with Etta went almost any hope of finding the other Barbers, unless I can get Fernando to help me. He invites me down once or twice a year, supposedly to check in, but we could do that electronically. I think he's just lonely. He trusts me, to an extent, but I can't get him to help me find Regina. He doesn't know exactly where she is—they correspond by email, now—and the FBI's had zero luck finding her.

"They did, however, track down Paolo in Sardinia and sent me there to make contact. He's even cagier than Fernando. Paolo insists Emilio is alive but won't let me talk to him. He wants information out of me, not the other way around."

Jim paused to take a drink of water, concluding, "He's an odd duck."

19

Saturday, January 2 to Sunday, January 3, 2021
Argentina

"Okay, wait," I interrupted, rubbing my temples as a headache began to creep up on me. "I'm getting lost again. We've got Etta in Argentina with Fernando and Marisol, Regina in Colombia with Francisco, and Emilio in Sardinia with Paolo, and none of them knew how to find each other, but Fernando managed to find you, and you found Paolo. Right?"

"Right. See, you're not lost at all."

"Who took them out of the house on the night of the fire? Why?"

"That's what I'm trying to find out. Paolo won't let me anywhere near Emilio, Etta is dead, and Regina's a ghost."

"So you're maintaining contact with Fernando on the pretense of keeping him hidden from his family while actually trying to find his family."

"Right."

"I can see why you wouldn't want him to know that. What I can't see is how I fit into this and what the Raphael has to do with any of it."

"You think that's frustrating? Keep thinking it through, and you're going to be climbing the walls by the time I get back."

"You psycho! Why can't you just *tell* me?"

"Because it would take hours, and because I don't want you to know yet."

"I hate you."

"No, you don't."

"Just tell me one thing: When did you realize what that painting was?"

"A couple years ago. Fernando finally let me see it, and even I could tell just from the way it's displayed that it's something special. I went home and started digging. The Art Crime team helped me confirm it was the real deal, based on a stamp—"

"On the back of the painting that only the Polish government and select law enforcement agencies know about," I finished proudly. "When I interned with the Art Crime Team, that painting was everywhere. They're obsessed with finding it. Why haven't they done anything about it? Do they know you found it?"

"Yes, but it's safe where it is. If someone swoops in and recovers it, who do you think Fernando will be looking to blame?"

"You could arrange an under-the-table sale, or better yet a theft."

"No one is supposed to know about it. Wipe the drool off your chin, it's not going anywhere."

"It's a priceless piece of world heritage," I argued.

"It's still going to be priceless after the rest of this thing is wrapped up. You just want credit for finding it."

"Well!" I started to protest, realizing he was completely right. "Isn't that why I'm here? Or was that a lie, too?"

"No, that's true. But not for the reason you think."

"Oh, my God." I paused to rub my temples again. "So you just get to skedaddle back home and keep your job and your life and everything, huh?"

"Don't expect me to feel bad about it."

"What are you going to say happened to me?"

"That you ditched me in Berlin and went AWOL."

"Is that what you're gonna tell my parents?"

He looked guilty again, but he insisted, "You know I can't tell them anything."

"They probably think I'm dead."

"Eventually they'll know you aren't."

"What do they think happened to Dude, then?"

"Stolen. Happens all the time, especially with purebred German Shepherds."

"Wow, you're really putting them through it."

"Sorry."

For the moment, I couldn't think of anything else to ask, and my brain felt like angry mush. We finished our picnic in mostly comfortable silence and were getting ready to head back into the house when Dude, who had allowed himself the small laziness of stretching out on the ground at my feet, suddenly rolled upright, ears quivering, focusing on a point about a hundred yards in front of us.

Jim had chosen a spot in the shade on the perimeter of a large clearing, and Dude saw something on the other side of the clearing, something that was invisible to us. I squinted in the direction that he was gazing, seeing nothing but dappled sunlight and shadow under a roof of gently stirring trees.

"What do you think?" I asked Jim without looking at him, sensing he was trying just as hard as I was to make it out.

"Could be nothing, could be a puma…"

"Let's just go," I pleaded, voice dropping to a whisper. "In case it's not nothing."

As if in disagreement, Dude lunged forward, breaking into a stiff trot across the clearing. He came trotting back at my call, and we all started toward the house at a forcibly measured pace. Dude tried several times to break away and investigate, his moving target making it clear that whatever was out there was trailing along behind us.

When I caught my first glimpse of the house looming up through the trees, the knot of fear in my chest loosened a tiny bit. Just outside the door, Dude's obedience hit a wall and he sat down, facing the woods, whining. As Jim and I watched him in mutual puzzlement, his tail began to sweep back and forth.

"Get him inside," Jim snapped, his demeanor shifting all at once from anxiety to annoyance. I grabbed Dude's collar and manhandled him through the door, glaring suspiciously at Jim.

"He's just looking out for me," I complained.

"I know. Do me a favor: Promise me you won't leave the grounds again."

"What—of course. You think I'm crazy?"

"Say you promise."

"Ugh." I rolled my eyes, intoning, "I promise I won't leave the grounds."

He studied me dubiously for a moment and then seemed to decide I was telling the truth. We put Dude back in his cage and headed upstairs to get ready for dinner. As soon as we got into the room, I went to the balcony to look down at Dude. He was sitting at attention, facing the wall of the courtyard and the woods beyond, his ears twitching every few seconds.

I was dismayed to learn that Fernando took family dinners very seriously. We were gently coerced into joining him and Marisol in the dining room at 8:00, a ritual I understood to be nightly. Having grown up on TV dinners eaten the way God intended, in front of the TV, I was deeply disaffected and made no effort whatsoever to hide it.

It was therefore a subdued hour and a half, Fernando and Jim talking sporadically while Marisol and I glowered at them. She was clearly at the table against her better judgment as well. Once or twice she shot a glance my way, less hostile than I would've anticipated, but she never spoke to me.

Eventually I consumed enough wine to see the humor in the fact that my behavior was a mirror image of the unruly teenage terror across from me. This loosened me up enough to join the conversation, which at that point was getting around to Jim's and my mystery encounter in the woods.

"What do you think it was, Fernando?" I asked lightly, as though the answer were of little interest.

"Probably a wild boar. We see them around sometimes, never too close to the house. Occasionally we hunt them, but right now it's too dangerous. They're far less picky about what they eat this time of year."

"Humans?"

"No, of course not. They'd only eat you if you were already dead, but they will hunt smaller prey if they need to. It makes them more aggressive, more mobile."

"I don't think it was a boar anyway," I shrugged. "Dude would've reacted differently."

Across from me, Jim's posture stiffened almost imperceptibly. I ignored him as best as I could, taking in Fernando's politely skeptical expression.

"What do you think it was, then?" Fernando asked.

"Another dog, maybe. He didn't seem to want to attack it. I wondered if maybe it was a stray, or a lost pet."

To general surprise, Marisol piped up to argue, "It's not like we have any neighbors." Voicing this fact seemed to deepen her bad mood. She polished off her wine and asked, "May I go?"

"Yes, please," Fernando answered testily.

"Anna is done too," she shot back, adding to me, "You don't have to sit here and listen to them talk. That's not one of the *rules.*"

"That's enough, Mari."

"Can I go, too?" I asked eagerly, finishing off my own wine in preparation.

Glaring at Marisol, who had risen to her feet and seemed to be waiting for me, Fernando explained, "You don't have to ask my leave, Anna. Mari does because she wouldn't even finish her dinner if I didn't make her stay."

Thinking of no useful response to this, I took the opportunity to retreat from the dining room with Marisol. As she shut the heavy doors behind us, I glanced back to see Fernando asking Jim something too quietly for me to hear, his hands gesturing in unmistakable frustration.

"He's such a tyrant," she spat, rounding on me and demanding, "You don't really think it was a dog, do you?"

"No."

"Why did you say that?"

"To see how Fernando would react."

Her eyes darted into abstraction over my left shoulder and she said, "I guess I messed that up."

"No harm, no foul."

"I don't think it was a boar, either. I think it was a person."

She managed to surprise me with that claim. I edged away from the dining room door and asked quietly, "Why?"

"I have seen someone. Come, I'll show you."

She cut a remarkably fast pace on her short little legs, back into the section of the first floor where most of the doors were locked. One door which had been locked earlier today now stood ajar, a cool glow of LEDs emanating from the opening.

I followed Marisol inside and marveled at the bank of monitors covering the right-hand wall, all of them showing some part of the house or immediately outside the house. Three screens at the bottom right were playing live, night-vision feeds of exterior areas I couldn't place. Marisol sat down at the desk in front of the monitors and pointed at the second from the right on the bottom row.

"I saw someone there, last night. Some man."

"Where is that?"

"The road leading here. About a kilometer from our gate."

"What did he look like?"

She shook her head, aggrieved. "I couldn't tell. It was just a flash, and then he was gone. Big, so I assumed it was a man. I can't play back the footage, only Fernando can. I didn't tell him about it, though."

Muscling past my bewilderment that she had chosen to share any of this with me, I thought of Marisol's parents, the crazy theory about who had killed them and why, and the reason her grandmother shut her and her brother up in this house in the first place.

A twinge of apprehension colored my response. "Maybe you should. Someone skulking around here at night can't be up to anything good."

"Fernando is paranoid enough. It was probably just some vagrant. But if your dog saw him again today, that means he's found the house and might not just go away like I hoped."

"Has this happened before?"

"A couple times. People wander across the border from Chile, from the coast."

"Why were you sitting here watching the security cameras last night?" I ventured, hoping against hope that my uninvited curiosity wouldn't anger her.

"I just do sometimes," she dodged. "Go ahead, take a look for yourself. I think you deserve to know when you're being watched."

She identified each video feed in turn: the front door, three back doors, a side door, several interior hallways, exterior shots of first- and second-floor windows, and each staircase, including one that looked dark and narrow as though strictly for servants' use. It was difficult to discern whether Fernando was more obsessed with intruders or escapees.

While I watched, Jim appeared in one of the hallways and moved from camera to camera, making his way upstairs to our room. I couldn't have asked for a better illustration of where I was visible, and more importantly where I was invisible.

"Do the cameras move?" I asked.

"No, they're all fixed."

"Thank you, Marisol. This is creepy, but at least now I know."

"You're welcome," she muttered, distracted as she gazed unblinkingly at the screen where the man had appeared last night. I left her there, probably hoping she'd see him again. Whether she was hoping to see him leaving or something else, I had no idea.

I went back to my room via the kitchen, grabbing Dude and taking him upstairs with me. Jim was in my shower when I arrived, his suitcase open on the bed and already half-packed. The sight made me equal parts angry and despondent. I extracted one of his neatly-folded t-shirts, rumpling up a good part of his careful packing, and requisitioned it to sleep in. When he got out of the shower, I was already in bed, turned away from the eviscerated suitcase I'd left on display like a disaffected cat pooping on the bed to advertise her displeasure.

"Anna, why?" he moaned, too quietly to really be asking me.

He repacked, trying not to make a lot of noise or jostle the bed too much. He thought I was asleep. When he'd been repacking for a minute or so, I turned over and upset the suitcase onto the floor.

I smiled at his wide-eyed disbelief from within a nest of blankets. "Oops."

"What was that for?"

"Why are you in my room?"

He lifted the suitcase off the floor, started piling clothes back into it, and explained, "There's only one other bathroom on this floor, and it's not nearly as nice."

"You let me have the best room?"

"It's only fair." He folded several pieces of clothing before adding, "I don't want to leave you here alone. I'd stay, if I could."

I nudged the suitcase with my toe, scooting it toward the edge of the bed again. His left hand shot out, trapping my leg by the ankle so that I couldn't move it an inch. Only the bulky blanket between my ankle and his hand prevented it really hurting.

"Ow," I complained, half-jokingly. From the open balcony, Dude gave a low *woof* of warning.

"Stop it," Jim said.

I waited until he'd let go before mumbling, "Sorry. I'm just… *really* mad at you."

"Really? I couldn't tell."

He finished packing in silence, moving his suitcase over by the door and leaving a stack of clothes for tomorrow on top of it. I didn't ask how he'd figured out I wanted him to stay, I simply scooted to the far right side of the bed and turned to face him as he climbed in.

"I'll be back," he promised. "You won't even miss me. You've got a job to do, remember?"

"Of course I'll miss you. Jerk."

▼

Pressure on the side of my face roused me partway from a deep sleep. I sighed, rolled over, and burrowed deeper into the blankets. In a chilly room, totally buried in warmth, I slipped back under as one last thought forced its way through the haze: If I could just press my back against Jim and steal a little more heat from him, this would be perfect.

When I woke up several hours later, sunlight was warming the room and ruining my hot-and-cold balance, and Jim was gone.

20

January to February 2021
Argentina

The effort I eventually made to get out of bed, get dressed, and find Fernando that morning was hardly worth it. Fernando was in the library Jim had shown me on his tour, and he told me Jim had left in the early morning hours to depart Alto Río Senguer at first light. Fernando passed along Jim's farewell and his nonsense excuse that he "didn't want to wake me."

Infuriated at Jim's cowardly departure, I took a detour to the kitchen on the way back to my room and grabbed a snack for me and a snack for Dude. He was perfectly content to sun himself on the balcony while I read. Fernando had plied me with a copy of a novel called *La Telaraña*, since he'd correctly guessed that one of my main problems was going to be boredom.

La Telaraña was a short, deeply disturbing book, and I finished up right about the time Dude started throwing me subtle signals that he was ready to go back outside. I dropped Dude off in the courtyard, not bothering to put him in his cage, and returned the book to the now-empty library. I exchanged it for a nice, dry history of Argentina and returned to the courtyard to find Dude teaching Mario his inane version of fetch. The two looked perfectly happy, so I left them to it. With my book, plus a bottle of wine and some more food stolen from the kitchen, I passed the remainder of the day in quiet isolation. Fernando didn't even make me come down to dinner.

▼

The next day, the gloves were off. I was jerked from a wine-in-duced coma by a series of insistent knocks, which merely paused rather than stopping when I hurled a handful of choice swear words at the door. I dragged the blanket off the bed to cover myself and cracked the door, squinting up at the now familiar face of one of Fernando's housekeepers.

"I'm so sorry, Miss. Mister Serna says it's time for you to wake up."

I absorbed this slowly, the young man shuffling uncomfortably as I stared at him. Eventually I mumbled, "Wha?"

"He… he said it's time to wake up."

"Well, you can tell him he's mistaken," I said churlishly, slamming the door in his face. I burrowed back into bed and was about to fall asleep again when the door opened, no knock this time. I poked my face out of the blankets to see Fernando in the open doorway, regarding me with a steely smile.

"We don't sleep the day away here, Anna."

I sat up slowly, convinced I'd misheard him. "We don't what now?"

"Sleep the day away. Come on, get up."

My instinct was to ignore him, curl up again, and try to fall back asleep, but I was awake enough to play that out in my head. It didn't end well no matter how I gamed it. Instead I stood up and stalked to the bathroom, trying to ignore him.

When I emerged, he was still there. He was standing in the open closet, flipping through the clothes Jim had scavenged for me. I watched, speechless, as he selected a dress and handed it to me.

"Wear this. Breakfast is in ten minutes."

I was studying the dress, trying to figure out what the heck just happened, when he stopped at the door and said, "Oh, and wear your hair down. It looks better that way."

He closed the door softly, and it took me a full ten seconds of open-mouthed silence to ask no one, "What was all that about?"

Despite my confusion and mounting anger, I sensed it was best to play along until I knew how serious Fernando was about this. I undid my braid, brushed my hair, and threw on the dress he had picked. At breakfast, I learned what I would be doing that day: German lessons with Fernando, Krav Maga with Marisol, swimming, reading, playing with Dude, and of course meals. He even scheduled in some free time.

The whole thing was presented as a polite suggestion, but one glance at Marisol disabused me of that notion immediately. She was tight-lipped, cheeks red and eyes downcast, her fork repeatedly stabbing a piece of sausage without any real purpose.

I closed my eyes and let my knee-jerk reaction wash over me like a tidal wave. I could imagine it. I'd throw my coffee in Fernando's face, give him a piece of my mind, and drag Marisol away for some margaritas or whatever we could scrounge up. Once that fantasy was dismissed, I focused on two bracing thoughts: One, I didn't need to be worried about boredom anymore, not with Fernando running the camp; and two, I was going to have fun paying Jim back for leaving me with this lunatic.

After a huge bite of food, I said briskly, "Well, I've never taught German before, but I'm sure we'll muddle through."

My falsely cooperative attitude lasted about half a day. It got me through two hours of starting Fernando on the basics of German via a lesson plan I pulled out of my butt, two more hours of trying to convince Marisol that learning Krav Maga was a great idea even if it was her pathologically bossy older brother's edict, and exactly one instance of being given a swimsuit and informed that it was time for a dip.

I dropped the swimsuit on the floor and returned to my room, earning myself a scant half hour of privacy before Fernando was back. I felt like kicking him through the third-floor window, but I let him barge into the room unchallenged and listened expressionlessly while he laid it all out.

"I was a little taken aback this morning at your lack of argument, given everything Jim has told me about you. This makes more sense."

"I am not your kid sister that you can boss around."

"No, you're my guest. I allowed James to bring you here as

the less objectionable of two options for how to deal with the fact that you were getting too close to inadvertently revealing my existence to James' and your employer."

Beneath my aggravation, I felt a dull surprise that Jim had been telling the truth about that.

"This was a huge concession on my part. Every person who knows where my sister and I live is one more person who can betray us. I brought James here because I trust him, and I allowed you to come here for the same reason. Is it so much to ask, then, that you show a little humility and allow me to run my own household the way I see fit?"

"You can do that without treating me like a zoo animal," I spat.

He shook his head, saying, "Please don't compare yourself to an animal. It's very offensive."

Ignoring that, I asked, "Are you really so concerned with the FBI finding out about you? This is Argentina. The FBI can't touch you here."

"Your government has a long reach, Anna," he retorted. "Surely you know this. You are correct that the FBI could do nothing under its own auspices, but I don't believe that would stop them. You don't either, really."

"But you haven't even done anything. At most you might be of great interest to the handful of people who still know and care about the Barber case. So what?"

"My family will be exposed. That can't be allowed to happen."

"I'm sure if they know how important it is that you stay

hidden, they'll be very discreet."

"No," he snapped. "Now listen, and stop arguing. You are not going to haunt this house like a malevolent ghost, pilfering food from my kitchen and appearing to Mari and me whenever the mood takes you. You will make yourself useful and stop being so disrespectful and ungrateful. It's that, or we go with option number two. Do I make myself clear?"

"Say what you mean," I snarled.

He smiled at me, a chilling, lifeless expression that didn't touch his eyes. "I care very much for my cousin, and he obviously cares for you. Nevertheless, if you continue to flout my authority, I will have your dog driven to the coast and left there to fend for himself. If you still don't behave after that, I'm sure I will have thought of some other means of convincing you. It will therefore be best for you, and for your dog, to cooperate."

He finished this diatribe by tossing me the swimsuit I'd left on the floor downstairs. I caught it, running my thumb across the ribbed surface.

"I'm sorry," I breathed, forcing him forward a step to hear me better. With a sinking feeling, I intoned, "I'm sorry. I'll do better. Please be patient. This is a different life for me."

"That's quite all right. I'll see you downstairs."

▼

In the shadow of the Andes, the days blurred together, one so much like the other that, though I could recall specific events—Marisol getting a front roll right for the first time, Fernando telling me about a dream he'd had entirely in German, Dude catching a mouse and leaving it at the foot of my bed—I couldn't have pinpointed the day or even the week in which they'd happened with any amount of certainty. As January faded away into February, I began to wonder if Jim really was coming back.

I hadn't figured anything out. Though I visited the Raphael as often as I had the time, no inspiration flowed from its surface into my brain. I wasn't sleeping well enough, or often enough, to really get the most out of my overworked brain, anyway.

After the first week, I'd taken to wandering the house at night, figuring that if I weren't allowed to, someone would find me and tell me. No one bothered, so I explored. It cut into my pre-appointed hours of rest, 9:30 to 6:30, but I didn't care. Every so often a door that had been locked the first dozen times I tried it would suddenly be unlocked, and I could explore a new room and fool myself that there was really anything new left to find. There were doors that were always locked, including one not far from my bedroom. I knew if there was anything interesting to find, it was concealed within one of those rooms.

Clearly it was the height of narcissism and the very depth of foolishness to let Jim leave without getting every last piece of information from him possible. The job of sorting out the lies from the truth would have been more than enough to occupy me. Starting with essentially nothing was an insurmountable task, and I was losing interest in understanding at all.

So the Raphael was the reason I was there. Big whoop. I was more interested in the when and how of the Raphael and me no longer being there, and the truthfulness of Jim's assertion that I was "going to feel very silly about this" when I found out what was "really going on here."

Nothing was going on here. That was the problem.

▼

On February fourteenth, I retired to my room more exhausted than usual. Marisol had long since tired of the inelegant, punishing nature of Krav Maga and had convinced Fernando she needed to learn French instead. The trouble was, after four days she had been unable to successfully enunciate even one French word. She was growing frustrated and was blaming my teaching for her inability to learn. I'd suffered through two full hours of back-and-forth, finally culminating in a very brief but hot argument over whether or not she was truly interested in learning French, or was just too much of a wimp to continue learning the vastly more useful self-defense techniques I'd been teaching her.

I didn't dislike Marisol, but she was exhausting to be around at the best of times. After a row like that, I felt like I should be awarded a finisher's medal for a marathon. Worst of all, she had Jim's eyes; true, they were brown rather than gray, larger, and framed by darker, fuller lashes; but they were his. They bore the same shape, the same focus, the same rage bubbling just beneath the surface.

By my count, there were eleven full-time residents of the house, not counting me. Fernando and Marisol of course; Dude's best buddy, Mario; his mother, Maria, who kept to the kitchen and whose existence I hadn't even guessed until my third week here when she'd emerged from her domain to scold Mario for letting Dude track dirt into the kitchen; and the aged, grumpy housekeeper, Martín. Apparently the community baby name book was down to the M pages.

There were five younger men—Ilan, Mateo, Daniel, Thomas, and Leandro—who all seemed to be related to each other but not to Fernando and who took care of miscellaneous tasks throughout the house but were there principally to protect Fernando and Marisol. Lastly I'd counted, but never exchanged a single word with, Luz, another older woman who looked after Marisol and was possibly Maria's sister.

I had no idea where they all slept or even which part of the house they could most accurately call home, but I knew they didn't leave at night. Like the Sernas, they never left. They never even spoke about leaving or about what might be going on outside the boundaries of the estate. The old man, Martín, was in charge of all the others, a logical arrangement since he had likely been with Fernando's grandmother since his youth. He took great pride in the upkeep of the house and frequently exhausted himself by reaming out the younger men for leaving doors open and lights on, messing up rooms he'd just tidied, and making too much noise while Fernando was in his study.

I didn't attempt to get close to any of them, not even Mario who was so smitten with Dude and truly struck me as a kindred spirit. I didn't need to attempt it to know Fernando wouldn't approve.

As much petty, vindictive pleasure as I would have taken in

striking up a romance with one of the many bored bachelors roving around, everyone but Marisol kept me at arm's reach so studiously that I knew it was Fernando's will. The only man who ever looked at me was Fernando himself, and though I was plenty mad enough at Jim to stoop that low, he only ever regarded me with an odd cross between curiosity and malice. Somehow I knew he was always on the lookout for a reason to simplify his life by killing me, burying me in the woods, and telling Jim I'd run away.

By Valentine's Day, my stubborn anger at Jim had ebbed to its lowest point ever. I looked around my empty room—Dude was no longer allowed to sleep anywhere but the cage—and wondered for the first time whether I could actually escape.

I hadn't given escape more than a passing thought for weeks. Tethered to the estate by the Raphael and by Jim's purported return, not to mention the specter of violent, wild boars roaming around out there, I'd been as determined to stay put as I was to stay mad. Now that anger had failed me, running away was looking like a viable option. In fact, I couldn't believe I'd stuck around so long.

The trick would be escaping unseen, with Dude. To do that, I'd need to climb down from my balcony, spring Dude from doggy prison, and set off through the small, padlocked door in the garden. That would require picking two different locks, which meant I needed two bobby pins. I had zero.

Could I wait until tomorrow, ask Marisol for help, and get her to obfuscate my escape from the security camera which I knew was pointed straight at the garden door? I could, but I wouldn't. It was now or never, and I'd deal with the camera once I'd cleared the first hurdle. Bobby pins, like pennies, are bound to turn up if you keep looking long enough, so I began to quietly tear my room apart in search of them.

What I found instead was so unlikely that I could only stare at it, perplexed, for a full minute. Squirreled away in the back of the bathroom cabinet, almost out of reach, was an old Nokia cell phone.

If I had any doubts about the purpose for which it had been placed there, they were dispelled by the tightly-coiled charging cable behind it. I pulled out the phone and the charger, blood pounding in my ears. A quick search of my room resulted in two possible places to plug in the phone: an outlet behind the bed and one behind the dresser. I elected to try the former, since I'd be able to leave the phone hidden under the bed and crawl underneath to use it. Prepared for what I'd likely find underneath the bed, I secured a shoe and only had to squish one small spider before the space was safe for me.

My escape plan completely forgotten, I plugged the phone in, made sure it was invisible from the doorway, and went to take a shower before turning in.

21

Monday, February 15 to Thursday, February 18, 2021
Argentina

My eyes popped open at 6:00 a.m., but that wasn't so unusual anymore. Rather than lazing around for a few minutes to catch the last few sweet kisses of sleep, I rolled out of bed and right back under it.

I'd barely been able to fall asleep, wondering how long the phone would take to charge and whether it even really worked. Of course, who had placed it there was even more compelling a mystery. If Jim had done it, why hadn't he told me about it? The question of charging was answered right away. I was able to power on the phone and could see by a rough, pixilated icon in the top right corner that it had service. If this was some trick of Fernando's, it was a good one. No way was I going to ignore this, and there was only one number on my mind: not my parents, not Jim, and not the FBI.

With one ear on the door for any sound of approaching footsteps, I dialed the number someone had written on a piece of blue paper and stuffed into my backpack somewhere between Berlin and the Cessna.

It rang, and rang, and rang some more, so long that I grew frustrated, hung up, and tried again, counting the rings this time. After 33 rings, someone finally picked up, but they didn't say anything.

"Hello?" I tested, holding my breath for the answer. I couldn't be sure if it was the crackling of the connection or something else, a human breath, but I heard something. "Hello? Someone put this number in my backpack. Please tell me who this is." When several more seconds passed without a response from the other side, I felt my pulse quicken again. "Just say something. Anything. I can hear you breathing, you sicko!"

Finally, a new sound, a chuckle. I held my breath again and was at last rewarded by the sweet, sweet sound of a voice.

"Such diplomacy. This can't be anyone but Anna Bowman."

I recognized Luke's voice at once, but instinct kept me from saying his name. "Did you put the number in my backpack?"

"Of course I did. Couldn't let Gumby have it all his way, could I?"

I had to assume 'Gumby' was his unaffectionate nickname for Jim. I asked, "Where are you?"

"In the middle of nowhere. Where are you?"

"Same."

"Same nowhere?" he asked.

"I have no idea," I admitted.

"You're being cagey. You think someone is listening in?"

"I think it's very possible. You might not even be—Tell me something only he would know."

"Uh… Kevin Bacon?"

I sputtered with laughter, pressing my hand to my mouth to stifle it. He was reminding me of the game we'd played in Colorado of arranging movie titles by actors in common, just to pass the time. "It's an older code, but it checks out."

"Dork."

"Why did you give me your number?"

"Because I knew he'd give you a phone. Didn't think it would take this long for you to find it…"

"He hid it from me! I might never have found it at all."

"Okay… I'm sure there was a reason for that. Keep the phone on silent, and keep it hidden."

"Gee, thanks for the tip."

"I'll text you next time we can talk. Delete the calls, delete the texts. You know the drill."

"Uh huh. Yep."

"What are you wearing?" he asked.

"Ji—Gumby's t-shirt."

"Ugh. Sorry I asked."

"You're not going to tell me the point of this, are you?"

"Not yet. Sorry, baby."

The line went dead, leaving me slightly out of breath. No sooner did the call end than I received a text message, not from the number I'd called but from a U.S. country code, a Virginia area code.

I smiled sourly at the texted complaint, "Took you longer than I thought it would."

"I figure things out faster when you TELL ME STUFF," I texted back.

It had to be Jim. Jim and Luke were up to something together. The mind boggled. I read Jim's next question and scoffed.

"Who'd you call?"

I replied, "You saw the call, you can see the number. Figure it out."

"What did he say?"

"He misses you."

"Cute. Behave yourself, keep your eyes open, and be patient."

"No, I always do, and no."

I silenced the phone, deleted the call and texts, and shoved it back against the wall as far as it would go. I barely had time to brush my teeth and throw on some clothes before rushing downstairs to breakfast.

▼

With a new spring in my step, I went about each day as instructed, taking every chance I safely could to check the phone for calls or texts. Three days after I found the phone, I finally woke up to a text from Luke that had come during the night. A rush of disappointment followed close on the heels of excitement as I read Luke's brief update.

"Haven't heard anything yet, keep it together."

After lunch, I checked again and found a text from Jim that said, "See you in a few hours."

I didn't know what a few hours meant, so I replied to ask for more specifics and received no answer. It turned out a few hours meant all day, and Jim failed to appear until midway through dinner. The wait gave me plenty of time to move from excitement that he was coming back, to irritation that he was taking so long, and back to excitement about how much crap I was going to give him.

He was ushered into the dining room by Martín, who had long since forgiven me for bringing Dude into the art gallery and, from what I could tell, thought I was some kind of genius for the humble feat of getting along with Marisol.

As Jim walked in, I stood up and bid Fernando and Marisol good night and swept past him to exit the dining room. As Martín closed the doors behind me, I heard Marisol announce with obvious glee, "I don't think she's very happy to see you, James."

Unfortunately, she wasn't quite right about that. The sight of him had sent a thrill of happiness through my whole body, and I was deeply annoyed about it. The very last thing I needed was to fall soppily in love with anyone, let alone James Camposanto, the architect of all my woes, but that appeared to be exactly what was happening.

I enclosed myself in the art gallery and took up a now-familiar position in front of the Raphael, letting the Italian boy's calm gaze and cheeky half-smile wash over me. Not for the first time, I spoke out loud to him, whispering, "Help me keep it together, will you? I can't just let him waltz back here and take me in his arms like some kind of Harlequin romance. Don't you smirk at me like that, you little punk."

The door opened and I fell silent, hoping I hadn't been overheard. As Jim approached, I turned around, arms crossed. He stopped a few feet from me, guarded expression warning me he'd already moved past any hurt feelings I'd been able to cause and was ready to defend himself.

"Well, get it all out," he said flatly.

I asked mildly, "What do you mean, Jim?"

"I thought you'd at least be a little happy to see me."

"I am," I said brightly, smiling up at him. "So happy."

"That's enough. I get it."

"Not yet you don't," I lilted.

Without waiting for his answer, I whisked past him and retreated to my bedroom. Whether because of my creepy attitude or some other business he needed to attend, he made me wait for a surprisingly long time. After brushing my hair and my teeth, changing into pajamas, and climbing into bed, I grew bored and started pacing around the room. Once more I was struggling to hold on to my bad mood like a recalcitrant toddler. I crawled under the bed to check for texts and found one waiting from Luke.

"Say hi to Gumby for me. Tell him I'm GTG."

I deleted the text immediately, jolted back to reality. GTG? Good to go? Go where? How did he know Jim was here? The door opened while I was still under the bed and I rolled out, jumping to my feet and brushing the dust bunnies off my shorts. He'd brought a bottle of wine and two glasses, which he placed carefully on the dresser on his way toward me.

"Oh good, *wine,*" I gasped.

Though outwardly calm, there was a distinct rigidity in his expression. He was livid. Perfect.

"Anna, enough. I expected some histrionics, but this is ridiculous. Grow up."

"Whatever you say, Jim."

His hands balled briefly into fists before he relaxed, returning to the dresser to pour two glasses of wine. He brought me one, which I accepted with a polite smile.

"How long are you planning to keep this up?" he asked.

"Keep what up?"

"I can't learn whatever lesson it is you're trying to teach me until you talk to me," he said, taking a drink of wine like it was medicine. Maybe he thought it would help him calm down. I followed suit, and it didn't work.

Abandoning the act, I snarled, "How creepy do I have to be for you to leave me alone?"

"*That's* what you want?" He took another drink too late to hide his smile.

"Don't you grin at me like that, like you've got something to be proud of. Do you have any idea how miserable it is here? Did you never wonder once why Marisol is such a handful, why she isn't happy? Do you even know your cousins at all, or just well enough to dump me here while you take care of your normal life back in the States?"

"I know Fernando is bossy, but—"

"*Bossy?* He's a dictator! He tells me what to wear, what to eat, what to do with my hair, when to wake up and when to go to bed, every blasted minute of every daggum day planned out for me! Your cousin is a sociopath, and *you* brought me to him."

He finally looked upset, realization sinking in. "What did he do to you?"

"I just told you!"

"How? God himself couldn't have made you fall in line like that."

"Oh yeah? Genius mastermind, you can't possibly conceive of some kind of leverage he might have on hand? Something you so helpfully supplied?"

"Something I... You mean Dude?"

"Eureka," I snapped.

I grabbed my wine and retreated to the balcony, the speaking of Dude's name goading me into checking on him. He was standing in the corner of his cage, food bowl visibly untouched, looking up toward my window. At the sight of me, he gave a low bark, tail wagging uncertainly.

"I'm fine, buddy," I called down to him, forcing a smile. "Eat your dinner."

When I turned back to Jim, I found him sitting on the bed, looking troubled.

"He told me he'd take care of you," he said quietly. "He told me you'd be safe."

"Well, I guess that was all technically true."

Jim's head sank, and he stared holes into the floor, giving no response. Apparently I'd convinced him he didn't really know his cousin, not if my news was that much of a shock to him. I felt a brief stab of pity and forced it away.

I said, "He didn't hurt me. He didn't have to. I've played the submissive housewife before. I was a little rusty, but it's like riding a bike."

"I'm so sorry."

"It's… it's not *that* big a deal," I lied, pity once more clouding my comfortable anger. "I knew you'd be back. I knew I'd at least get a break."

"I'll talk to him…"

"Why? To give him a reason to not trust you, to make him think you might be turning against him? Why don't you just literally throw gasoline on a fire and skip the allegory?"

"These last few weeks must have been a nightmare."

"Sure, they were awful," I agreed lightly. I stood in front of him and ran one hand through his hair, trying halfheartedly to comfort despite my resolve not to. "Buck up, Jim. We're together now, that's what matters."

He looked up at me, his tender expression making me regret the sentiment at once. He reached up to stroke my cheek, then my hair, whispering, "Is it?"

"To me."

"I love you, Anna."

"Aw, for crap's sake," I cried, turning out of his arms. "Please don't say things like that."

"It's not my fault Jackson stole my thunder. I loved you first, I just didn't want to admit it."

"That sure sounds like your fault."

"Yeah, I guess it is."

I sighed. "I don't want to be loved, not by either of you. Not like that."

"Well… sorry."

"Just keep it to yourself, please."

"You got it."

I looked unwillingly at him and detected a hint of laughter in his otherwise sober expression. I hadn't succeeded in hurting his feelings, not even a little bit.

"He says hi, by the way," I snapped, as though it might upset him.

"Just hi?"

"He's good to go. Whatever that means."

He nodded, apparently satisfied by that answer. I sat down on the bed next to him and said wearily, "Can't you give me some hint about what's going on? Since when are you two in cahoots?"

"We found ourselves united in an unexpected way, in Miami."

"Wow, that was almost one-quarter of a whole fact."

Sliding one hand onto my knee, he lowered his voice and said, "When I leave again, it won't be for such a long time. You're almost done."

The sadness in his voice took me off guard. I stared at his profile until he turned to me and forced a smile onto his face.

He asked, "That's good news, right?"

"Uh… sure."

"Can I stay with you tonight, or were you planning to go all Stepford Wives on me again? That's got to be the most unnerving thing I've ever seen."

"Guess you'll find out."

As we settled into bed, Jim stretched one arm over me and I turned away from him, scooting up against him and staring out through the open balcony doors. I could easily imagine a shadow looming across the pale balcony, a silhouette blocking out the stars.

If it had just been the phone, the texts from Luke, and the titillating non-information that he was once again in the "middle of nowhere," I might have been comfortable with the assumption that Luke was out there, right now, waiting for his chance. Fernando had to be his target; who else could it be?

Jim was the detail that didn't fit, the infuriating puzzle piece that doesn't connect anywhere and turns out to be from a completely different puzzle. Luke could have killed Jim, yet another scion of the Barber family, a dozen times over already. Instead, he was clearly cooking something up with Jim, and somehow I didn't believe it was the cold-blooded, contract murder of Jim's own cousin.

When Luke had finally admitted to me who his target was, hadn't he said drugs were involved? I'd seen no evidence that Fernando was up to anything at all, let alone anything related to drugs. As far as I could tell, he was just hiding, protecting his family's ill-gotten horde like Smaug smoldering away in his mountain. Drug trafficking required, well, traffic. Fernando had hosted visitors the entire time I was there. He never left the estate. The possibility remained that he was masterminding some faraway operation, maybe branching out after all those years in demoralizing boredom. Maybe managing a burgeoning cartel headquartered in Tres Islas, Colombia was how he chose to pass the time.

Still mesmerized by the blank canvas of the open balcony, I asked Jim, "Is Fernando the head of the Tres Islas Cartel?"

He took so long to answer that I thought he'd fallen asleep. Finally he whispered, "You can do better than that, Anna."

22

Friday, February 19, 2021
Argentina

I wasted one of a limited number of chances to sleep in the next morning by snapping awake at 6:00 a.m. on the dot, like a trained pet.

I turned over, half expecting to see an empty bed next to me, but Jim was still there. He had rolled away from me and was sleeping on his stomach, his long arms wrapped around his pillow, the blanket pushed down to his waist. In that attitude it was more apparent than ever that swimming was his favorite form of exercise, and it looked good on his lanky frame. After the predictable wave of lust triggered by my study of him, I felt it again, that rush of happiness, that childlike affection and trust. They comingled so easily, the hot, sticky desire and the unquestioning contentment. I knew what he would call the combination, but I also knew better.

"Get a grip," I breathed.

I eased out of bed and took a long shower, risking a missed breakfast. I hoped Fernando would push back breakfast time, accommodating Jim's sleep schedule and obscuring his own dictatorial ways as he'd clearly been doing for the entirety of their association.

After my shower, I went straight back to bed to snuggle up next to Jim until the sky brightened and I started to hear activity elsewhere in the house. Down in the courtyard where Dude spent his nights, Maria was singing some folky song to herself as she puttered around. Maybe everyone got to sleep in when Jim visited. The smell of breakfast in the works didn't begin to drift up through the open doors until the criminally late hour of 9:00 a.m.

As I listened languidly to Maria's song and breathed deep of the promise of coffee and breakfast meats that floated up from the kitchen, a new sound, farther away and yet earsplittingly loud, broke through it all. Jim and I sat up in alarm as a rapid succession of eight or nine distinct popping sounds shattered the peaceful morning atmosphere.

We looked at each other and wordlessly agreed not to question whether it was gunfire. There was no other reasonable explanation. It wasn't just any gunfire, but a fully-automatic rifle. The shots came from no further than half a mile away, if I had to guess. Gunfire wasn't an inherently worrisome sound to me. Growing up in rural Texas, I'd been woken up by that distinct popping noise more times than I could count, and it was usually of an innocent nature. In Argentina, out here where no one else was supposed to be, it was downright alarming.

We rushed down to Fernando's study, meeting Marisol at the door. I hadn't breathed a word to Jim and could barely breathe at all with the thought that it was Luke out there, that something was happening that I wasn't ready for because no one told me *anything*.

Marisol's eyes were round, her skin unusually pale. One look at her told me nothing like this had happened before, or at least not for a long time. I gave her a bracing smile.

"Dove hunters, maybe?" I ventured, while we waited for Fernando to answer Jim's knock.

She shocked me by retorting, "I know what an AK-47 sounds like. You don't hunt doves with that."

The doors burst open and Fernando waved Jim inside, stepping in front of Marisol and me when we tried to follow.

"This doesn't concern you," he said harshly, though his expression softened at the sight of his sister's face pinched with worry. "Please go down to the wine cellar and wait for us. Mari, perhaps you can show Anna some of the more valuable bottles. I'm sure that will be interesting."

My mouth fell open as he shut the doors in our faces. I turned to Marisol, asking, "Wine? Seriously? Who gives a fart about wine right now?"

"The cellar is our safe room," she whispered to the impenetrable wood of the study doors. She turned, not toward the cellar below the kitchen, but toward the room with the security camera monitors. "Come on, let's see if there's anything."

"Why aren't these in his study?" I asked as Marisol locked us in the tiny room filled with screens. She looked them over once before answering.

"They were, but he didn't like them there. Too bright and hot, he said. He can see the individual camera feeds from his computer, anyway."

"Hey," I stopped her, seeing her hands shake as she gripped the chair in front of her. "Remember combat breathing?"

"Sure."

"Try it. Close your eyes and breathe. Think about what you'd do if someone came in here right now with an AK-47."

She did as I instructed, saying at length, "This is not helping."

But her hands became still, and a little color returned to her cheeks. She continued to breathe and really seemed to be calming down when we heard it again, unmistakably closer: at least a dozen shots, horribly loud even within the walls of the windowless room. Marisol backed into the wall opposite the monitors, her chest heaving.

"It's the people who killed my parents, I know it is," she squeaked, not seeing the screens at all. "They're coming for me and Fernando. They're coming…"

"Look," I said, taking her by the shoulders and moving her closer to the center screen, where a camera angled down at the front door was feeding us a very clear picture of nothing happening. "There's no one here. I don't see anyone on any camera. Those shots could be a lot farther away than they sound. It could have nothing to do with us."

"Someone followed James here. I know it." Suddenly her hand gripped my upper arm so hard it hurt as she pointed with her other hand to a screen near the bottom. "Look! That's him, that's the man I saw. I think…"

Fully expecting to see Luke, I peered down at the screen and nearly laughed with relief. It was a small, wiry man, alone, wielding an AK-47 just as Mari had identified. A hat pulled low over his face revealed only a graying beard and a mouth set in a hard line as he crept heel-to-toe along the side of the road leading toward the hidden estate, his rifle at low ready.

As we watched, a massive boar appeared behind him and must have made some telling sound. He whirled, gun rising, and we heard the burst of shots before we saw the muzzle flash on camera. The feeds were delayed significantly. This time he got the boar. It slumped over, dead, in the middle of the road, and Marisol laughed.

"It's just a poacher. It's just some old man."

"We'd better get down to the cellar," I warned. "Fernando expects to find us there."

As she led the way, I recalled her description of the man she'd seen on the camera the night I'd arrived. In just a flash, the size of him had given her the impression of a man, not a woman, but the poacher we'd just seen didn't fit that description. He was diminutive, slight, easily mistaken for a woman unless his beard was visible. There was no way this could be the same person.

I kept my thoughts to myself and feigned interest in the wine selection while we waited for Fernando to come fetch us. In the meantime, another troubling thought occurred to me.

"Where do the others go in an emergency?" I asked, noting

the clear absence of anyone but Marisol and me in the cellar safe room. Somehow I knew where Martín had gone, instructions or no: straight up to the art gallery to stand guard over the Raphael. If anyone in this house knew its worth, it was him.

"I don't know," Mari answered, frowning. "This has never happened before, not since I can remember. I'll ask Fernando. Maybe they don't know."

Fernando and Jim found us in the cellar, where we pretended to be surprised that the gunman had turned out to be nothing more sinister than a lone man hunting boar with a weapon of convenience. My facsimile of relief didn't fool Jim, not for moment, and I could tell from his suspicious half-smile that I'd soon be explaining how Marisol had introduced me to the security cameras.

We ate breakfast together, relief and humor at the overblown situation creating an uncharacteristically cheery mood. Afterward Fernando and Jim disappeared into the study again, presumably to get one another up to speed on all their self-important business.

Marisol and I elected to go swimming, where I had little trouble convincing her to ditch French in favor of Krav Maga, now that she saw how much more use the latter could be. With a waterlogged stick serving as a stand-in for a rifle, I taught her a few disarms, and then we took advantage of the buoyancy provided by the water to work on her kicks. She was never going to be a kickboxer, but I thought she could do some damage given the right motivation and opportunity.

Thoroughly exhausted after just over an hour, she stretched

out on a chaise and announced she would be sunbathing now. I rolled my eyes at her, annoyed. Since joining her would soon have my skin the same color as my red roots, I elected to pay a visit to Dude instead. He was overjoyed to escape from his cage after hearing the gunshots, and he led me on a frantic tour of the house, sniffing everything twice and thoroughly inspecting each door and window to make sure it was secure.

He led me to the third floor, to the one door tucked away in a corner that I usually passed over because it was always locked. Dude nosed at the door and revealed it was slightly open, the latch sliding free even as it swung inward at his touch. I leaned sideways to look inside, fearful he'd barged into some sanctum sanctorum that we could get in trouble for even knowing about. I couldn't see much, as the light was off and the windows were covered by heavy blackout curtains. As I dithered about whether or not to go inside, Dude's ears flew to attention, alerting me to someone coming down the hallway toward us.

I started to close the door but paused, immobilized by curiosity, as voices became clear long before their owners appeared around the corner. The first I could hear was Martín's.

"… will probably kill us if he finds out. How could you be so stupid?"

"You told me to check all the outside windows. You didn't say to skip that room!"

"Keep your voice down. It was understood, no one goes in there."

"I'm sure I closed it."

"I want to be sure."

Martín was with either Leandro or Daniel; their voices were nearly indistinguishable and I felt certain they were brothers. Torn now between raging curiosity and fear that getting caught in front of this open door would come with consequences I wasn't prepared to face, I finally made up my mind and looked down at Dude.

"Go find Jim," I whispered, so quietly that I couldn't hear me, but I knew Dude could. He stared at me, trying to understand. "Go find Jim," I repeated, waving my arm in the general direction from which the voices were approaching. He took one tentative step away, and I decided that would have to be good enough. I backed into the dark room and closed the door softly behind me, making sure the door latched. No more than a second later, I heard footsteps.

"Did you hear that?"

The voices rounded the corner that had mercifully blocked me from view. "It's just the dog," Martín answered, dislike evident in his tone. "What's he doing up here by himself? If Mario let him out again…"

"I'm sure he's just looking for his lady," Leandro (or Daniel) cooed. "Look," he said, and I jumped in alarm as the doorknob rattled loudly. "See, I told you, it's locked."

The whole door rattled as Martín checked for himself. "Fine," he relented. "Next time I tell you to check the rooms, skip that one."

Their voices and footsteps were already retreating as the young man answered wearily, "I know, I get it. Come on, doggie."

With a whimper, Dude galloped after them, his paws pounding across the thick carpet that covered the middle of the hallway.

I turned on the spot, tingling with excitement. What had I found? Rather than flipping on the light, I edged carefully through the murky room and moved one of the curtains just enough to let in a blinding ray of sunlight.

At first sight, without a second thought, I knew where I was: Etta Serna's bedroom.

23

Friday, February 19, 2021
Argentina

Every piece of furniture within the spacious room was covered in white sheets, giving me the impression of so many oddly-shaped ghosts frozen in fear at my sudden intrusion. The very air was old, sharp with the scent of slow decay. The gentle folds of each sheet were gray with accumulated dust, and with a jolt of dismay I looked down and saw clear tracks through the dust on the tiled floor that I'd made with my bare feet, mingled randomly with larger tracks that I assumed were made when Leandro or Daniel had checked the window.

I hesitated again, thinking… Since I couldn't hope to hide the fact that I (or someone) had been in here, would it be so much worse if I snooped around a little? A chest under the window, a tall wardrobe, a closet, all promised something interesting to be discovered.

I started in the closet, a built-in place to hide from anyone peeking into the room who was too thick to notice my foot-prints. Moving the curtain aside a little more for adequate light, I opened the closet door and was surprised to find it was more than large enough for me to walk inside. I found a dangling string near the center of the space and tugged on it, flooding my vision with sickly yellow light as the bulb swung back and forth from the force of my overenthusiastic tug.

I nearly passed out at the sight of two bare feet standing be-hind a row of dresses hanging on the far wall, my breath catch-ing in a pre-scream before I realized I was looking at a long mirror leaning against the wall behind the clothes. I moved the dresses aside and looked at my full reflection, shaking my head at myself.

"Calm down," I whispered. My reflection looked dubious until I turned away to find something more appealing than the musty garments of a long-dead grandmother.

Down the center of the wall to the right of the door was a column of long, narrow drawers, all closed, two near the bottom bearing small, round locks in a muddy brass color that put me in mind of a skeleton key. I nudged at the bottom drawer with my toe and was rewarded with a slight movement; it wasn't locked.

Inside were a lifetime's worth of letters, postcards, maga-zines, to-do lists, and all the sundry bits of paper one might collect in the course of a normal life. Certainly the postcard addressed by, I assumed, Fernando's mother from Barcelona, Spain predated Etta's retreat to this isolated, self-imposed pris-on. The address for Etta was in Buenos Aires, where she must have lived before coming to this house.

I tried to picture Etta, couldn't, and rooted around the assorted papers for a photo. A drawer higher up held exactly what I'd hoped to find: a photo album. I flipped breathlessly to the first page, where I was greeted by an unsettlingly crisp, black-and-white image of two girls. One was in her teens, the other younger, and they were sitting on a bench above a rocky beach, their hair frozen in the grip of a light breeze. Their unsmiling faces stared the camera down, all four of their hands entwined, knees touching beneath voluminous skirts as they angled possessively toward each other. The cars parked on the street behind them made me think of Cuba, but I knew the photo had been taken in Colombia. No preternatural intuition informed me on that count; the Colombian flags billowing away from a building on the far right were enough.

The elder was Etta, I was certain. She was a World War II Era Marisol. Who was the younger, a hawk-faced girl who looked like she'd never learned to smile? I eased the photo out of the plastic corners that held it in place, turned it over, and read one word: "Regina."

I slipped the photo back into place, fighting a wave of sadness. They were just kids, and God only knew how or why they'd ended up so far away from home. At least they'd been together, at least then. I wondered if Fernando's grandfather had been behind the camera, and the Etta in the photo held so tightly to her little sister because she knew that soon they would be parted, and the parting might be forever.

The rest of the album was no cheerier a spectacle. It chronicled Etta's life until Fernando's parents' wedding and then ended abruptly. No sequel appeared to have been made. Etta was featured more in the earlier photos, less and less as time wore on, but not in one single picture had she cracked so much as a half-smile. Either she was just a stoic person, or she'd been miserable for most of her long life.

At the back of the album, tucked carefully behind a large wedding photo, was a single piece of notebook paper folded twice. It was yellow with age, warning me to take care as I pulled it free and unfolded it.

"Dear Etta," I read, "How I've missed you. I was awfully broken up that you couldn't come to the wedding, but by now I figure you understand why just as well as I do. Still, you could say hello to your *esposo* from me and I'll do the same, as though it will matter.

"My Spanish is coming along okay, but I still feel like a toddler sometimes. Alejandro is very patient, though, would you believe he really seems to want me to learn? He's mostly kind and terribly handsome, and sometimes I wonder whether you and I are the luckiest girls in the world or the absolute sorriest. Can we be both all at once?

"I saw the American news on a television in the hotel lobby, and would you believe there's another war already? This time in Viet Nam. At least we're far away from all of that.

"I'll write you again as soon as I'm home, so you can have my address. Alejandro doesn't see any harm in us writing, do try to make Victor see it his way. They'll never meet, will they? Funny, because I just bet you they'd get along like a house on fire.

"Well, now I've done it. I'm too pressed for time to start

over, so you'll have to feel that the same way I did. Give your baby boy a kiss from me, and keep your chin up—After all, who can doubt that the worst is over for you and me?

"All my love, Regina *Lira.*"

With measured movements, I folded the letter and replaced it behind the wedding photo, then returned the album to its drawer. I sat down heavily by the door, leaning my head against the doorframe. Many deep, slow breaths passed my lips while I struggled to contain myself. All I wanted, in that moment, was to cry, to really, really cry like I hadn't cried in at least a decade. I didn't even know why, but the thought of the girl who'd written that foolishly optimistic letter, and the thought of her sister reading it, made me so deeply sad I couldn't remember the last time I'd been happy.

Those two girls were Jim's grandmother's sisters. Had Bettina met Jim's grandfather already? Did she hold out even the tiniest shred of hope that her siblings were alive? Had Regina ever tried to write to her, too?

Sluggish with misplaced grief, my mind jerked away from Regina to Jim's assertion that the Raphael was the reason I was here. I would bet my life Jim was telling the truth about that. Just like that, another of Jim's rare moments of frank honesty popped into my mind, some of the first words he'd ever spoken to me. When I'd asked why he'd yanked me from the running for agent, he'd said, "You were a great fit—for me."

I leaned forward, pressed the heels of my hands into my eyes, and groaned. This had to be a bad dream. I was running for my life from a deadly foe, my feet sucked into the ground with each step as though I were running through quicksand. I could scream with the force of my desire to run faster, to sprint, to risk my lungs exploding just to get there half a second faster; but I couldn't get there at all. I couldn't put the pieces together. I needed more information, and not the sort I'd likely find among Etta's personal possessions.

In less than a minute I'd done all I could to return the bedroom to the state in which I'd found it, including sweeping my feet back and forth across the footprints so at least it wasn't obvious I was the one who'd been in there. I left the room, closed the door, and made sure the handle locked behind me. I rushed to my bedroom and shook the dust out of the borrowed sarong I'd wrapped around myself as a swimsuit cover up. After thoroughly checking my reflection for any more dust—a dead giveaway I'd been in the one room of the house that Martín didn't clean—I decided to tuck myself away in the library and act as though I'd been there since leaving Marisol downstairs.

Whatever Fernando and Jim had to talk about, it took them all day. I didn't see either of them until I wandered down to the dining room for dinner, not even certain there would be a dinner until I caught a whiff of food. The last one to arrive, I slipped effortlessly into the browbeaten compliance I'd been feigning for weeks. I took my seat and apologized to Fernando for being a few minutes late, and he waved away the apology with a patient smile.

"There's no need to stand on ceremony, we've all had a stressful day. Mari tells me you helped her to calm down after we heard the gunshots. I'm very grateful."

"Yeah, no prob."

I took a bite of food, thinking the conversation was over, and was overcome by that ineffable sensation that someone was staring at me. Glancing at Fernando again, I locked eyes with him and shuddered involuntarily at his expression.

He knew exactly what I'd done.

I glanced at Jim, wondering if he noticed any of this, but even as my gaze moved away from Fernando's face it changed, relaxing, not even a ghost of the anger and accusation remaining for Jim to perceive. I forced down another bite, my throat tightening.

If I'd thought for a second that Martín had been exaggerating about Fernando finding out that someone had been in his grandmother's room, I now knew better. Praying to God it was mere sentiment, and not a desire to protect something tangible in that room that I might have stumbled across, I ate as much as I could stomach and excused myself, rushing out of the room too quickly to hope to hide my distress.

Jim found me in the bedroom ten minutes later, buried in blankets and attempting in vain to force myself to sleep just to keep panic at bay. My little Nokia hadn't received any messages since Luke's "good to go" text. Hoping the battery would hold a charge, I'd stashed phone and charger back in the far corner of the bathroom cabinet.

I felt the bed sink with Jim's weight as he sat down next to me. "Anna, what's wrong?"

Muffled by the blankets, I answered sadly, "I did something I probably shouldn't have."

"That doesn't narrow it down much."

I poked my head out of the blankets to get some air and gave him a brief summary of the apparently unforgivable thing I'd done, leaving out the insignificant discoveries I'd made and making it sound as though I hadn't nosed around the room at all. When my tale was over, Jim didn't look nearly as upset as I felt.

"That's it?" he asked, grabbing the edge of the blanket when I tried to disappear under it again. "You're overreacting."

"No, you didn't see his face. You still don't know what he's really like. Jim, I think… I think he might kill me for it."

"That's absurd."

"Just trust me, for once!" I erupted, infuriated that he could so easily dismiss my terror. "You *have* to take Dude and me with you when you leave this time. I might have forgiven you for the first time, but now you know how he treats me when you're gone. You can't possibly leave me here again…"

He lay down next to me, putting his lips to my ear. For a moment I thought he was about to get tender at the worst possible time, but he said so quietly that even with his lips tickling my ear I had to hold my breath to hear him, "You know what Luke is here to do. You have to be here for it. I'm begging you."

"Why?"

"Not here."

"Argh!" I rolled over, dragging the blankets with me so that I was entirely twisted up in them. I was fed up with Jim and his half-truths, his stupid master plan. I wanted to slug him, but I settled for trying to pretend he wasn't there.

He made this impossible by saying, "I need to talk to you about your parents."

24

Friday, February 19, 2021
Argentina

I was so taken aback by Jim's pronouncement that it took me several seconds to extricate myself enough to sit up and stare at him. Anxiety and anger forgotten, I asked breathlessly, "What about them?"

"You're going to be mad at me for not telling you sooner."

"I'm always mad at you for not telling me sooner."

"Just try not to freak out."

"Jim!"

"All right," he sighed, standing up and planting himself about a yard away from the foot of the bed. Was he trying to put distance between himself and my fists? "Back on January twenty-fifth, I got a call from your mother. I guess she'd written down my number when I called you back in July."

"Okay, and?"

"She wouldn't tell me what she wanted. She demanded that

I meet her at a coffee shop in DC. Apparently she was already there when she called me."

"Oh, boy…"

"Quiet, let me get this out. I went to meet her and of course she wanted to know what was going on, where you were, whether you were okay. She said she wanted to tell you someone had stolen Dude, and she was getting pretty upset that she couldn't reach you. I told her I'd already let you know about Dude, but she kept insisting she needed to know where you were and wanted to talk to you. She's, um… Well, she got under my skin a little bit. I just wanted to reassure her, get her off my back and out of DC, so I showed her this."

He handed me his cell phone, unlocked and open to a grainy selfie of Alice and me in front of the Brandenburg Gate in Berlin. I studied the photo, glaring hatefully at it, knowing exactly what my mother had seen. She'd been to the Brandenburg Gate herself.

"You imbecile," I snapped, tossing the phone back to him.

"It's not like I didn't know she'd place it. I just wanted to convince her you were alive, and well, and working on something for me in Germany, long term. She promised me she wouldn't tell anyone, not even your father, that she'd just sit tight and wait for your assignment to be over. I didn't know what was really going on until a couple of days later, when Dom came into my office and unloaded on me, totally unsolicited.

"Apparently your mother stayed at your apartment instead of returning to Texas. She met Dom, they got to talking, and Dom told her she might find you at your boyfriend's house, since you hadn't been coming around at all for the past few months."

"Oh, no…"

"Oh, yes. Dom told her about our little subterfuge last New Year's Eve. Your mom was understandably confused that Dom thought I was your boyfriend, since you'd told her I was your boss. Dom set her straight about me, but couldn't tell her for sure if Philip Levin was your real boss because obviously Dom doesn't know about any of that. Your mom was the one who dropped Levin's name. Oh a hunch, I checked Philip's visitor logs and lo and behold—guess who paid him a visit on January fifteenth?"

"A skinhead with a shiv, I hope."

"Your mom, Anna."

For a full minute I just stared at him, asking and answering my own questions as the full meaning of what Jim was telling me slowly became clear. I finally choked out, "She played you."

"Yes, she did. Your father flew to Berlin a week after I met with your mother. He's still there."

"What did Philip tell her?"

"I don't know. I got the call logs from the prison and found two calls from Philip to your parents' house. The first one they didn't answer, but the second one your mom picked up. All he told her was he had some information about you, and he wouldn't tell her anything over the phone. I paid Philip a vis-it myself as soon as I could, but I couldn't get anything out of him. He seemed pretty pleased with himself, though. I tried your mom's number, but she wouldn't answer, and I went to your apartment to try to talk to her, but Dom said she'd left the previous evening. I have no idea where she is now. She didn't fly anywhere, that much I know. Your father isn't answering his phone. I don't think he took it to Germany with him."

"You get yourself to Berlin and get my dad," I gritted. I could feel my face turning red with the effort of staying angry and keeping the next emotion at bay. "If anything happens to him, I'll kill you."

"There's no way he's going to find anything. If I go over there and track him down, it'll just convince them there's something to find."

"I don't care! What if Marcel finds out he's there? Have you given any thought at all to what will happen to my dad then?"

"There's no reason for Marcel to worry about him, even if there was the slightest chance they'd cross paths."

"Call Ingrid. Tell her to ship my father home in handcuffs if she has to, just get him out of there. She owes you one, doesn't she?"

He nodded, way ahead of me. "I already called her. I had to leave a message, and she hasn't called me back yet."

"Try again!"

"Look, you've got to calm down. Obviously Philip is up to something, and I think we can assume it's not good. But we don't know anything else yet. Your parents are just—"

"Excuse me, but we know a heck of a lot more than that! Let's start with the fact that my parents aren't stupid. They wouldn't knowingly interfere with my work, not if my mom believed one word of your 'long term job in Germany' nonsense. This is a rescue operation! They think you're putting me in danger, and who do you think gave them that idea?"

"Philip."

"Just like he told Tommy you were a cartel asset, and that you'd recruited me."

"Why? What possible benefit to him?"

"Well that's what I've been trying to figure out this whole time! For all you've put me through, I still haven't figured out what Philip is really up to, let alone why. Guess I've been a little too kidnapped!"

"You're stressed, and you're seeing imminent danger where there is none. I understand you're worried about your parents—"

"Like heck you understand."

"—but I am working on it. I shouldn't have told you."

"Oh, don't even go there," I warned. "All you ever do is not tell me anything until you have no other choice."

"What can I say? You do your best work in the dark."

"You better find somewhere else to sleep, Jim. I'm abut this close to throwing you a blanket party."

He frowned, not understanding, and rather than stooping to asking me what I meant, he Googled it. His mouth twisted in disappointment. "That's not nearly as much fun as it sounds."

"Get out!"

He relented, pointedly grabbing pajamas and a toiletry bag out of his suitcase before departing without another word. He didn't slam the door behind him, which I decided to interpret as a sign that he was at least a tiny bit sorry. The heated exchange had chased away my earlier fear, but as soon as Jim closed the door, it all came flooding back: the look on Fernando's face, that promise of swift and sure retribution, the knowledge that soon, possibly as soon as tomorrow, I'd be left alone again for Fernando to deal with as he saw fit.

One thought allowed me to finally, mercifully, slip into the blissful ignorance of sleep that night: Luke was here, and Jim plainly wanted to be gone before he made his move. The sooner Jim left, the sooner Luke could swoop in to do his thing.

▼

When I came to, not only was Jim in bed with me, but I was draped across his chest, his right arm curving down my back so that his hand rested comfortably on my waist. I had no memory of him coming back to the bedroom, let alone of snuggling up to him, but I was cool with it.

I already regretted my terrible reaction last night and wanted to mirror Jim's calm assurance that my parents weren't in any real danger. Even with all I didn't know or understand, I convinced myself that things were proceeding more or less exactly as Jim wanted them to. I had no reason to believe they hadn't been since the day he'd plucked my ill-fated file out of the FBI's latest pool of agent hopefuls.

With renewed fortitude, I made my way down to breakfast without waking Jim, hoping I could corner Fernando and dispense with all this suspense. I planned to tell him exactly what I'd done and ask him, point blank, what he was going to do about it. It was only seven in the morning, and the dark, cold kitchen foretold another late breakfast. I changed course for

Fernando's study instead.

I knocked on the door, waited a few seconds, and received no answer. I turned to go and bumped right into Fernando.

"Gah," I gasped, backing into the door. "You scared the crap out of me."

"I thought I told you not to be so crass," he said, his voice so level and cold that it was worse than a scream. He stepped closer, too close, bearing down on me as I pressed myself against the door. "Why are you trying to get into my study?"

"I'm not. I came to talk to you."

He considered me briefly, not unlike a cat deciding which part of the human he most wanted to bite. At a sudden movement of his right hand I flinched automatically, but he merely extracted a key from his pocket and reached around me to unlock the door. He opened it and motioned for me to go inside. I backed in, wondering where all that fortitude from this morning had gone so quickly. He closed and locked the door behind us.

"Talk."

I skipped the confession. He so clearly already knew what I'd done. I said, "I'm sorry, Fernando. If I'd known how important it was to you, I wouldn't have gone inside. You have to believe I didn't mean any harm…"

"I don't have to believe anything."

"I know you know I wander around at night. I've been in almost every room of this house. I thought by now if you'd wanted me to stop, you'd've told me to."

"That room is *different*," he hissed, starting to lose control. An unhelpful surge of curiosity distracted me: What could possibly be so important about that room?"

"I understand that now. I'll never go near it again. You have my word."

"What did you see? What did you disturb?"

"I saw the inside of the door," I defended. "I just waited until the coast was clear, then I left. I wasn't trying to find out what was in there, I just didn't want Martín to find me there."

"Why not, if as you say you had no idea what you were doing was wrong?"

"The door was ajar. It was always locked before. I heard him coming and I just panicked."

"You saw nothing?"

"Nothing."

"If I find out you're lying to me, no amount of affection for my cousin will save you. Is that clear?"

"Crystal."

"Get out."

I slipped past him and experienced a fleeting moment of panic when the door wouldn't open, but I managed to unlock it and slip through. I was breathing hard under a retreating wave of adrenaline. Never in my life had I been so convinced that someone wanted to snuff me out, right then and there.

I ran into Jim on his way down, and without having time to compose myself I knew my face was an open book. He looked startled by the very sight of me.

"What happened to you?"

I shook my head, tight-lipped. I was tired of trying to convince him not to leave me here, tired of failing to make him understand the danger in which he was placing me and everyone I loved.

A thought occurred to me, one last desperate gambit, and I asked, "Can you take Dude with you when you leave?"

"Why?"

"Don't make me explain the obvious. Just tell Fernando that my nieces aren't getting over him being stolen, and you've got to take him back for their sake. Can you do that?"

"Sure, of course."

"Thank you."

25

Wednesday, February 24 to
Thursday, February 25, 2021
Argentina

Jim stayed three more days before departing once more for Washington. How he'd managed to convince Fernando to let him take his biggest bargaining chip, Dude, with him, I couldn't guess. I said goodbye to both of them in the chilly, early morning hours with a sick, sinking feeling in the pit of my stomach. I knew I had until they drove out of sight, and then the other shoe would drop. I just didn't know how heavy it would be.

No one but Fernando and I had dragged themselves out of bed to see Jim off. I turned to him as Jim's borrowed Land Rover was finally lost to view, not wanting the blow to come from any direction but face-on. He was already looking at me, a faint smile playing around the corners of his lips.

"Curiosity is a dangerous thing," he said absently, looking

over my head at who knew what. "I've come to a decision."

"About what?"

"Come with me."

I trailed behind him, silent on bare feet while his heels clicked officiously on the terra cotta tiles. I hadn't even bothered to change out of my pajamas, a set purloined from Jim's suitcase, and had long since begun to feel the cold air around me leeching the warmth from my very bones. I thought he was leading me back to my bedroom, so when he passed my door and continued walking, I stopped.

"Where are we going?"

"To my grandmother's room. I want to show you what's in there."

"I don't want to see what's in there."

When he withdrew a compact revolver from his pocket and directed it casually at me, I realized I had lost my capacity to be shocked. I just frowned at him, not understanding.

"You're gonna shoot me? Why?"

"I wasn't actually planning to shoot you, it's simply a useful alternative to you doing as I say." He jerked the gun to his right, toward the corridor which led to Etta's room. "Go."

"All right. Jeez."

I began to lead the way, walking slowly, mentally begging him to prod me in the back with that goofy little revolver. If he would just get close enough… But he kept his distance, no doubt aware of my intentions.

"Open it," he breathed when I stopped at the door. "I've already unlocked it for you."

I did, realizing what he was about to do less than a second before he did it. As the door swung inward, I felt two hands on my shoulders pushing me forward with such force that I had to run into the room to keep from falling flat on my face. By the time I'd recovered and turned around, the door was closed, plunging me and the room into inky darkness.

"Enjoy your stay," he called through the door. "I imagine it will be no more than three days long."

Footsteps carried him away. I stood still where the light had left me, waiting for my brain to catch up.

The room was different. I could sense it without needing to see it. The scent of decay was stronger, sweeter, menacing. I felt my way to the window and twitched the curtains aside, but it was too dark outside still to reveal anything. I sat down under the window, facing the room, and waited with uncharacteristic patience for the sun to rise and show me the full extent of the horror.

Long before the sun was fully risen, my eyes had adjusted enough to the scant moonlight and starlight to make out basic shapes. The bed and all the other furniture was where I remembered it, still cloaked in ghostly white, but on the other side of the bed, on the floor, something large and opaque blocked my view of the stretch of floor between the bed and the closet. Whatever it was, it made neither sound nor movement, and with increasing desperation I told myself over and over that something that inert couldn't possibly pose any real threat.

At some point I lay down with my back pressed against the wall and drifted to sleep. When my eyes crept open, light had penetrated the dark room and I could no longer excuse my failure to investigate the source of the room's new, nauseating aroma. I stood up, opened the curtains as far as they would go, and coughed as dust rained down from the heavy fabric and filled my nose and mouth.

Turning from the window against every inclination in my body, I steadied myself as my gaze was drawn like a magnet to the bed. Now that I was specifically looking for something sinister, I couldn't believe I'd missed it before.

At the foot of the bed, barely visible because of the sheet that sloped down from the headboard to rest over the lower corners of the footboard, two tiny peaks broke the otherwise smooth, white surface. Feet.

I got close enough to grip the sheet by one corner and started to back away, dragging it with me.

The sight of Etta's desiccated corpse didn't frighten me even half as much as it should have. She looked like a cheesy Halloween decoration, right down to the old fashioned dress and intact, carefully coiffed hair. Her withered hands were crossed and had melted into her now-hollow abdomen. She'd been dead for so long that not even the vague suggestion of decay I'd smelled when I first intruded on her resting place had been enough to make me suspect she was there. She was just bones, clothes, and mummified skin. I felt bad for her, staged there to rest in prolonged ignominy rather than being properly buried.

Fernando was farther around the bend than I'd guessed.

It wasn't Etta that I was afraid of, anyway. The smell of death was powerful and recent. Already it had permeated my hair and clothes and clung to me like syrup. I had to take a moment.

"I know we don't talk anymore," I whispered, trying to breathe through my mouth, "but I've got to ask you for something: If that's Luke, give me some sign now, otherwise I'm going to have to see for myself."

I waited, looking around. No writing on the wall, no gusts of air, no loud noises or flashes of light warned me off. I took a deep breath, regretted it because then I tasted death too, and stepped around the bed. Disappointment erased fear, for the moment: The object on the floor was a crisp, black body bag, its contents unknowable unless I could convince myself to open it. I'd already guessed it was a body; I needed to know whose it was.

It was large, that much I could tell. That ruled out the boar hunter and Marisol, as well as Maria and Luz. This didn't help much, though, because I hadn't believed for a moment that it was any of those people. From the first moment of acceptance that there was something there, that it was the source of the smell, I'd linked it inextricably to the fact that I hadn't received any texts from Luke since before Jim arrived.

I paced back and forth in front of the bed for a long time, working myself up. Did I want to know, or did I not want to know? Better yet, once I knew, what the heck could I do about it?

It was nearly noon before I made up my mind: I couldn't stand not knowing. It would make me as crazy as Fernando. I knelt down next to the head of the body bag, pulled my t-shirt up over my nose, and began working the stiff, clumsy zipper down.

The first thing I saw was a shock of dark hair, followed by a forehead adorned with a single, dime-sized dot the color of raspberry jam. I moved the zipper down enough to see the eyes, wide open and completely white, and the nose, before I whipped the zipper back up and sealed him back inside. The smell was too much.

I stood up, retreated to the window, my safe space, and gave vent to a single, bark-like laugh of relief and shame. It wasn't Luke, but it was someone, someone who probably didn't deserve to die for an innocent mistake, just so his corpse could be used as depraved punishment against another: Daniel.

Without really thinking about it, I wrapped my right fist in one side of the blackout curtain and punched through the lower pane of the window, showering glass daggers onto the hedges below. It was too far to jump, and I didn't intend to downclimb it, not yet. I just needed air. Thinking of the view from the security camera somewhere to the left of this window, I knocked out the rest of the glass so that, on camera, it wouldn't be immediately obvious that the window was broken.

I dragged the body bag into the closet and shut it inside, hoping that would keep the smell somewhat contained. After that, I was out of things to do. Now that I knew Luke was still alive, or at least had no proof he wasn't, I intended to wait for him. How long, though?

Fernando intended me to dehydrate to death in here, or my interpretation of 'three days' was wrong. Well, I'd show him. I still wasn't acclimated to this desert air, and I was already dehydrated from drinking too much wine with Jim last night. I gave myself no more than two and a half days, including time served. At least I wouldn't have to pee in the corner.

That first day, it wasn't the thirst that plagued me but the hunger, a bizarre urge to feel when a body is moldering away in the closet. The hunger cramps faded away around nightfall, replaced by a persistent, hollow ache. My body had finally realized it needed water, not food.

The energy deficit allowed me to sleep, curled up under the window, but not for long. With darkness came plummeting temperatures, and I shivered myself awake long before sunrise. The only blanket I'd spotted was underneath Etta, and I certainly didn't intend to use it, so I trembled away until the sun rose and I was able to find a blanket in the chest that sat next to me under the window.

I wrapped myself up in it, rhapsodizing over the scents of cedar and moth balls that burst out of it with each movement, until the room warmed up so much that I had to take it off. I found a handkerchief in the chest and wrapped it around my nose and mouth. Soon I was dizzy from the fumes. Or maybe it was the hunger and thirst.

I sat under the window and stared at the closet, wishing I hadn't moved Daniel's body in there. That was the cache of diverting discoveries, the letters, the photos, the clothes; and now it was off limits because to open the door would surely redouble the power of the malodorous scent it was containing. Still, I was considering it right up until the moment when I blinked and realized the room had become so dark I couldn't really see anything. Night had come again, and by my estimate I wouldn't survive the next day unless I got some water.

Gunfire shattered my restless sleep soon after that thought. I couldn't even remember laying down to go to sleep. I sat up too fast, making my head spin, and peeked over the windowsill to see what was going on. The window faced the woods, the view offering nothing remotely informative. Another burst of five shots caused me to look all around, unable to even guess at the direction from which they came. Someone began to scream, and a mighty crash shook the very floor on which I crouched. If I didn't know any better, I'd think someone had driven a truck or van straight into the house. More gunfire erupted, overlapping, the shots contending with one another.

My mind snapped into action when I heard footsteps outside the bedroom door. Knowing that couldn't mean good news for me, I stood up halfway and leaned out the window, trying to assess the outside of the house for footholds and handholds to climb down. It was no good. I wasn't a champion climber at the best of times. To try anything in my current state wouldn't be functionally different from jumping out the third-floor window.

As the telltale sound of keys rattling in the lock reached my ears, I made up my mind and dashed to the bedroom door. As it began to swing inward I leaned against it, and as soon as the force from the other side began to topple me I stepped away, letting the person outside overbalance and stumble through the door.

Without even seeing who it was, I brought my hands together into a tight ball and swung them down like a club, landing a solid blow right at the base of his neck. As he crumbled to the ground, I flipped on the light switch, something I couldn't believe I hadn't thought to do sooner. Idiot.

Splayed out on the floor at my feet was Mario, his brows pinched together in unconscious puzzlement.

"Sorry," I mumbled, stepping over him to gain the hallway. He'd probably be okay. I had no quarrel with him, and I wondered belatedly if he'd come to let me out. Disregarding this, I stopped first at the nearest bathroom and drank greedily from the tap in the dark, not wanting to give away my position by flipping another light switch. I drank too much and made myself woozy, so I sat down on the cold floor and pressed my cheek to the tiles until the feeling passed. I drank more water, then moved on.

All the while, gunfire filled the house with mounting urgency.

26

Thursday, February 25, 2021
Argentina

I slipped into my bedroom and found the Nokia in the bathroom, hoping a missed text from Luke might give me some clue about what to do next. It was dead. I changed out of my death-scented pajamas and, since I didn't have time to do anything about my hair, I tucked it up under a beanie from my suitcase and called it good. Creeping along silently and praying I wouldn't take a stray bullet, I found a window that faced the front of the house and peered down toward the front door.

Sure enough, half a red-and-white, 1980s-era Ford F-350 was sticking out of the wall just to the right of the door, smoking delicately. I smiled at it, unaccountably cheered by the sight.

Even as I watched, headlights rounded the other side of the house and a sleek, black Escalade screeched around the corner, gravel flying. As it passed the house on its way toward freedom, I tried to make out who was inside, but the windows were tinted so dark that it was impossible to tell.

Mario was unconscious in Etta's bedroom, and Daniel was dead in the closet. Two down, nine to go. Maybe after seeing what happened to Daniel, the rest had fled. I just hoped it wasn't the other way around, with Fernando making his exit in his Caddy while the rest of the household battled away.

"There you are!"

I whirled around at the voice, a smile ready for Luke that died on my lips as I looked once more down the snub nose of Fernando's revolver. I raised my hands, not sure what else to do.

"Come here. It's time you made yourself useful."

"Why don't you go eat a fistful of worms instead?" I asked, in German, as seriously as I could. He cocked his head like a puppy, processing my words.

"A fistful of worms?" he repeated incredulously.

"See, I've already been useful."

"Get over here," he hissed, pulling back the hammer to underscore his words. I complied, moving at a glacial pace, eyeballing his trigger finger with roiling apprehension.

"Your finger's on the trigger," I said conversationally, nodding toward it. "Watch it."

"Don't even speak," he snapped. "Walk, that way—slowly!"

This time he couldn't resist the impulse to jab me in the back with the weapon to goad me into walking faster. With the hammer back and his stupid finger inside the trigger guard, this was more than a mere annoyance.

I paused at the top of the stairs and reached for the banister to steady myself, and he couldn't have timed his next jab better—or worse, depending on the perspective. I spun, my right arm batting his away while my left hand made a grab for the gun. He hadn't fired when I moved, and I didn't comprehend why until I'd twisted the revolver away from him, pointed it at his chest, and squeezed the trigger no fewer than seven times. The series of impotent clicks that resulted were deafening to my ears. He started to laugh at me, so I overhanded the gun at his face and dashed down the stairs while he recoiled and recovered.

The gunfire had ceased completely, the house deathly silent except for my thunderous descent down two flights of stairs to the ground floor. Once I was down, I stopped, listening for the sounds of pursuit, but silence had fallen again. Eventually I heard the sibilant hiss of steam escaping from the F-350's radiator, and another sound, even fainter, coming toward me. More footsteps, nearly obliterated by the caution of the person making them.

They were approaching from the wide hallway that led to Fernando's study, and I could either run back up the stairs, leave through the front door, or dash across the hallway to take my chances through the back of the house. I chose to dash, skipping across the opening about a foot ahead of a burst of gunfire.

Pressing my back to the inadequate cover of the corner, I called, "It's me! It's Anna!"

"Aw, dang it—did I get you?"

The sound of Luke's voice, the casual way he'd asked if I was currently dying of a bullet wound, made me laugh out loud.

"No, I'm good!"

"Am I clear that way?"

"Fernando's upstairs. He's out of ammo. I don't see anyone else."

As my words echoed into silence, the power cut out, plunging us into total darkness.

"Well, great."

Luke appeared around the corner, looking positively alarming in black fatigues, black ski mask, and matte black boots. Even his weapon was a dull black, a built-out AR-15 that was smoking gently from the barrel.

"Are you okay?" he asked, voice dropping to a low whisper.

"I'm fantastic. This is literally the best day of my life."

He flipped on a flashlight attached to the underside of the AR-15's barrel and directed it up the stairs, complaining, "I thought you were dead. You didn't answer my texts."

"Fernando locked me in a room with a dead body after Jim left. Well, two bodies. I couldn't get to the phone."

"Um. Wow."

"So, what's the plan? What can I do?"

He looked me over, his expression hidden beneath the ski mask, and I thought I heard him sigh. "Here." He passed me a gun and two spare magazines. "You have pockets, right?"

"For once, yes," I answered, feeling the weapon to see what I was dealing with. "Glock?"

"M and P. You've got forty-five rounds—don't make me regret giving you that."

"As if."

A bullet ricocheted off the tiles an inch from Luke's left foot, forcing us both back down the hallway away from the stairs.

"I guess he reloaded," Luke growled. "At least he can't hit anything with it."

"Are you here to kill him, or rescue me?"

"Baby, you know I didn't expect you to need rescuing."

"Does Jim know about this?"

"Sure, we're best friends now. Watch it," he said suddenly, grabbing my arm and hauling me further back, around another corner, as Fernando advanced. I had to give Fernando credit for bravery, going after an assassin with nothing but a six-shooter, but I was distracted by confusion.

"The FBI helped you plot and carry out a contract killing on foreign soil for your human trafficker boss? Sorry, Luke, I'm not buying it. Sounds more like the CIA."

"I'm not looking a gift horse in the mouth, and neither should you. Help me out here, we need to stop retreating."

"Follow me," I said at once, backing toward the kitchen.

My foot bumped into something soft and heavy, and I glanced down to see a man's body face-down on the floor, blood pooling under his face. I couldn't tell who it was. We edged around it, one of us feeling very sick all of a sudden, and gained the kitchen without being spotted by Fernando.

Barely audible, I told Luke, "He'll expect me to go back up-stairs. The safe room is through that door, that's what he's going for. I'll break for the stairs, and you wait here for him."

"Got it. Don't get shot."

He slid into deep shadows across the hall from the cellar door, and I didn't pause to consider what I was doing. I ran flat out toward the stairs, betting my life that Fernando had gone around the dining room the other way and wasn't waiting around the corner to pick me off.

I dashed across the same hallway from which Luke had inadvertently shot at me and received much the same greeting, except Fernando wasted only one shot which missed me by an even more comfortable margin. I ran back upstairs as fast as my legs were willing to carry me, stopping at the second floor to peer over the banister. He hadn't followed. I listened, pulse hammering in my ears so hard I feared even the report of a gunshot wouldn't get through.

It did, though. Three shots rang out, two much louder than the other. I retraced my steps and found Luke standing over Fernando's body, studying the revolver with casual interest. Luke nudged at Fernando tentatively with one toe, garnering no reaction, and pocketed the pillaged revolver. His next words chilled me to the bone.

"He's down. Where the sister?"

"What?"

"Marisol Serna. She's part of the deal. Where would she be?"

I forced my gaping mouth closed, not trusting it. I couldn't have heard him right. He was going to kill Marisol? He'd actually agreed to that? I didn't have to speak, though. He got there on his own.

"Safe room's down there?" he asked, impatient, directing his gun toward the cellar door.

I found my voice and stammered, "No—down the hall further. This way."

"You're a lousy liar. Just stay up here and watch him. I'm not sure he's dead."

"She's just a kid."

"Stay up here."

I followed him anyway, stooping to check Fernando's pulse by way of fulfilling my guard duty. I felt nothing. Luke eased open the cellar door and directed the beam of his flashlight down the stairs. Some safe room. Silent as the grave, he started down. I trailed behind him, too keyed up to attempt to dissuade him again, my mind riddled with doubts. This wasn't right, he wasn't about to do this.

Just as Luke reached the bottom of the stairs, I pushed past him and stepped in front of his gun.

"Don't you dare," I snarled.

He didn't answer, the light from his gun moving from my chest into the corner, where Marisol was crouched, her arms around her knees, her face buried between them. A sob tore from me and she raised her head slightly, roused by the sound. She took one look at Luke, a creature straight out of her nightmares, and began to shake violently. I stepped in front of the gun again.

"You can't be serious."

"I thought I told you to stay upstairs."

"I thought you didn't kill women."

"She'll be her brother in a few years. Doesn't matter if she's a girl, she's got to go."

"No."

"Get out of the way, Anna!"

While I silently refused, Marisol choked out, "Please… please don't hurt me."

She began to cry, almost soundlessly, only her desperate gasps for air giving her away. Even through the ski mask I could tell Luke was turning green.

"You know you can't do this," I whispered.

"It's like you think I have some other choice," he argued, stepping around me for a clear shot again. "Marcel knows I helped you escape. This is the price. It's her or me."

"What about a hundred million dollars instead?" I gasped, inspiration striking me like a slap to the face. "Would that console him?"

"What are you talking about? She doesn't have that kind of cash."

"It's not cash. It's a painting."

The barrel of the AR-15 dropped almost imperceptibly, only the beam of the flashlight making it obvious that Luke was now aiming at the floor to Marisol's left.

"What painting? Here?"

"It's a lost Raphael. It's worth nine figures easily."

"Come on."

"Hey, this is me you're talking to! It's a Raphael."

"There are papers in the study," Marisol said, her voice quavering over each word. "From when my grandfather got it. I'll show you where they are."

"There you go, provenance and all. Marcel will be thrilled."

Luke shook his head, arguing, "He can't sell a hot painting."

"He can't sell that fetish hotrod either, so why should that matter to him?"

His answer seemed to take an eternity.

"Take her upstairs, I want to see these papers. Slowly!" he barked as Marisol began to rise to her feet. I edged toward her, holding out my hand.

"I'm not going to let him hurt you," I said confidently, staring Luke down. "Come on, just pretend he's not there."

We made it to the top of the stairs where I paused, realizing what Marisol was about to see. My stomach turned, nearly making me sick. Fortunately, it was completely empty.

"Mari, come here." I pulled her into a hug and pressed her face into the hollow of my shoulder, whispering, "Don't open your eyes until I tell you to."

We got past Fernando's body, which I could have sworn had moved a bit since Luke and I had gone into the cellar. Maybe he wasn't dead. I decided not to point that out to Luke, choosing instead to hobble as best as I could with Marisol in tow until we turned the corner toward the study, her brother's body hidden from view.

As soon as I let her go, she shot off like a deer, racing toward the study at impressive speed. I gave chase automatically, sensing one possible reason she'd make a move like that: Fernando had another weapon stashed in there. Exhaustion and hunger slowed me down considerably, and Luke passed me, reaching the study doors half a second ahead and crashing into them to find they were locked.

"Thanks a lot, Anna!" he cried, shouldering the doors so hard they shook.

"Hey, the painting's this way," I snapped, jerking my thumb toward the stairs. "Just leave her."

He groaned. "Look, that Escalade was my getaway car. I have to see if I can get the truck started. Just get the painting and meet me outside. It better be impressive."

"Promise me you won't—"

"She's off the hook," he assured me, yelling through the door, "as long as she doesn't leave this room!"

Deciding that would have to do, I hightailed it to the art gallery and arrived gasping for air, my body just about ready to give up on me. I caught my breath in front of the Raphael, cast in ominous crimson tones by emergency lights tucked into the four corners of the gallery's ceiling. I had a problem.

The painting itself wasn't large, but the frame was massive. It probably weighed over a hundred pounds. I considered it desperately, totally at a loss for how to get it off the wall without damaging the canvas. After what felt like an hour of staring, immobile, unable to act, I wrapped my hands around either side of the frame and lifted, trying to judge how much it really weighed. It got up about four inches before the wire slipped off the hook with a *twang*, and the full weight of the piece was in my hands for a millisecond before my grip failed. I barely got my feet out of the way of the frame as it crashed to the floor, splitting into three pieces. The freed canvas fell forward and I caught it, swearing as my palm smacked across the boy's face. I moved my grip to the sides, wishing I'd thought to bring some gloves.

Far below, a distinct roar told me Luke had managed to get the truck started. Without so much as a towel to drape protectively over the seriously fragile, centuries old painting, I carried it out of the gallery.

Just outside I stopped, my progress arrested by a man standing in the middle of the hallway.

"Martín?"

He had a wad of clothing pressed against a wound on his forehead that seemed to be bleeding freely. Wobbling slightly on his feet, he asked, "Where are you taking him?"

"Back to Poland," I said at once, thinking I could at least try to make it true. Marcel would get his grubby little hands on this painting over my dead body.

Seeing that he had no answer to this, I started to walk around him, giving him a wide berth and, to my lasting personal shame, using the Raphael as a kind of shield. He turned with me, holding up the hand that wasn't occupied with trying to staunch the blood pumping out of his head.

He begged, "Wait. You can't take him like that. He's too fragile."

"Well, I'm taking him. If you've got some kind of cover…"

He staggered into the gallery and returned with a bundle of cloth tucked under his arm. He tossed it to me.

"Better than nothing," he sighed.

He half sat, half fell by the gallery door. I wrapped the painting in the unused drop cloth he'd given me, keeping one eye on him the whole time.

"Thank you. Marisol is in the study. Fernando is outside the kitchen."

"Are they…?"

"She's okay. He's dead."

"Good."

I glanced over my shoulder at him as I retreated, but he didn't move from his post by the gallery door. I experienced a flash of concern that there was something else there, something else he was guarding; but for all I knew it was just a fingerpainting by Marisol.

I found Luke in the battered Ford in the driveway, poised for flight. He honked the horn when he saw me, which I thought was pretty petty. I scowled at him before climbing into the back seat with the Raphael.

"Took you long enough!" he groused.

"Only seventy years," I laughed, my sparkling wit utterly lost on Luke as he floored it.

I buckled the passenger-side seatbelt around the Raphael and lay across what remained of the back seat, flattened by a crushing wave of fatigue. The jerking, bouncing pickup cab couldn't keep me awake. My body was done, and I passed out in an instant.

27
Thursday, February 25, 2021
46°58"S, 71°50"W

When I woke up, everything was new: the light that suffused the cab with heat, the stillness, the subtle suggestion of live fish in the air, the dull ache from the crown of my head to the tips of my toes. I hadn't felt the passage of time one bit, and my first thought was for the Raphael's safety.

Lying in the fetal position, facing the back of the seat, I had only to crane my neck backward to see him still buckled in just as I'd secured him, the layers of white drop cloth both disguising and protecting him. Still, the light was too harsh.

I unbuckled him and slid him between the passenger seat and the back seat, shielding the canvas as much as possible from the sunlight. Again, I felt myself at a loss for what else to do. I finally glanced toward the driver's seat to see that it was empty. The truck wasn't moving, and Luke wasn't in it.

Through the windshield I could see water, but nothing else.

I had to lean forward to see the beach on which the truck was parked. It stretched as far as the eye could see in either direction, and behind the truck it sloped upward to a crown of scrubby bushes that blocked the rest of the world from view. I couldn't see an opposite shore, but far to the right I saw a shoulder of land rising from the water to form a small peak covered in green. I didn't see or hear any other people, not even any other cars.

I climbed out of the truck and spotted Luke sitting in the sand at the edge of the water, posture thoughtful, still as a statue. I came around him at a wide angle, not wanting to startle him.

"Where are we?" I asked when I appeared in his peripheral vision and his gaze shifted temporarily from the water to me.

"Forty-six degrees, fifty-eight minutes south; seventy-one degrees, fifty minutes west," he recited stiffly. "Give or take."

"Is that… significant?"

"Sit down already, you're making me nervous."

I did as I was told, scooting as close to him as I dared. The sand was coarse and dark gray, lighter-colored shells and rocks mixed in. I joined his silent study of the water for a minute, trying to answer my own next question so I didn't sound like idiot; but, in my defense, I had no idea how long we'd been driving or even exactly where we'd started.

"Is this the ocean?" I ventured. His quick, breathy laugh confirmed I'd guessed wrong.

"It's just a big lake. Chile's about five miles that way," he jerked a thumb over his left shoulder.

"Oh, cool. Do you have any water?"

He turned to fix me with a puzzled expression. "Anna…

it's a lake."

"Oh, right. My brain is… not working so well right now."

"Hold on a sec." He climbed to his feet and stomped back to the truck, returning with a huge pack that looked like it weighed about seventy-five pounds. He let it fall into the sand and began rooting around in one of the outer pockets, extracting a small, blue tube that looked like most of a bicycle pump. "Here. Stick this end in the water, and suck on it from this end. It's not easy, but you seem pretty motivated."

I wasn't too far gone to get the picture, helped along by the word "LifeStraw" decaled onto the side of the tube. I waded chest-deep into the lake, shuddering as the cold water wrapped its arms around me. Getting water through the filter and into my mouth was no picnic, but after the first couple of swallows I felt myself reviving somewhat. I drank as much as I thought my stomach could safely hold, then dragged my soggy self back to Luke and sat down again.

I passed the straw back to him. "Thanks, I hate it."

"Why'd you go so deep? Trying to die of hypothermia before you die of thirst?"

"I don't know. I didn't expect it to be that cold."

That nonsensical answer earned me another strange look. The pack rustled some more, and Luke pressed an energy bar into my hand. "This is literally the last scrap of food I have."

"Thank you," I gasped, tearing into the brick-like quasi-food as though I hadn't eaten in weeks. It tasted of artificial bananas and stale chocolate chips. I hummed with pleasure.

"Don't eat it so fast, you'll be sick."

"'Kay, Mom," I mumbled around a mouthful of food.

"Well, as long as we're being rude… I'm sorry, but you smell like death."

"It's my hair," I answered, not caring. "If you've got shampoo in that thing, I'll do something about it."

He had to dig a lot deeper in the pack to get to it, but eventually he presented me with a small, hazy plastic bottle filled with turquoise liquid. I took it hesitantly.

"This the best you got?" I grumbled.

"I'm not giving you the good stuff." He stood up again, pulling me up with him. "Think you can handle another ice bath?"

"At this point, I think I can handle just about anything."

I didn't bother checking for other people again. The beach had such an air of loneliness and isolation that we could've been the only two people on earth for all I knew. I stripped down to my underwear and waded into the water again, followed by Luke.

While I worked the harsh, tea tree-scented shampoo into my hair, Luke scrubbed himself down with a bar of soap; then we switched. In the back of my mind I knew this wasn't kosher. Suds floated all around us, contaminating the lake, but I pushed this thought away. Desperate times called for desperate measures, as they say. Once he was done shampooing, Luke pressed his nose to my hair.

"Ah, that's better," he sighed. "Tea tree death."

"Rinse and repeat?"

"Let me."

He worked a gratuitous handful of shampoo into my hair,

making me wait a full three minutes before he rinsed it out. I started to get grumpy. It wasn't my fault I'd been locked in a room with a recently-dead corpse for two days! Sensing my shifting mood, Luke gave me an apologetic smile when I emerged from the water the last time. He worked his fingers through my hair, searching for stray soap suds.

It was the most natural thing in the world to rest my head on his broad chest while his fingers worked, and soon enough he stopped combing through my hair and wrapped his arms around me.

"I don't know what I would've done if you hadn't been there," he confessed. "I can't stop thinking about it."

"I do. You wouldn't have… There's just no way."

"Wish I could be as sure as you are."

"I know you," I insisted, wondering even as the words formed whether that were true. "I know you would've let her live."

"Marcel told me she was older, that she was dangerous. I expected—I didn't expect that."

"Why are you still whacking people for Marcel?" I asked, pulling away from him to watch his face. "I thought you burned that bridge when you helped me escape."

"He gave me a way back in. Said he understood, love makes people do stupid things, and he got what he wanted anyway. If he takes the Raphael… not likely, but I'll try… then I'll be two-thirds of the way done."

"Who's number three?"

"Paolo Barbato."

I frowned. "Man, he's really got it in for that family."

"You'd think." He sighed. "Let's get out of this water. I'm freezing my butt off."

I was still bursting with questions, but they could wait until we were warm and dry again. Luke didn't have much in the way of clean clothes stuffed in that massive pack, but a t-shirt and a thin camping towel fashioned into a sarong were plenty good enough for me.

I washed my unmentionables in the lake and laid them out to dry on the hood of the truck, settling onto Luke's sleeping bag in the open bed. While he kept watch, waiting for who cared what, I tried to sleep some more; but sleep evaded me. As the sun neared its zenith, I traded places with him and kept my eye on the landward side of the beach while Luke snoozed.

My stomach began to grumble around one o'clock (assuming my watch was still keeping correct time), temperatures rising into the low seventies. I made several trips back to the water with the LifeStraw, each trip less satisfying than the last, until by three in the afternoon I was hungry enough to wonder what we were waiting for and what was on the other side of the beach.

I climbed up the sloping sand into the bushes, cresting the beach to find a flat expanse of low foliage stretching before me for at least a quarter mile, bordered by a grayish strip that might have been a road. Even as I watched, shading my eyes with one hand and standing on the balls of my feet to try to see better, a car appeared on the road driving east. I watched it come closer, mildly interested. When it should have passed me, it veered left and headed straight for me. I half-ran, half-rolled back down the beach.

"Luke, wake up," I cried, fighting back panic. I reached the truck and shook the tailgate urgently. "Hey, wake up! Someone's coming."

He groaned, raised himself on one elbow, and pulled a phone from his pocket. He studied it for a moment and then lay back down, sighing, "It's just Jim."

"Oh… You couldn't have told me he was coming?"

"You didn't ask."

I paced back and forth behind the truck, my fingers twisting together on their own accord, guts writhing in discomfort. Surely Jim knew what had happened. Surely I wouldn't have to be the one to tell him his cousin was dead. I tried and failed to take my cue from Luke, who actually fell back asleep in the few short minutes between me spotting the car and it rolling cautiously over the crest of the beach to park next to us in the sand. He obviously wasn't too concerned.

Jim was still driving the Land Rover in which he'd departed Fernando's estate. As soon as he stopped, the car began to shake violently as joyous barks erupted from inside it. Jim hopped out of the driver's seat and released Dude from the back. He tackled me to the sand, licking my face, whining piteously. Had we only been apart this time for a few days? It felt like a month.

Luke roused himself again and sat up, and when Dude caught sight of him he leapt straight up over the tailgate and into the bed of the pickup to greet Luke like a long-lost friend. I took the opportunity to stand up and brush myself off, looking around for Jim. He'd wandered down to the edge of the water, hands in his pockets.

"Oh, boy," I grumbled. "When did you both become the moody, contemplative type?"

"Couldn't have anything to do with you," Luke suggested under his breath, as though I wasn't meant to hear.

I trudged down to where Jim stood and tentatively touched his arm, halfway afraid he'd lash out. When he looked down at me, his haunted expression asked the question he couldn't seem to articulate. I squeezed his arm.

"Marisol is okay. We have the Raphael, too. That's what you wanted, isn't it?"

He wrapped his arms around me, resting his chin on top of my head. I could feel relief coursing through him as he choked out, "Thank you."

"I wish you hadn't put me through that, Jim," I scolded in an ineffectually gentle tone. "But I think I'm starting to understand."

"I meant for you to save them both. I didn't realize…"

"Don't mention it."

We fell silent, comfortable in each other's arms, until Luke and Dude joined us, the latter pausing only to sniff my hand before dashing into the water. Nothing could keep his spirits down for long. Jim let go of me and took half a step back, his face a featureless mask as he looked at Luke. When he finally spoke, his words were flat, all business.

"You can't keep the painting. You know that."

"What a surprise."

"I considered having a fake made, something for you to give

Marcel. But we have to give it back. It's going to be all over the news for months. There's no way."

"Whatever. It was a long shot anyway."

Which meant, I saw in a flash of clarity, that Luke had killed Fernando for nothing. So why wasn't Jim more upset? Would that come later? I mentally amended my claim that I was starting to understand: I was starting to *start* to understand.

"Do you need help getting to Italy?" Jim asked.

Over Luke's response, I asked, "Italy? Why Italy?"

"Not really," Luke answered, ignoring me. "But you could get me as far as Albuquerque."

In the years to come, Jim would swear my hair had turned back from blonde to red in that instant, as my last ragged nerve snapped and I hit my limit, as every moment of confusion and every unanswered question reached critical mass and imploded with nuclear consequences.

I couldn't decide quickly enough which one of them was more deserving of my wrath, so I closed my eyes and screamed, *"Whattheheckisgoingon?"*

When my outburst gained me nothing but tense silence, I opened my eyes and looked at them both in turn. Luke seemed appropriately abashed, but I could've sworn Jim was fighting back laughter. At least it helped me decide who to scream at.

"Both of you wretched weasels have been lying to me and using me and lying to me some more for as long as I've known you! Tell me the truth right now or I swear I'll strap you both into that truck and set it on fire and roast marshmallows while you burn to death!"

Jim could contain himself no longer, asking in mock surprise, "Who's got marshmallows?"

I kicked him in the shin as hard as I could, then whirled around to do the same to Luke. A wave of dizziness hit me and I sank to the ground, nerveless, narrowly avoiding a head injury thanks to Luke's quick movement. He caught me, supporting my head as he lowered me to the ground.

"What did you do to her?" Jim asked, all traces of humor gone. His voice sounded far away. Luke's response was tight, defensive, but I couldn't make it out. Darkness blotted out both their faces, and the last thing I remembered was a cold, wet nose pressing against the back of my hand.

28

Thursday, February 25, 2021
Chile

I twitched my hand away, mildly annoyed. A big, warm hand closed over mine, squeezing lightly before slacking off, as though worried my bones would break.

Luke asked, "Anna?"

"Hng."

"You in there?"

Refusing to open my eyes, I felt the soft sheets surrounding my body and the calming hum of a ceiling fan whirring at low speed above me. "Where are we?"

"Some lodge in Chile."

I made a tiny noise of distress. "I passed out and you didn't take me to a hospital?"

"Jim didn't think you needed a hospital, just rest, and food eventually when you're up to it. Apparently his lordship already had a reservation here."

"How about a scotch?"

My eyes crept open to enjoy Luke smiling down at me, puzzled but happy enough.

"I'll see what I can do…" he said.

"Where's Dude?"

"Playing in the water. Jim's keeping him company."

"So you get to answer my questions. You drew the short straw."

His expression became grave. "No. You'll have to hear it from him. I only know bits and pieces."

"Where's the Raphael?"

He nodded toward one corner of the room. "There. I figured you'd want to keep it close."

I struggled upright and leaned against the headboard, gazing adoringly at the mummy-wrapped rectangle propped against the corner farthest from the door. As much as I adored him, it was starting to feel like a crime that he hadn't been returned to his rightful owners yet.

"That painting is why I joined the FBI," I whispered, as though Luke had asked why I felt so strongly about it. "I watched a documentary when I was ten years old, and they said the FBI's Art Crime Team was still trying to track it down. I didn't think I'd actually find it. I just wanted to be a part of the story."

"Well… mission accomplished."

"This really isn't what I had in mind."

"At least it hasn't been boring." I felt something smooth and cold against my hand and he instructed, "Here, drink this."

I drank all the water he foisted on me, then ate half a sleeve of stale crackers some hungover tourist had left behind months or years ago. It was enough to get me to the shower, where I scrubbed away the last of the dirt and grime and worked up a proper appetite. Wrapped in a complementary robe embroidered with the name of the lodge in flowing, royal blue script, I left the bedroom in search of something better than crackers to eat.

The wide double doors in front of the bed were open to reveal a breathtaking view of the lake a stone's throw away, the sun sinking into it already. This was the only exit I could see, so I went outside onto the porch and followed the smell of food into an outdoor kitchen situated between the room I'd left and another that looked just like it on the other side.

Two of my three companions were in the kitchen already. Dude was half-sitting, half-leaning against Luke's legs while Luke busied himself with something on the stove. I would've been content to hover around the corner, watching the homey scene as long as it lasted, if Dude hadn't caught sight of me and given away my position by trotting over to check on me. Luke glanced up, then returned his attention to the pan he was minding.

"What's for dinner?" I asked, sliding onto the bench seat of the kitchen table.

"I'm trying to make rice. It's not going very well. Jim left to find something more substantial."

"Is he avoiding me?"

"You'd have to ask him."

His flippant tone didn't fool me. That was twice now he'd volunteered Jim's whereabouts. I studied Luke's profile, wondering what that could mean. Nothing occurred to me.

"How long are we staying here?" I asked.

"I'm leaving tomorrow. I don't know how long you're staying."

I almost asked where he was going, but I decided I couldn't handle another non-answer. Instead, despondent, I asked, "Will tomorrow be the last time I ever see you?"

"I hope not." He dished out a bowlful of rice and set it in front of me, sliding into a seat across from me. "There's another option, though."

I had already jammed a huge spoonful of rice into my mouth and was huffing urgently as it burned my mouth. "Argh—what other option—*hffff*—what do you mean?"

He pointed at something behind me and I twisted in my seat, looking up at a wooden canoe hanging from the exterior wall of my room.

"We drag that down to the lake, row across, and get lost in Chile for as long as we can."

I swallowed painfully and turned back to him, heart thumping with excitement as I realized he was completely serious. While he waited for me to say something, I looked out over the lake and tried to picture it: Luke rowing, Dude curled up in the bottom of the canoe, me skimming the water with my fingertips and watching the sun set. It would be dark by the time we reached the other shore, if we could find it at all. Luke would pitch a tent, and I'd gather firewood while Dude established a protective perimeter. Maybe Jim would come back to find us gone and spot our campfire across the lake. Maybe he would stand out on the porch for a while like Gatsby gazing hopelessly at that green light. I laughed to myself at this, and Luke, who had been leaning forward, sat back and crossed his arms.

"I'm not trying to be funny."

"I know. I was just picturing… Never mind. No. I'm sorry, I can't do that. I'm not finished."

"Finished with what?" he argued.

"This thing with Philip. The FBI. Jim…"

"He's been jerking you around since day one, and you know it. Why are you okay with that?"

"I'm not okay with it. I've just accepted it."

"You don't know the half of it, just you wait. It's a miracle he hasn't gotten you killed yet. He's a liar and a manipulator and a terrible human being."

"Whatever," I said lamely, already tired of this conversation. I took another bite of rice and chewed thoughtfully, concluding, "It's a little crunchy."

"Sorry."

"I know you think I'm choosing him. That's not what this is."

"No, you're choosing his bank account," Luke shot back, seeking to wound.

I kept my eyes on my bowl, refusing to take the bait, letting him have it out.

"You actually think when all this is over, you get to be the queen of the castle, be his arm candy at fancy parties, maybe get a shiny new Lexus for Christmas every other year? As soon as he's done with you, you'll be on your own again and you know it."

"You horse's rear end," I spat, standing up so that I could look down at him. "You can believe all that if you want to, but I don't have to sit here and listen to it."

Dude gave a low bark, and for a moment I thought he was scolding me for being mean to Luke. Then I heard the Land Rover returning.

I waited until we could both hear Jim's footsteps coming toward the kitchen, then whispered, "I actually considered it, you know. Thanks for making it easy."

Luke stood up and walked away, out onto the porch, as Jim rounded the corner. I sank back down, resting my elbows on the table and my face in my hands.

"Hey, Dude," Jim mumbled. "No, this isn't for you. *No.* Hey." His tone changed and he asked solemnly, "What happened to you?"

I looked up at him, dry eyed, and shrugged. "Just tired."

"Here." He deposited several grocery bags on the table and rooted around in them, coming up with a white paper bag about the size of a greeting card, the bottom corners translucent with grease. "Try this. I promise you won't regret it."

He returned to the car to unload more groceries. I peeked inside the little bag and found a golden-brown empanada inside. My stomach gurgled greedily at the sight, and I wolfed it down way too fast. I was licking my fingers when Jim dumped a second pile of bags on the table.

I looked over the accumulated mass of groceries and asked, "How long are we staying here?"

"A while. You need a break. Do you happen to know how to

cook Chilean sea bass?"

"You mean Patagonian toothfish?" I asked.

"Ugh, no. What the heck is that?"

"Chilean sea bass."

"Oh—Wow, that's some effective re-branding."

"Did someone say Chilean sea bass?" Luke asked, reappearing in the kitchen to inspect the groceries. He'd pulled himself together, and the quick transition was jarring. I stared warily at him, but he refused to look at me.

Jim said, "Yep. Get cooking, you two, I've got some business to take care of."

With that, Jim disappeared into my bedroom. I heard the doors close behind him and asked, "Is he serious?"

"Come now, Anna, we mustn't keep his lordship waiting."

"Stop calling him that," I said, unable to completely hide a smirk.

If Luke wanted to pretend that nasty little exchange hadn't happened, that was fine by me. We whipped up a respectable feast of sea bass, rice (which improved greatly after Luke's first failed attempt), and some green beans and carrots that Luke artfully sliced into long strips à la fancy restaurant. I mostly just watched him work and tried to stay out of his way.

As he was adding the finishing touches, I had to ask, "Where did you learn to cook like this?"

"Dad was a chef," he said, distracted. "I helped him out whenever I could."

That simple statement made me realize that everything I knew about Luke wouldn't fill a postcard. I busied myself by opening a bottle of wine, perturbed by some non-specific emotion I couldn't quite get a handle on. I drifted away, still fighting with the simple corkscrew, to kick on the bedroom door.

"Dinner's ready, Milord!" I called, not waiting around for Jim to answer.

I poured myself a glass of wine, filled a plate, and settled in for what I profoundly hoped would be at least a couple of hours' worth of long-awaited answers from Jim. He didn't disappoint, though I could tell right away as he dived in that I wasn't going to like most of what he said.

"Guess I can't put this off any longer," he remarked wryly, taking in my impatient expression. "Any chance I could get a few bites first?"

"Make it quick," I said. I gave him five minutes, sipping delicately at my wine and watching him eat while he did his best to ignore me. At the five minute mark, I snapped, "Time's up, let's have it."

"Jeez, Anna."

"Information, please, or I swear I'll pass out again."

"Fine. I've been wondering where to start, and I think… I think we have to go back to nineteen forty-five. Anna, you already know some of this, but I don't think Luke does. But you both know about the fire, right?"

I nodded, and Luke said, "Sure."

Jim launched right in, Luke absorbing the information with far greater interest than I could summon. I kept one ear on the tale while I ate, if only to make sure Jim told Luke the same thing he'd told me. It all jived: the family diaspora, the organized crime, Paolo's murderous vendetta. It matched Jim's earlier rendition so well, in fact, that I realized he'd rehearsed it. What a control freak.

"The first thing you need to understand and accept, Anna, is there are no coincidences." Jim finally said, alerting me that the history lesson was over. We were getting to the meat and potatoes now. "This has been about the Raphael from day one. There have been a few wild cards, things I couldn't control, but the damage was minimal."

"Like Luke being up a creek without a canoe?" I challenged.

"Yes."

I turned to Luke. "Is the damage minimal?"

His gaze was fixed on Jim, his expression mildly terrifying. "Let's find out."

29

Thursday, February 25, 2021
Chile

Jim took a fortifying drink of wine and said, "When I found out Fernando had the lost Raphael, I confirmed it with the Art Crime guys as soon as I got home. Overnight I had too many cooks in the kitchen: my boss, the Cold Case Unit, the Art Crime Team… a cluster of mutually exclusive priorities. Art Crime wanted the Raphael, Cold Case wanted the Barber kids, I wanted both, and meanwhile my boss and I had a real job to do that had nothing to do with either. Rich—my boss—told me he'd stay off my back and hold them all off for one month while I tried to figure out what to do.

"I had Fernando eating out of my hand, thinking I was pirating FBI resources to keep him safe. I had Paolo stringing me along, trying to keep me away from Emilio while hounding me for information about the Sernas and the Liras. Turns out I also had a leak, but I'll get to that.

"I decided to look into the Lira branch of the family tree, try to get a feel for where Regina Barber-Lira fit into all this. Knowing her husband's name helped a lot. I found the record of their marriage in Barranquilla and followed the couple through records until Alejandro died in eighty-nine and Regina dropped off the face of the earth. By then she'd had Francisco, so I picked up his trail. However and whyever his mother chose to live like a ghost, Francisco didn't appear to share her concerns. He moved to Miami in two thousand and started getting really, really rich.

"I first learned about the Tres Islas Cartel in late twenty eighteen. Thinking I'd found a path to Regina, I started poking around the organized crime units for the agent in charge of keeping tabs on them. That's how I almost met Philip Levin.

"I wanted to start a conversation immediately, but Rich convinced me to take a step back and assess the guy first. I'm glad we did. When we found out what he was up to, I opened an investigation into him. That's what Rich and I do. The Continuous Evaluation Unit. It doesn't get us invited to many parties, but it keeps us entertained.

"While I was still trying to figure out how to use Levin to get what I wanted, I picked up an assist to keep me busy. I was asked to look over recent applicants for agent and make recommendations. I'd done it several times before, and I guess I had a reputation for having enough time on my hands to take care of it." He looked right at me and said, "You caught my eye immediately."

"Why?"

"At first it was the hair. Imagine me sitting there, thumbing through file after file of average Joes and suddenly you pop out at me. There's no science to it, kiddo, I just thought you were hot."

"Real professional."

"I decided to take a closer look at your file, you know, see where you lived, where you were currently assigned…"

"Jim!"

"I wasn't going to do anything with it. I was just curious and bored. It wasn't your full file anyway, just your application for agent, your test results, basic demographics, that sort of thing. I read over your education history and it hit me like a ton of bricks. Art History. Art Crime. The Raphael."

"I don't get it," I admitted, impatient.

"You started the wheels turning, that's it. I asked myself, how much damage could a face like that do? I thought about what would happen if I added a female agent to the mix. I wasn't getting anywhere with Paolo. I hadn't even considered tempting him with a honeytrap."

"Jeez, Camposanto," Luke complained. I took a drink of wine, not sure whether to laugh or kick Jim again.

"Hey, I'm just explaining how I arrived at my conclusion. I didn't even know Anna."

Over Luke's continued objections, I said, "I don't care. I want to hear the rest."

"Let me back up," Jim said, causing Luke and me to exchange an exasperated glance. "Since before I met him, Paolo has been looking for Regina Lira and Etta Serna, and not so he can send them birthday cards. Etta went into hiding after Emilio visited her in Buenos Aires, and Regina dropped off the map when her husband died. Regina is *hiding* from Paolo. Fernando was as well, at Regina's insistence. Paolo knew I was in touch with Fernando and figured out I wasn't going to help him. Paolo found a weak link in my organization and exploited it."

"This leak you mentioned," Luke said.

"That's right. The bad news is, we don't know yet who it is. Rich and I are the only ones who know about the whole thing—the Barber descendants, the Raphael. We've told Cold Case and Art Crime what they need to know and nothing else, as it's beyond Top Secret. Someone in our office got word to Paolo that Regina Lira's son was in Houston. That's where Frères Enterprises comes in."

"Okay, stop," I snapped, making the Time Out gesture with my hands. "You knew about them before I went to London?"

"Frères Enterprises? Sure. I told you, there are no coincidences here."

"You absolute donkey. Do you have any idea how long it took me to put that together, to find Luke again? Why didn't you tell me?"

"Because of the leak, Anna. Are you even paying attention to me?"

The haze of confusion was making me grouchy, and I snarled, "Yes!"

"If you're getting frustrated, maybe we should take a break."

"No," Luke cut in. "I want to hear it. Now."

"Okay. Paolo and his Sardinian associates—and yes, Anna,

before you interrupt me again, he still works with them and as far as I know has zero appreciation for the irony of it—they wanted into the American market and started making overtures to Marcel Marchand. He's already established, the infrastructure is there, it's a match made in hell. Paolo had this juicy info on Regina's son, and Marcel had a top-notch assassin who could take care of him. Luke killing Francisco Lira was Marcel's gesture of friendship to start a relationship with the Sardinians."

"They know about Paolo's vendetta?" Luke asked. "Aren't they his family, too?"

"They know nothing about it. Lira was high up in an organization that would become a competitor of the new March-and-Sardinian alliance. It made sense to get rid of him. That doing so would grievously wound Regina Lira was the icing on the cake for Paolo. Paolo picked out the target, Marcel picked out the man for the job, and Luke and Paolo began communicating directly to make it happen."

"You know Paolo, too?" I asked Luke.

"We've talked on the phone. Never met him."

"Anyway. Rich lost patience with Paolo and decided to try to get information the Hoover way—tapping his phones. That's how we found out about the plan to kill Lira. Rich saw an opportunity. I'd told him we needed to get a female asset working on Paolo, and Rich thought we could sneak her in through the back door. I never dreamed it would be you, Anna, you just gave me the idea.

"Since we ran the risk of Paolo finding out through the leak that we'd sent in another agent, we decided to take the long way around. We knew Levin was recruiting agents to go undercover with the Tres Islas Cartel. If we could get an agent into *Levin's* operation, make sure she was there when Lira was killed, and send her after Luke on the pretense of gathering information about the hit, we could get around every official information channel and have an asset inside Marcel's operation that could get to Paolo through him."

"That wasn't the pretense," I argued. "It was to find out who gave up Tommy and me to the cartel."

"Obviously I didn't know that would happen. You—she—whoever—was never supposed to be in that much jeopardy. Wild card number one.

"Rich and I had to pick a female agent, fast, because Philip was already looking for fresh meat to throw at the TIC. We put together a short list and pulled their files, and I added your name to the list, Anna, because you'd given me the idea in the first place. I got a lot of resistance. We had other prospects who had experience doing that sort of thing, and you were just a lowly intelligence analyst. I argued that you were ideal—you had the looks, you spoke every single language you'd need to, you were clearly agent material, and your background made it clear we wouldn't run the risk of you getting too close to the criminal element."

Luke gave a grunt of laughter. "How so?"

"You know what I mean. While Rich and I were still debating, Philip ran through his first round of possible undercover operatives and rejected every last one of them. Word was, he wanted someone fresh. Philip's hunt for inexperienced candidates brought your file up to the top of the stack in a big hurry. I could see you were going to make agent, which put you at Quantico when I needed you in Houston. I had to sort of… steal you.

"I told them I'd reviewed your file and you weren't a good fit for agent, and they rejected you. I called your boss, Christopher King—one of the few people I trust implicitly—and told him to send you to the assessment office as soon as possible. I thought it would be best if you went along with someone you knew, in case you were nervous. But you didn't have many friends…"

"Yes, it's been remarked on, thank you."

"But King thought you were getting along pretty well with your trainee, and you don't get much fresher than a blonde haired, blue-eyed, twenty-two-year-old kid, so Tommy went with you. I headhunted your neighbor, Dominique, as soon as I could. Once you'd made it through training, I had Dom help me set up a meeting."

"You didn't tell her why, though," I pointed out. "Do you think she's the leak?"

"It's unlikely. She wasn't in the picture until well after the leak passed information about Lira to Paolo. She likes to talk, though, and I couldn't be too careful. But back to Houston. We knew the TIC was running that warehouse and decided it had to happen there to minimize the possibility of collateral damage. I had to get you two and Lira there at the same time. Since we'd opened the investigation on Philip, I got authorization to tap your phone and Tommy's, too. I saw the text inviting you to the warehouse, knew Luke was already in Houston waiting for the right moment… so I just called Paolo and told him where Lira was. I called it an act of good faith: I help you connect with your sister's son, you let me talk to Emilio. Obviously the latter never happened.

"Someone, presumably Philip, tipped Lira off that you were FBI. We think he was trying to build trust with the cartel, which was why he wanted inexperienced agents who might not see the warning signs in time to get away. Philip didn't count on you being so hard to kill, and I made the mistake of believing he wouldn't send his own people to their deaths. You were just supposed to be an accidental witness to Lira's death.

"It didn't change much, though. You came back to Washington a complete wreck—no offense—and I had a choice to make. You'd already been through hell, thanks to Tommy, and—"

"Why thanks to Tommy?" Luke asked. "What happened?"

I shook my head, and Jim said only, "Let's not get into that now. Philip almost got you killed, and I was this close to sending you back to King and starting over at square one. But you changed my mind, Anna. You told me you wanted Philip to burn. I thought the only thing worse than pulling you out right then would be telling you the truth. I told you Jackson might have information that would help us nail Philip and sent you to Colorado to cultivate a relationship."

"Oh, she sure did," Luke snapped. "Are you kidding me with this, Camposanto? You threw her at me like a piece of meat on the *slim* chance she could get through me to Marcel and then to Paolo? You're a sociopath."

Jim absorbed the blow without any apparent damage. "Maybe it runs in the family."

"None of this has anything to do with the Raphael," I reminded Jim. He stared at me, calculating.

"Aren't you upset?" he asked at length.

"How can a piece of meat be upset?" I shot back.

"Okay. Should I go on, or…?"

"Finish the story," Luke hissed.

Jim went on. "The next snag came when Philip tracked you down too, Luke. He messed everything up, or so I thought, by spooking you into running back to Marcel before Anna could get anywhere. Imagine my surprise when Anna told me you'd invited her to follow you to London."

I shot a hooded glance at Luke, whispering, "I wasn't going to tell him. I had to."

Luke shrugged. "My fault for being such a sap, I guess."

"It kept things moving, and it told me I was right about Anna. We sent Anna to London to find you again, getting her even closer to Marcel, but I couldn't tell her about Frères Enterprises. She had to work it out on her own, because all of my information about them came from Paolo.

"Yet again, things went pear-shaped. Marcel smelled a rat. He knew about me from Paolo. He knew who I was, knew there was a blood connection. He believed I'd turned Paolo into an FBI asset, that he'd helped Anna find Luke both times. He took Anna just to see what Paolo would do. Unfortunately, Anna, I think your little Italian friend with the Lamborghini screwed the pooch on accident. When he tried to—uh—acquire you from Marcel, that was all the proof Marcel needed that you were on

Paolo's payroll. He thought the kid was trying to get you back to Paolo without garnering suspicion. Marcel actually called Paolo to gloat that his plan hadn't worked. There was no way you were getting imbedded in Marcel's or Paolo's operations after that.

"I had to get Anna to Argentina, to the Raphael, because Luke was on his way there in search of Paolo's next target—Fernando. I knew it would happen eventually. My regular trips to Argentina could only stay hidden for so long. Luke and I started comparing notes."

I perked up and asked, "When?"

"In Miami, while you were asleep," Luke answered. "I called Paolo and told him I was on the way back to the States with Camposanto, that I was planning to shadow him next time he went to Argentina so I could find Fernando. Paolo didn't like that plan. He told me not to trust Jim. As if I need reminding… but I thought, hey, Paolo's a bad guy, he doesn't trust Camposanto, so maybe I should give it a try. So I found Jim getting tipsy at the bar and told him everything."

"Tipsy?" Jim echoed.

"Yeah, you were all butthurt, drinking alone, don't you remember?"

"No."

"I do." Luke returned his attention to me, ignoring Jim's steady gaze. "I told him Paolo wanted me to kill Fernando and Marisol Serna and that they were somewhere in Argentina. I didn't know they were his cousins. I was asking for Jim's help, I figured what does he care about a couple of strangers in South America? He owed me one for helping get you away from Marcel."

Of Jim, I asked, "Why didn't you just ask Luke to lie to Paolo, to tell him he'd done the hit and call it a day?"

The taunt came from Luke this time. He said, "You keep asking about the Raphael and you still don't get it."

Before I could erupt, Jim explained, "I wanted Luke to take the Raphael in exchange for their lives. I wanted them to survive, Anna, both of them. If Luke just showed up and stole the painting, who do you think Fernando would blame? You had to be there, to make sure it seemed unplanned. For you, it was."

"So you didn't know, either?" I asked Luke.

"Never would've come down here if I had. It was a dirty trick. I'm glad I killed your sick cousin," he hurled at Jim, calm façade vanishing in an instant. "Do you know what he did to her? Are you still gonna sit there and tell us you didn't know how messed up he was?"

"I never saw that side of him," Jim assured me.

"He locked her in a room with a rotting corpse! She smelled like death when I found her!"

I met Jim's alarmed gaze for a moment, then found a very interesting pile of rice on my plate and stared at that. "He killed one of his man," I intoned. "He locked me in the room where he'd put—where Etta was."

"*Etta?*"

"She was basically mummified. I don't think Mari knew. Fernando didn't let anyone in that room."

"Unbelievable," Jim breathed. He ran a hand over his face. "I don't know what to say."

"How about 'sorry'?" Luke suggested.

"This isn't what I intended."

"Does it still constitute minimal damage?" I asked.

"You tell me," Jim said. "Now that it's done, was the Raphael worth it?"

The obvious answer, at least to my haywire brain, was a resounding yes. I'd have given my left nut (so to speak) for the painting; but I was too angry, mostly for Luke's sake, to give Jim the answer he wanted. I crossed my arms on the table and rested my head on them, gazing silently at Luke.

Jim pressed, "I wanted you there to give him a way out. I didn't want my cousins to die just because Paolo is obsessed with pruning the family tree. I thought they were innocent."

"Marisol is. I guess you did the wrong thing for the right reason. That's on brand."

"Yeah, and I'm left holding the bag," Luke groused. "The painting instead of the girl, that's the deal I made. And now I've got nothing."

"Well maybe you shouldn't have agreed to murder a nineteen-year-old girl in the first place," Jim shot back.

"Paolo told me she was older."

"Someday she will be. You gonna kill her then?"

"No!"

"Paolo will still want her dead."

"Well, I'll tell him she is dead. It's not like I have anything to show for letting her live."

"Good." Jim leaned back, rolling his shoulders back to loosen them up. "Guess it's too dark for a swim, huh?"

30

Thursday, February 25 to
Friday, February 26, 2021
Chile

Night had fallen while Jim spilled his guts. We all gazed auto-matically out at the lake, now a black void below us. I spotted what looked like a covered hot tub on the porch and said, "How about a soak instead?"

"Pass," Luke said, standing up. "You two have fun."

We both watched him stomp away to the other bedroom and heard the door snap shut. Dude, just a fluffy blur in the pitch dark beyond the kitchen, drifted over to sniff at the door. I could sense his concern for Luke and couldn't help but relate.

Jim cleared his throat. "Well. Did I at least explain every-thing to your satisfaction?"

"No. What about Dude? You dragged him down here so Luke could use his GPS tracker to find the house, right?"

"That's right."

"So why'd you steal my passport in Miami? Wouldn't it have been easier to let me keep it?"

"Sure, if I'd wanted Rich to know. He didn't sign off on any of this."

"What are you going to tell him?"

"When the painting surfaces, I'll tell him you ditched me in Berlin and slipped your passport into my luggage. I'll say I lost it in Miami, which is technically true. I tossed it in a trashcan, so it's definitely lost now. And your dad's in Berlin… Maybe he'll get a kick out of helping me cook up a lie about the two of you being in Berlin this whole time."

"Why?"

"Why don't I want to tell my boss I used an untrained asset and an international assassin to con my cousins out of a painting without damaging our relationship? Or why don't I want to tell my boss that I failed spectacularly and got one of the last living Barber descendants killed?"

"Well when you put it that way…" I sighed, pushing my plate toward Jim. "These dishes aren't going to do themselves."

Without waiting for his response, I left to hunt down a food bowl for Dude and the dog food I sincerely hoped Jim had been feeding him for the past few days. I found both against the wall on the landward side of the cabin, where the Land Rover and the severely mangled pickup were parked.

Dismal thoughts sprang unbidden into my head at the sight of the pickup's damage: front bumper and grill missing, hood crumpled and curling away from the engine compartment like a snarling lip. It was a miracle the thing had gotten as far as it had after being used as a battering ram, but I guessed Luke hadn't chosen the solid steel, multi-ton monster for its charming appearance.

I imagined Marisol and Martín surveying the damage while Mario mopped up the bodies. Would they leave the house, or patch it up and carry on? I suspected the former, since at least one person had flown the coop and probably wouldn't be trusted to maintain the secret of the house's location and its hunted occupants. I wondered if Marisol would seek Jim out as her brother had, and if she did whether it would be for solace or vengeance. I wondered if she had known all along that her grandmother's body had been in the upstairs bedroom or if she only learned of it yesterday. Did she love me for pleading for her life, or hate me for aiding the man who had killed her brother?

Standing there, staring vacantly at the pickup, I jerked in surprise as Dude nosed at my hand. I set the bowl down and ruffled his ears. "Sorry, buddy, I zoned out there for a sec. Sitz."

I put him through the normal pre-dinner routine, comforted by the familiarity, then returned back through the kitchen. Jim was up to his elbows in dishwater. Rather than helping him, I headed to the bedroom to get ready for what I hoped would be a deep, dreamless sleep.

Jim's laptop was open on the bed, the screen dark. I gave the touchpad a quick poke and the screen woke up immediately, but it was only to ask for a password. After considering the keyboard with half a mind to try out a few stupid guesses and deciding not to waste my time, I closed it and moved it to the desk by the door. Jim appeared in the doorway, frowning.

"What?" I asked, giving myself away with nothing but my guilty tone. He showed me his phone, which was displaying a stalker-type shot of my torso. I had to stare at it for several seconds before I realized what it was. "Whoa."

"My laptop takes a still from the webcam every time it wakes up and sends the image to my phone."

"Space-age."

"That laptop is Bureau property."

"So maybe you shouldn't walk off and leave it sitting by an open door."

"My bad. Anything I can help you find?"

"I was just curious, Jim, take it easy."

"Uh huh," he grunted, disappearing to finish the dishes.

I rolled my eyes at him and left the door open, letting in the crisp, chilly night air. I went through the whole bedtime routine properly, even washing my face, and climbed into bed. Since I'd once again been separated from my meager stock of ill-fitting clothes, I stole enough from Jim's suitcase to cover myself up. A few minutes passed before I realized that my body wasn't in the mood for sleep. I found a deck of cards in the desk and was lying on my stomach, playing a losing game of solitaire where my pillow should have been, when Jim came in.

"How are you still awake? You must be exhausted."

I half-turned, raising an eyebrow at him. "You wanted me to be asleep so you wouldn't have to find out exactly how mad I am at you."

"Was that a question?"

I turned back to my game. "Nope."

He took his sweet time getting ready for bed, sliding under the covers and turning to face me. I ignored him, laying out another game of solitaire as though I were enjoying the seesaw of rigmarole and defeat. He grabbed the tail end of a lock of my hair and tugged on it again and again until I finally looked at him.

"Are you five?" I snapped, thawing a little at his impish expression. His hand slid down my back.

"You're can't be that mad at me. You're here."

"Non sequitur," I said haughtily, stacking up the cards and moving them to the nightstand. "I have to sleep somewhere. Good night."

Though I turned away from him, he refused to be ignored. He laid one hand on my waist and said nothing, letting me think. I should have been slapping his hand away and banishing him to either share a bed with Luke or sleep on the porch with Dude, but I was fighting the urge to pull his arm over me and fall asleep against him.

He ended my internal struggle by asking, "He told you he's leaving tomorrow, right?"

"Yeah."

He took a while to reply, and I could almost hear him debating whether or not to speak. Finally, "I understand if you'd rather be with him tonight. I'm not saying I like it, but—"

"Are you serious?"

"You know you may never see him again," he pressed, adding, "I know you love him."

"I legitimately cannot think of a response to that." I sighed, rolling over to face him. "I can't believe you think I could— You're nuts. I'm not doing that. He doesn't want anything to do with me, anyway."

"When was the last time someone turned you down?"

"Fine." I stood up and threw my robe back on. "If you want me out of here that badly, I'll go."

"That's not what I want," he protested, but I was already on my way out of the room.

Indignation faded as I stalked across the porch in darkness, its flame too weak to contend with the chilly breeze. I stopped at Luke's door and raised my hand to knock, pausing as an unusually sober thought occurred to me. I did love Luke, and saying goodbye to him tomorrow was going to sting. I might even shed a tear or two. Doing this would make it that much harder for both of us. He had probably come to the very reasonable conclusion that if I did love him, I loved Jim more. He may even have convinced himself that I never cared for him in the first place.

Let him believe that. It would be a sort of mercy, just about the only thing I could do for him now.

I returned to the other bedroom, slipped under the covers, and silenced Jim's question with a kiss. As soon as I stopped he tried to speak again, and I pressed my hand to his mouth.

"What you really want is for me to say I forgive you, and you're going about it all wrong. I don't want to hurt you back."

He pulled my hand away and asked, "What do you want?"

"Heck if I know. Let's start with this." I rolled over and spooned up next to him, pulling his arm over me.

▼

The next morning came far too soon, not just because I was dreading it so much but because I hadn't fallen asleep until nearly two in the morning. I woke up and stumbled out of bed at six, summoned by the sound of Luke loading his stuff into the pickup. Dude's claws were click-clacking over the wooden slats of the floor outside as he followed Luke around, probably freaking out. Jim was already up. I hesitated at the bedroom door, listening as they conferred in hushed tones.

Jim was saying, "You shouldn't have any trouble getting into Denver. Your passport's been cleared already. But if you do, call me. I'll get it sorted out."

"Thanks. I guess the whole FBI knows I'll be in Albuquerque."

"And we would appreciate it if you didn't commit any crimes. You know, speeding, drug use, murder for hire."

"You're pretty pleased with yourself, aren't you?"

"Yeah, I am."

"Tell Anna bye from me, if it's not too much trouble. See you, Dude."

I darted out, crying, "I don't think so. You're not sneaking away like that. Who does that?"

Jim slipped past me, back to the bedroom, pressing his hand briefly to the small of my back. I followed Luke to the pickup, already fighting back tears. This was going to be ugly. He tossed the last item—a bag of chips—into the passenger seat through the open driver's side window and turned to me slowly, as though the preferred option was to drive away without even acknowledging me. His expression was shuttered, a little angry that I hadn't allowed him to skip this.

I could think of nothing else to say but, "What's in Albuquerque?"

"It's just a place to get lost for a while. 'Til I get a few things sorted out."

"Will you go to Paolo, in Italy?"

"Sure." He didn't sound thrilled at the prospect.

"You know I didn't mean to use you like this. I thought—"

"You thought you were using me a different way."

"I'm sorry."

"I'm sorry, too. I fell for it, made an idiot out of myself, Marcel is gonna kill me, and I didn't even get the girl."

"Paolo should take care of you…"

"Yeah, it's the least he can do."

"I don't want this to be the last time I ever see you."

"What about our lives seems compatible to you? Why can't you just cut me loose already? You really are greedy aren't you?"

Somewhere beneath my anger and grief at the way this was going, I sensed that he might just be trying to make it easier for me. I tried to return the favor by not throwing myself into his arms like a blithering idiot, but I couldn't keep the tears in my eyes any longer. I looked away from him as the first two fat, hot tears tumbled out, hoping it was too dark for him to see. His massive hand rose to my face, his thumb wiping away one tear. When he spoke again, his voice was gruff, every word seeming to cost him more than he was willing to pay.

"Sorry. Those better be the last tears you cry because of me. I mean it."

"Please don't hate me," I whispered, stopping the next three words just in time.

He wrapped his arms around me, breathing, "I don't."

31
February to March 2021
Chile

The echo of Luke's last insult was enough to keep me from kissing him goodbye, but only just. I watched, arms wrapped protectively around myself, as he climbed into the truck, started it up, and trundled noisily away across the uneven dirt road.

Rather than returning to bed, I picked my way down to the beach and sat at the edge of the water. Luke and Jim both seemed to think this was a logical place to contemplate one's vicissitudes, so I gave it a try. It worked, in a way. The regular, monotonous slap of tiny waves against the wet sand made it impossible for my thoughts to coalesce. They tumbled around uselessly, driving me half-crazy, but at least I stopped crying.

I shivered thinly until the sun rose, when Jim saw fit to show himself. He appeared next to me, sat a cup of steaming coffee in the sand next to my hand, and said gently, "I'm not trying to bug you. I just wanted to go for a swim."

"You're not bugging me," I intoned.

"Yeah. Okay…"

He trailed off, dropped a towel in the sand, and waded into the lake. It must have been positively frigid. He hesitated for a long time before going all the way under. I felt myself perk up a little as a bemused smile crossed my face. I couldn't summon the appropriate level of anger over what he'd done. I was already over it, as he knew all along I would be. It's not every day you recover a lost Raphael.

Sooner or later I would have to tell Jim I loved him, but Luke's harsh words before dinner yesterday made me afraid to do it. I didn't bother denying it to myself: The man had a point. Granted, he was just lashing out at me, but that didn't mean he was wrong.

That afternoon, as Jim had warned me over breakfast, two representatives from the Chilean government arrived at the cabin to take possession of the Raphael, the first step in what was likely to be a long, slow journey back to Poland. I said goodbye to him with a much lighter heart than the last goodbye, feeling a weight leave my chest as the Chileans loaded the naked canvas into a protective, hard-shelled case and locked it up like a nuclear football. I listened and watched from an open window in the bathroom that faced the back of the cabin, at Jim's insistence. Dude was sequestered with me and had the good sense not to bark at the strangers.

They thanked Jim for recovering the painting in a way that clearly bespoke their ignorance of how it had come about. I assumed that information would remain a closely guarded secret for a while yet. My spirits soared at the thought of visiting Kraków someday and seeing the Raphael returned to the frame that had been hanging there, empty, for so many decades. I wondered what the museum would write on the wall next to it, and I resolved to learn Polish so I could read their own words in their own language.

When the Chileans departed, they left Jim, Dude, and me to what had finally, officially, become a vacation. We had the cabin through the first week in March, and I had Jim's solemn promise that he wouldn't conduct any business at all except his continued efforts to track down my dad in Berlin with Ingrid's and the BKA's assistance. He swore he'd pay for my parents' own extended vacation afterward, to begin to make up for what they'd been through in the past year.

Three days in, Jim received confirmation that Ingrid had located my dad at his hotel, met with him, and convinced him to call Jim. He took the call and quickly passed the phone off to me as if it had turned into a venomous snake. My dad was not a happy camper, but at least I was able to convince him to head home. In turn, he was able to confirm that my mother, who had been screening Jim's regular calls this whole time, was safe and sound in Texas with the girls.

▼

On our last night in Chile, the weather finally got cold enough to fire up the hot tub after dinner. We sat, soaked, and stared up at the stars for a while, but soon I became much more interested in Jim than in the stars.

I sat across Jim's lap, kissed him, and admitted, "There's something I've been trying to figure out how to tell you, and on balance I've decided that you should just guess. I don't think I can say it."

He didn't need to guess. He smiled knowingly at me, looking so smug that I couldn't bear it. I kissed him again.

"Why can't you say it? Too mushy?"

"No, it's because…" I sighed, sitting back a little so I wouldn't be distracted. "It's because I'm afraid to. Because of something Luke said."

I related his accusations verbatim, Jim's smile collapsing into an aggrieved frown. "I'm sorry he put that thought in your head," he said when I'd finished. "Obviously, he's full of crap."

"He didn't put that thought in my head. That's why it scared me so much."

For a moment he looked insulted, but he recovered quickly and shook his head. "I'm buying you a Lexus the second we get back to DC."

"I'd prefer a Challenger, actually. Blue. Widebody. You know what, make it a Hellcat."

"I'll pay every speeding ticket with a smile on my face." He pulled me closer, kissing me contentedly. After a while he added, "I just thought of the perfect way to prove him wrong."

"Oh yeah? Better than a Hellcat?"

"Way better. When we get back home, move in with me."

I stared at him, searching his expression. He seemed like he already regretted his offer.

"Seriously?" I asked.

"Don't leave me hanging."

"You think that's a good idea?"

"Why not? I told you, I'm not letting you out of my sight again. This would be way more civilized than locking you in the basement."

"True…"

"And Dude will love the back yard."

"Jim…" I started, not finding the next words fast enough. His eyes fell and he started to change the subject, but I cut across him with, "It's definitely appealing."

"Just forget I asked, okay?"

"No. I worked so hard to be on my own. I'm not ready to give that up yet."

"The one time you decide to be mature."

"Is this a limited-time only, act now, supplies are running out offer?"

He perceived what I was actually asking and grabbed me by the waist, just a little too hard, just jealously enough to make my heart flutter. "It's there whenever you want it."

We went to bed early so we could start the long drive back through Argentina to Comodoro Rivadavia, a city on the Gulf of Saint George out of which Jim had arranged a charter voyage up the coast to Buenos Aires. The capital was the closest city from which he'd been able to book a private flight back to Washington. That was for Dude's sake, as he wouldn't have been able to fly in the cabin on any commercial airline, if he'd been allowed on board at all.

I learned on the day-long voyage that I was not a huge fan of the open ocean. More specifically, it scared the pants off me. The few times we left off hugging the coast to catch this or that current to speed up our trip, I fell to pieces and had to take Xanax-muddled naps below decks where I couldn't see that I couldn't see land. I'd never been happier to board an airplane than I was in Buenos Aires. The reality of how far away I still was from home had started to wear on me, and even though thousands of miles still lay ahead of us, flying would certainly speed things up.

We landed at Reagan in the wee hours of Sunday morning, the seventh of March, and took a cab the short distance to Jim's house in Arlington. We had flown from summer into the last desperate throws of winter, and Dude was the only one dressed appropriately for the weather. Snow had fallen recently, and mounds of it still lurked in shady spots around the city through which we drove.

After I fed Dude and let him out into Jim's back yard, he rolled around in the snow like a madman and refused to come back inside. He insisted on sleeping in front of the back door like an incompetent night guard.

Unlike Dude, I preferred to spend the night snuggled up next to Jim in his enormous bed. If I was going to spend these coming hours of darkness with my mind incessantly whirring, I figured I might as well be comfortable.

A less selfish woman would have been agonizing over Luke: Where was he? Was he safe? Was he happy, or at least not miserable? Was he thinking of me? Did he despise me? But I was me, and my thoughts had already turned to how all of this was going to impact my future at the FBI.

Jim and I had to report to his boss, Rich, in just over a week to explain ourselves. Jim had informed me we'd spend that time preparing, getting our story straight, rehearsing it, and generally doing our best to hedge against the all-too real possibility that my misdeeds, real and fabricated, would end in my termination from the Bureau. I can't claim that specter was all that terrible to me. After all, with the outstanding Raphael exception, working for the FBI hadn't gone at all as I'd hoped.

The fact remained that I still needed to understand how Philip Levin fit into all of this, and Jim was going to help me whether he liked it or not.

Thanks for reading! Don't forget to read the bonus content at the end of this book: the first chapter of the sequel, *Bigger Fish*. If you enjoyed *House on Fire*, please take a couple minutes to leave a review or rating. Reviews help readers decide whether to buy my books, and every single review helps so much—even the bad ones.

Want to be the first to know when new stories come out? You can sign up for my mailing list on my website, akweller.com. You'll get my occasional newsletter, and you'll receive a link to download a free short story.

▼

About the Author

AK Weller was born and raised in Texas, moved to New Mexico, and now lives in Montana with her husband, four cats, and three dogs. She mostly enjoyed brief careers as a technical writer, private investigator, social worker, and pet sitter before finding her calling as a semi-employed writer. AK writes mysteries and thrillers while running her own graphic design business. Her favorite books to read over and over again were written by JRR Tolkien, Stieg Larsson, Sue Grafton, Michael Crichton, and JK Rowling.

▼

Also available from AK Weller

The Anna Bowman Thrillers: a 5-Book Thriller Epic

Book 1: Enemy Closer

On the run from her ex-husband, a powerful federal agent, Abigail takes shelter in a cabin in rural southwest Colorado with her trusty German Shepherd, Dude. When she learns someone else has been using the cabin to hide out too, she'll find herself stuck with a shady, surprise roommate for the summer. While they figure out how to get along, they'll learn their stories were intertwined long before they met. *Enemy Closer* is a suspense thriller that allows you to experience each new piece of information along with the characters right to the end, when you realize everything you thought you knew was a lie. A deeper story has only just begun to unfold.

Book 2: House on Fire

Thanks to her boss, shady FBI Agent Jim Camposanto, Analyst Anna Bowman finds herself the target of two different international criminal cabals. With no obvious way out of the mess she's just beginning to understand, she'll have to drag the truth out of her secretive boss and a hitman who just can't seem to shake her. Will Anna ever get to relax and feel safe with her beloved German Shepherd, Dude, or will she become addicted to Camposanto's dangerous games? Anna Bowman's misadventures continue in *House on Fire*.

Book 3: Bigger Fish

Home from her unlikely triumph in Argentina, Anna thinks her life is getting back to normal until a surprise visit from David March and sets her on a collision course with Luke Jackson once again. With a little help from two people straight out of Anna's past, they'll unravel a mystery that takes them out of the frying pan and into the fire.

Book 4: No Port in a Storm

After unraveling a murderous family feud, FBI castoffs Anna and Jim travel to Italy to deliver a final peace offering. Amidst their fraught romance, they find no shortage of ways to make new trouble. While fostering unlikely friendships against an idyllic Mediterranean backdrop, they provoke dangerous enemies closer to home. Emily, Luke, and Dude were supposed to be safe in Texas, but suddenly they're in the crosshairs again. As tensions escalate, Jim's clever schemes are put to the test. When generations of hostility erupt into all-out war, will Jim's cunning save them, or will Anna's fighting spirit be their only way out?

▼

Coming soon from AK Weller

<u>2.15.2020</u>

In the prequel to *Enemy Closer*, Anna Bowman escapes her boring hometown and joins the FBI. After a few years as a quiet but efficient cog in the machine, she tries to achieve her childhood dream of becoming an FBI Agent, only to be rejected and bewildered. Ensnared instead in the intrigues of Agent James Camposanto, Anna will embark on an unexpected assignment in Houston, Texas with her protégé, Thomas Holladay. What really happened on February 15, 2020, in Houston, and how in the world did a divorced art historian from Manchester, Texas end up there?

<u>Friday the 14th</u>

Anna Bowman and her older sister, Emily, just wanted a fun night out to celebrate Anna's twenty-fifth birthday. While enjoying some much-needed time away from their significant others, the sisters accidentally pick up a new friend at a casino in Oklahoma. When a tongue-in-cheek plan to burn down each other's houses and collect the insurance money falls into the wrong hands, Anna and Emily will have to band together to stop an arsonist… if they decide they want to. Find out who's left standing on *Friday the 14th*.

A Last Time for Everything

A Last Time for Everything tells the tragic and unbelievable origin story of 17-year-old Anna Bowman and the events that set her on the path to joining the FBI.

Sam Walsh, PI Mysteries

Prequel - Tiger by the Tail

Private Investigator Samantha Walsh has been in denial about her true identity for 25 years. When a terrifying figure from her past explodes back into her life, Sam will have to decide how much she's willing to sacrifice to stop running from her father's killers in *Tiger by the Tail.*

#1 - Sam vs. the Black Hat

Newly independent PI Sam Walsh needs clients, and she can't afford to be picky. When her old boss sends a prospective client her way, Sam takes the case - a classic cheating spouse - against her better judgment. Caught between a dishonest client and a dangerous, shadowy foe, Sam will either solve her first case or die trying. Sue Grafton's iconic Kinsey Millhone is catapulted into twenty-first century Texas suburbia in book one of the Sam Walsh, PI Mysteries.

Short Stories

Underworld: A Short Suspense Thriller

Underworld follows mystery woman Seffy Nix as she moves into a 140-year-old mansion that seems to be haunted by a slovenly, inconsiderate ghost bent on distracting her from the mission that brought her to small-town Helena, Montana.

The Beast and the Books: A Short Monster Story

All alone one night, Rodney is clearing out a storage unit. His biggest problem is his wife's massive book collection, at least until the lights go out and he realizes he's not alone. Something is living deep in the bowels of the storage facility, and it's about to make a break for freedom. Unfortunately for Rodney, he's right in the creature's path.

Anywhere But Home: A Memoir

A short memoir about budding author AK Weller's increasingly nonsensical attempts to fill a void in her life caused by an abusive relationship. From Oklahoma to Texas to Colorado, she hops from one distraction to another until she realizes the answer to her problem is starting over.

350

<u>The Institute: A Short Story</u>

High school junior Miguel thought getting an underage drinking charge would derail his life at New Mexico Military Institute in Roswell, but when his new friends draw him into their world of pranks and mischief, he'll discover there's a lot more going on at NMMI than he ever imagined. Will Miguel maintain his hard-won GPA and graduate with a diploma that will open doors for him to wherever he wants to go, all while learning how to mix a little fun into his busy life? Will his new friends have his back when things start to get spooky?

▼

Keep turning for a sneak peak at the next
chapter of Anna's story: *Bigger Fish*.

1
Saturday, March 13, 2021

I sat with pencil poised over the blank answer sheet, battling the double vision that threatened to make my writing illegible. After a few seconds, I realized no one was providing me with an answer to write. I looked up from the paper and saw my four companions watching me expectantly.

"You guys think *I* know?" I asked.

It was a dismal realization, but not the end of the world. After all, bar trivia at the Hamilton in Washington, DC wasn't exactly the Paris Peace Conference. Thinking this, I zeroed in on Sharen directly across the table from me. She'd pulled "Paris Peace Conference" out of the hat in the last round, so why not this?

"Fear of being happy," I prompted. She shrugged. My ears began to seek out telling whispers from nearby tables in the packed bar, but no one was blabbing.

Dominique Danes, my neighbor in life if not at our booth, startled everyone by smacking Sharen on the arm and urgently, silently, motioning with both hands for me to pass her the pencil and paper. I complied, taking the opportunity to sip at my fourth—fifth?—something-th martini. If I played it right, Dom would keep the answer sheet and I'd be off the hook. I had no idea how I'd been elected the smart one in the group, anyway.

While Dom scribbled, erasing and correcting a couple times, I gazed serenely around at the bar in general and my four companions specifically. Speaking of being happy. The atmosphere was drunkenly exuberant, I was among friends, and as far as I knew, no one wanted to kill me.

One short week had passed since FBI Agent James Camposanto and I had returned to Washington, DC after rescuing a lost Renaissance masterpiece, Raphael's *Portrait of a Young Man*, from a hidden estate in Argentina. The painting was back in Poland now, where a welcome-back exhibition was in the early planning stages. We did that. For all the screw ups and cataclysms and downright unconscionable behavior that got us there, we did it.

Three days ago, I'd returned to my long-forsaken Krav Maga class, which ended in an invite to bar trivia. I'd asked Dom to join me, even though she knew none of my classmates, because she was the only person with whom I could imagine enjoying a night out. My three classmates were nice enough, but I only remembered Sharen's name because her job as an OPM Accountant was the inspiration for a long ago lie that no longer mattered. I couldn't even remember the other two people's names.

Again Dom smacked Sharen, who didn't seem to mind the attention at all, which yanked me out of my reverie. She slid the paper back to me, and I silently mouthed, "Cherophobia."

"I'm ninety percent sure that's it," Dom explained. She took a drink of her scotch—I do admire a woman who drinks scotch—and amended, "One hundred percent. How I know, I don't know, but I know."

"Good enough for me," announced the woman to Sharen's right, whose name might have started with a K. She grabbed the answer sheet and took it to the emcee, sashaying just enough that the man sitting to my right became unnaturally still as he appreciated the view.

Sharen and Dom were getting along like peanut butter and jelly, and intuition told me my other two classmates would be leaving together. They were cute. K Something and M Something. They'd met at class, and the two had been orbiting one another like satellites for as long as I was aware of them.

You'd think being a fifth wheel would upset the apple cart of contentment I had going, but it only made me more comfortable. Once our team was finished losing trivia, I'd find my way back to Jim's house in Arlington, Virginia where rested my dog, Dude, and my Jim, whatever he was.

James Camposanto. If he were the answer to a trivia question, that question would probably be, "Who does this guy think he is?" A mastermind. An intriguing if infuriating romantic partner. The reason my life wasn't boring. The gleeful control freak who'd had the absolute gall to suggest the clothes I wore tonight might be too skimpy. Because the weather may turn, he'd insisted. But he'd had that spark in his eye, and I knew he'd only said it to provoke me. It had worked, which meant I'd been a few minutes late to trivia.

Lost in the pursuant memories, I scoffed aloud, "Fear of being happy. How is that even possible?"

"It's when you think something bad is about to happen because you can't be happy forever," Dom sagely explained. "Take you, for instance."

"Me?" I squeaked.

"Yeah, you, Space Force. You had to sit at the end of the booth facing the door. What'd you think is gonna happen that you need to be guarding the door?"

M Something piped up in my defense. "No one thinks something is going to happen. Doesn't hurt to be cautious."

"Oh okay mhm," Dom mumbled. "So you didn't snap up that seat to be next to our girl Anna. You just wanted to be on deck in queso emergency."

I distinctly heard her say "queso." Maybe I'd had a bit too vodka much.

M Something glanced unwillingly at me, then caught K Something's eye as she meandered back to us through the crowd.

"I plead the fifth," he concluded.

While we waited for the scores from the last round to be announced, Sharen and Dom folded together into a whispered conversation. M and K made awkward small talk across the table. I sat back and enjoyed the entertainment, sipping at martini number who-the-heck-cared and wondering how I was going to get from DC to Arlington without ending up in a ditch.

Jim had dropped me off, insisting he'd be happy to come get me no matter how late I stayed out; but he was probably asleep by now, and I didn't want to wake him up. I could ride the Orange Line almost all the way to Jim's house, but I'd still have to walk about a mile, and I really didn't care to.

I decided to take an Uber, recalling my mostly unused salary as an FBI Intelligence Analyst that had been piling up for months and months. Might as well spend some of it. I opened the app on my phone, then glanced toward the door, wondering if it had started raining again.

My curiosity could not have been timed worse, because I locked eyes with a man walking into the bar. Automatic embarrassment shifted at once to recognition. I knew him, and he knew me, and he wasn't supposed to be there. He wasn't even supposed to be on this side of the Atlantic Ocean. Was I seeing things?

Too drunk to look away, I stared brazenly at the familiar face with a mixture of puzzlement and discomfort. He matched my gaze for what felt like an eternity, then settled into a seat at the bar with clear line-of-sight to me, took off his coat, and ordered a drink. I tried to ignore him, part of me hoping I was seeing things, that he'd disappear if I played it cool.

For a few minutes I feigned interest in the others' conversation, but soon my eyes drifted back to the bar. The man was still there. He'd received a pint of beer and was, unfortunately, solid and real enough to pick it up and drink it.

I watched him sip his beer and only snapped out of it when the emcee turned down the music to announce the winners. Our team took the round, but we didn't even place in the overall scores.

"Anna, why don't you go claim our prize?" Sharen suggested. "You look like you could use a free beer."

"Yeah, Anna, let's see the legs that launched a thousand ships," Dom put in, causing Sharen to erupt with laughter.

I was too focused on the man at the bar to appreciate her assessment, but I did slide out of my seat. Knowing I wouldn't be back, I dropped some cash on the table and waved a half-hearted farewell to my confused companions.

"Say hi to Jim for me," Dom called after me.

At the name, the man at the bar glanced up and saw me walking toward him. As I passed his seat, I heard his mostly-empty glass clink as he sat it down and knew I had about eight seconds to form some kind of plan. Eight hours wouldn't have been enough, not in my state of advanced inebriation. I turned a corner, reached the door to the women's restroom, stopped, and turned around.

David Marchand stood in front of me, too close, his face passing in and out of focus in the poor lighting as I tried to decide if I was the kind of person who saw things when she drank too much.

David couldn't be here. He was the youngest brother of Marcel Marchand, a French crime boss whose clutches I'd escaped back in December in London. David may have turned traitor to help me escape, but that didn't mean I was happy to see him.

"I'm sorry to surprise you like this, Anna," he said in a low voice, his accent more apparent than ever in the sea of American conversations providing background noise. "Are you all right?"

"I'm very drunk. Very, very, very."

"I can see that. However, I need to talk to you, and it can't wait." He pushed open the door to the family restroom and waved me inside.

"Ew," I complained. "Can't we go outside?"

"Oui, if that suits you better."

He offered me his arm and I sputtered with laughter, demurring, until I took a wrong step and nearly broke my ankle. I grabbed his arm and mumbled, "Friends are gonna think you picked me up."

"They can't be dumb enough to make such an obvious error in judgment."

"You're a funny little French guy, you know that?"

He waited until we were outside on the sidewalk to reply, "I worry you might not be able to understand what I'm saying in your current state."

"No, no, being drunk makes me normal smart."

"You are flirting with alcohol poisoning."

"I flirt with everything. Just say what you came here to say."

He started to, but before he could get the first word out his gaze shifted to a spot over my right shoulder. I turned around, not even considering whether that was his intention, and found myself looking up at all six feet, seven inches of James Camposanto.

I backed up, dizzy with indignation and liquor, and saw my dog, Dude, tethered to Jim's right hand by a slackened leash. Dude's tail began to wag as soon as I noticed him, but I was too surprised to greet him properly.

"Did you *follow* me here?" I demanded of Jim.

"I was at your apartment and wondered why you hadn't

called yet." He smiled at me and then looked over my head, narrowing his eyes at David to ask, "Is this guy bothering you?"

Over my own fit of laughter at this, I heard David ask, "Are you James Camposanto?"

"Jim, Jim," I gasped, turning again and backing into Jim's non-dog side for support. "This is David Marchand. This is Marcel's baby brother. He helped me escape from the house with all the dogs!"

Of course, Jim already knew this, as he'd masterminded said escape; but again, I was very drunk. Shoulder-to-shoulder with Jim, I felt him tense up. David took a half-step back.

"I'm not here to cause trouble," David preempted. "I need your help."

Jim's arm slipped protectively around my waist anyway. I rested my head on his shoulder, as it seemed to have suddenly doubled in weight, and closed my eyes as Jim asked, "With?"

My eyes popped open at David's low answer of, "Luke."

Luke Jackson. Had it really been less than a month since we said goodbye in Chile? The intervening weeks had seen Jim lavish me with affection and distractions, all to heal the wounds caused by his own Machiavellian hand. Luke was out of my life and down on his luck. His former boss, David's brother Marcel, wouldn't take him back. Luke was supposed to have found safe harbor in Italy with a new benefactor, but if Jim knew whether he'd made it there safely, he wasn't telling me.

It seemed to me that Jim took several minutes to answer, "Luke who?"

"Don't be a jerk, Jim," I snapped. "What happened?"

"Anna," Jim said sharply, fingers digging into my side. "Maybe it's best if you don't talk right now."

"Ugh. You're so bossy."

"Let's go to Anna's apartment," he bossed, adding most reluctantly, "If that's okay with you, Anna."

"It's closer," I agreed. "Why'd you bring Dude? Not that I'm complaining."

Jim didn't answer, but as we fell into step on the sidewalk heading toward my apartment on Dupont Circle, David asked, "This is your dog, Anna?"

"That's my boy."

"He's magnificent. The largest Alsatian shepherd I've ever seen."

"I like you, David. How's Penelope doing?"

"She grows less like a Malinois and more like a person each day."

"Next time you see her, please inform her that I love her."

David chuckled, and I thought I heard Jim force a reluctant breath of laughter. I knew I'd be getting a lecture soon enough, some hogwash about being careful and whatnot.

The ten-minute walk helped me sober up enough to realize it was way too cold outside for the ten-minute walk, and I was shivering miserably by the time the three of us and Dude slipped into the warm shelter of my apartment building's lobby. Jim, comfortable in his light jacket, was kind enough not to say, "I told you so."

We climbed into an elevator, I swiped my key card to get us moving, and Jim judged the time was right to ask David, "So what does Luke want? What happened to him?"

"I don't know what happened. He won't tell me. Marcel sent me to Atlanta to take care of some business at our international office. I then traveled to Denver to meet Luke, at Luke's request, and we rented a car and drove down to Alquer—Alqubur—uh—"

"Albuquerque," I supplied.

"Yes, New Mexico. He wanted to speak to you but was wary of contacting you directly, so he sent me. He mentioned a leak at the FBI."

"So he wants to chat," Jim concluded. "Is that all he told you?"

Jim's carefully-worded question elicited information without giving it, unlike what I wanted to ask David ("Did Paolo find out he didn't kill Marisol?"). I decided to follow Jim's advice and shut up, though my feathers were still a little ruffled about it.

Before David could answer, the elevator doors opened on my floor and we filed out, not speaking again until I'd locked my apartment door behind us. I invited the men to make themselves at home while I took a quick detour to the bathroom, calling, "Don't talk, I don't want to miss anything!"

I hurriedly did my business, washed my hands, and returned to the living room to plop down on the floor, leaning against Jim's long legs.

"As to why Luke didn't come here himself. He doesn't know who to trust," David explained. "He thinks Marcel wants to kill him, and he might not be wrong about that.

"He told me Marcel asked him to kill Fernando and Marisol Serna on Paolo Barbato's request, then to kill Barbato himself. I have no idea why Marcel would ask for this, but for Luke it was a way back in after helping Anna escape.

"Luke told me he planned to seek refuge with Paolo in Italy rather than returning to Marcel in London, but he no longer believed it was safe to do so."

"So why not go back to Marcel?" Jim asked. "Bridge too burned?"

"I haven't discussed any of this with Marcel, obviously. I'm not an imbecile."

If it was clear to me that David was losing patience with us, it must have been clear to Jim, but he pressed, "If Luke's so worried about a leak, he can get over it. We stop the leaks we want to stop. If he wants to talk, he knows how to reach me."

"Why do I feel I have wasted my time coming here?"

Jim didn't answer. I squirmed, wondering if he were going to ignore David's news. When I couldn't keep it in any longer, I asked, "What are you gonna do, Jim? You can't do nothing."

"I guess it can't hurt to humor him," he answered, plainly unhappy about it. "Where is he?"

"I don't know," David admitted. "Probably still in Al— uh—New Mexico. He told me Anna would be able to find him."

Jim asked something that made so little sense to me I didn't even hear real words. That convinced me I was going to be missing the rest of this conversation. I excused myself to the kitchen to make coffee, brought three steaming mugs back to the living room, and tried my best to tune in. After the tenth time I nodded off and almost struck my head on the coffee table, Jim sent me to bed with a bottle of water and a trashcan.

* 9 7 9 8 9 9 9 1 6 3 0 8 8 7 *